Praise for the *USA Today* Bestseller *THE SECRET MOTHER* and Shalini Boland

"Shalini Boland is without a doubt the queen of twists and she never disappoints."

—BytheLetterBookReviews.com

"Utterly gripping to the last page and full of twists and turns to keep the reader guessing. A fantastic thriller!"

—Sarah A. Denzil, author of the *Wall Street Journal* bestseller *Silent Child*

"Absolutely loved this amazing book! One of the best psychological thrillers I have read!"

—Renita D'Silva, author of *Monsoon Memories*

"A roller-coaster of emotion until the very end. *The Secret Mother* is the first book I have read by Shalini Boland, but it won't be the last."

—TheBlondePlotters.com

"I loved the way Boland created tension here...so nailbitingly good! This was an excellent psychological thriller filled with uneasiness, doubt and a huge pack of lies."

—NovelGossip.com

THE SECRET
MOTHER

THE SECRET MOTHER

SHALINI BOLAND

GRAND CENTRAL
PUBLISHING

NEW YORK   BOSTON

Copyright © 2017 by Shalini Boland
Cover Design and illustration by Emma Graves
Cover copyright © 2019 by Hachette Book Group, Inc.

Grand Central Publishing

Hachette Book Group
1290 Avenue of the Americas, New York, NY 10104
grandcentralpublishing.com
twitter.com/grandcentralpub

Originally published in 2017 by Bookouture in the United Kingdom

First Trade Paperback Edition: June 2019

Grand Central Publishing is a division of Hachette Book Group, Inc. The Grand Central Publishing name and logo is a trademark of Hachette Book Group, Inc.

The publisher is not responsible for websites (or their content) that are not owned by the publisher.

The Hachette Speakers Bureau provides a wide range of authors for speaking events. To find out more, go to www.hachettespeakersbureau.com or call (866) 376-6591.

Library of Congress Cataloging-in-Publication Data has been applied for.

ISBN: 978-1-5387-6436-7 (trade paperback)

Printed in the United States of America

LSC-C

10 9 8 7 6 5 4 3 2 1

For Pete.
Your name means "rock"
and that's what you are to me.
My rock.

CHAPTER ONE

The street lamps flicker, illuminating the grey pavement mottled with patches of dirty snow and slick black ice. Slushy puddles hug the kerb, cringing away from the hissing, splashing car tyres. It takes all my concentration to keep my balance. My hands would be warmer if I jammed them into my coat pockets, but I need them free to steady myself on walls, fences, tree trunks, lamp posts. I don't want to fall. And yet would it really be so terrible if I slipped on the ice? Wet jeans, a bruised bum. Not the end of the world. There are worse things. Far worse things.

It's Sunday: the last exhale of the week. That uncomfortable pause before Monday, when it all starts up again—this lonely pretence at life. Sunday has become a black dot on the horizon for me, growing larger each day. I'm relieved now it's almost over and yet I'm already anticipating the next one. The day when I visit the cemetery and stand above their graves, staring at the grass and stone, talking to them both, wondering if they hear my inane chatter or if I'm simply talking into the empty wind. In burning sunlight, pouring rain, sub-zero temperatures or thick fog I stand there. Every week. I've never missed a Sunday yet.

Sleet spatters my face. Icy needles that make me blink and gasp. Finally, I turn off the high street into my narrow road, where it's more sheltered and the wind less violent. A rainbow assortment of overflowing bins lines my route, waiting for collection tomorrow at some ungodly pre-dawn hour. I turn my face away from the windows where Christmas tree lights wink and blink, reminding me of happier Christmases. Before.

Almost home.

My little north London terraced house sits halfway along the road. Pushing open the rusted gate, I turn my face away from the neglected front garden with its discarded sweet wrappers and crisp packets blown in from the street, now wedged among long tussocks of grass and overgrown bushes. I thrust my frozen fingers into my bag until they finally close around a jagged set of keys. I'm glad to be home, to get out of the cold, and yet my body sags when I open the door and step into the dark silence of the hall, feeling the hollow of their absence.

At least it's warm in here. I shrug off my coat, kick off my boots, dump my bag on the hall table and switch on the light, avoiding my sad reflection in the hall mirror. A glass of wine would be welcome about now. I glance at my watch—only 5:20. No. I'll be good and make a hot chocolate instead.

Strangely, the door to the kitchen is closed. This strikes me as odd, as I always leave it open. Perhaps a gust of wind slammed it shut when I came in. I trudge to the end of the hall and stop. Through a gap in the bottom of the door I see that the light is on. Someone's in there. I catch my breath, feel the world slow down for a moment before it speeds back up. Could I have a burglar in my house?

I cock my ear. A sound filters through. Humming. A child is humming a tune in my kitchen. But I don't have a child. Not any more.

Slowly I pull down the handle and push the door, my body tensing. I hardly dare breathe.

Here before me sits a little boy with dark hair, wearing pale blue jeans and a green cable-knit jumper. A little boy aged about five or six, perched on a chair at my kitchen counter, humming a familiar tune. Head down, he is intent on his drawing, colouring pencils spread out around an A4 sheet of paper. A navy raincoat hangs neatly over the back of the chair.

He looks up as I enter the room, his chocolate-brown eyes wide. We stare at one another for a moment.

"Are you my mummy?" the little boy asks.

I bite my bottom lip, feel the ground shift. I grasp the counter top to steady myself. "Hello," I say, my heart suddenly swelling. "Hello. And who might you be?"

"You know. I'm Harry," he replies. "Do you like my picture?" He holds the sheet out in front of him, showing me his drawing of a little boy and a woman standing next to a train. "It's not finished. I haven't had time to colour it in properly," he explains.

"It's lovely, Harry. Is that you standing next to the train?"

"Yes." He nods. "It's you and me. I drew it for you because you're my mummy."

Am I hallucinating? Have I finally gone crazy? This beautiful little boy is calling me his mummy. And yet I don't know him. I've never seen him before in my life. I close my eyes tight and then open them again. He's still there, looking less confident now. His hopeful smile has faltered, slipping into a frown. His eyes are now a little too bright. I know that look—it's the one that precedes tears.

"Hey, Harry," I say with false jollity. "So you like trains, huh?"

His smile returns. "Steam trains are the best. Better than diesels." He scrunches up his face in disgust and blinks.

"Did you come here on the train? To my house?"

"No. We came on the bus. I wish we did come on the train,

the bus was really slow. And it made me feel a bit sick." He lays the sheet of paper back on the counter.

"And who did you come with?" I ask.

"The angel."

I think I must have misheard him. "Who?"

"The angel brought me here. She told me that you're my mummy."

"The angel?"

He nods.

I glance around, suddenly aware that Harry might not be the only stranger in my house. "Is she here now?" I ask in a whisper. "Is there someone else here with you?"

"No, she's gone. She told me to do some drawing and you'd be here soon."

I relax my shoulders, relieved that there's no one else in my home. But it still doesn't help me solve the problem of who this little boy is. "How did you get into the house?" I ask, nervously wondering if I might find a smashed window somewhere.

"Through the front door, silly," he replies with a smile, rolling his eyes.

Through the front door? Did I leave it open somehow? I'm sure I would never have done that. What's going on here? I should call someone. The authorities. The police. Somebody will be looking for this child. They will be frantic with worry. "Would you like a hot chocolate, Harry?" I ask, keeping my voice as calm as possible. "I was going to make one for myself, so—"

"Do you make it with milk?" he interrupts. "Or with hot water? It's definitely nicer with milk."

I suppress a smile. "I agree, Harry. I always make it with milk."

"Okay. Yes, please," he replies. "Hot chocolate would be lovely."

My heart squeezes at his politeness.

"Shall I carry on colouring in my picture," he says, "or shall I help you? Because I'm really good at stirring in the chocolate."

"Well, that's lucky," I reply, "because I'm terrible at stirring in the chocolate, so it's a good thing you're here to help me."

He grins and slides off the stool.

What am I doing? I need to call the police right now. This child is missing from somewhere. But, oh God, just give me ten minutes with this sweet little boy who believes I'm his mother. Just a few moments of make-believe and then I'll do the right thing. I reach out to touch his head and immediately snatch my hand back. What am I thinking? This boy has to go back to his real mother; she must be paralysed with worry.

He smiles up at me again and my chest constricts.

"Okay," I say, taking a breath and blinking back any threat of tears. "We'll do the chocolate in a minute. I'm just going to make a quick phone call in the hall, okay?"

"Oh, okay."

"Carry on with your drawing for a little while. I won't be long."

He climbs back up onto the stool and selects a dark green pencil before resuming his colouring with a look of serious concentration. I turn away and pad out to the hall, where I retrieve my phone from my bag. But instead of dialling the police, I call another number. It rings twice.

"Tess." The voice at the other end of the line is clipped, wary.

"Hi, Scott. I need you to come over."

"What? Now?"

"Yes. Please, it's important."

"Tessa, I'm knackered, and it's hideous out there. I've just sat down with a cup of tea. Can't it wait till tomorrow?"

"No." Standing by the hall table, I glimpse Harry through

the doorway, the curls of his fringe flopping over one eye. Am I dreaming him?

"What's the matter?" Scott says this the way he always says it. What he really means is, *What's the matter now?* Because there's always something the matter. I'm his damaged wife, who's always having some new drama or make-believe crisis. Only this time he'll see it's something real, it's something not of my making.

"I can't tell you over the phone, it's too weird. You have to come over, see for yourself."

His sigh comes long and hard down the phone. "Give me twenty minutes, okay?"

"Okay. Thanks, Scott. Get here as soon as you can."

My heart pounds, trying to make sense of what's happening. That little boy in there says an angel brought him. He says I'm his mummy. But he's not mine. So where on earth did he come from?

I take a breath and go back into the kitchen. The air is warm, welcoming, cosy. Nothing like the usual sterile atmosphere in here.

"Can we make hot chocolate now?" Harry looks up with shining eyes.

"Of course. I'll get the mugs and the chocolate. You open that drawer over there and pass me the smallest pan you can find."

He eagerly does as I ask.

"Harry," I say. "Where are your parents, your mummy and daddy?"

He stares at the pans in the drawer.

"Harry?" I prompt.

"They're not here," he replies. "Is this one small enough?" He lifts out a stainless-steel milk pan and waves it in my direction.

"Perfect." I nod and take it from him. "Can you tell me where you live?"

No reply.

"Did you run away from home? Are you lost?"

"No."

"But where's your house or flat? The place you live? Is it here in Friern Barnet? In London? Close to my house?"

He scowls and looks down at the flagstone floor.

"Do you have a last name?" I ask as gently as I can.

He looks up at me, his chin jutting out. "No."

I try again, crouching down so I'm on his level. "Harry, darling, what's your mummy's name?"

"You're my new mummy. I have to stay here now." His bottom lip quivers.

"Okay, sweetie. Don't worry. Let's just make our drinks, shall we?"

He nods vigorously and sniffs.

I give his hand a squeeze and straighten up. I wish I hadn't had to call Scott. And yet I need him to be here when I ring the police. I can't deal with them on my own, not after what happened before. I'm dreading their arrival—the questions, the sideways glances, the implication that I might have done something wrong. I haven't done anything wrong, though. Have I?

And Harry…he'll be taken away. What if his parents have been abusive? What if he has to go into foster care? A thousand thoughts run through my mind, each worse than the one before. But it's not my place to decide what happens to him. There's nothing I can do about any of it, because he's not mine.

I don't have a child. Not any more.

CHAPTER TWO

Harry and I bustle about the kitchen together, and it's so easy. So natural. Like we're doing something we've always done. Like I really am his mummy and he really is my son and it's perfectly normal to be making hot chocolate together on a Sunday evening after a walk in the rain. We'll enjoy our drinks while watching a film, and then we'll have to get his things ready for school tomorrow. I'll run him a bath and wash his hair before tucking him up in bed and reading him a bedtime story. *No!* Stop it. Stop it right now. Why am I torturing myself with these ridiculous thoughts?

My throat is tight with tears, and all of a sudden, I'm crying into the bubbling pan of milk.

"Are you okay, Mummy?"

I swipe at my tears with the sleeve of my sweatshirt. "Yes, yes, I'm absolutely fine, sweetie. I can't wait to take a great big slurp of this when it's ready."

"Me too."

Harry kneels on a chair and I supervise as he stirs in the chocolate powder with a wooden spoon. Then I pour the drink into two mugs and we sit together at the tiny kitchen table. I only have a few minutes left to enjoy this snapshot of how my life could have been.

I know I should try harder to find out where Harry is from.

To ask again who his real parents are, where he lives, and all those other important things. But he wouldn't answer them the first time and I don't want to upset him. I'll leave those questions to the professionals.

Harry takes a noisy sip of his drink and grimaces. "It's hot."

"Careful, don't burn your tongue. Blow on it, cool it down a bit."

"Do *you* like trains?" Harry asks. He's acquired a hot-chocolate moustache, which makes me smile.

"I love trains," I reply. "Once, I took the train right down through France and then on through Spain and Portugal."

"Wow! How long did that take?"

"Days and days."

"And nights, too? Did you sleep on the train?"

"Sometimes," I say, remembering the cramped carriage Scott and I shared, back when we first got together. Those hazy, beautiful first days of love.

"Can *we* do that?" Harry asks, his eyes wide at the thought of such an adventure. "Can we go on a train through all those countries and sleep on there with our sleeping bags?"

I want to tell him yes, of course we can. I want to say that tomorrow we'll book tickets and travel across the world by steam train together. That we'll see amazing, exotic sights and wave to all the passers-by. We'll chat to interesting people and have a cabin of our very own. I'll buy him an engine driver's cap, and the conductor will let him blow the whistle. It'll be the best fun in the world.

"I'm sure that one day when you're older you'll be able to do that, Harry."

"Brilliant," he replies with his nose in his mug, making his voice sound all echoey.

The doorbell rings and I give a small start.

"Who's that?" Harry asks with a frown, placing his mug back on the table.

"That will be Scott," I reply, getting to my feet. "Don't worry, you'll like him. He's nice."

"Okay."

"I'm going to let him in," I say, "and then I'll be back. Just stay here for a moment, all right?"

Harry nods, his face suddenly serious.

I leave the kitchen, closing the door behind me. Scott refuses to use his keys any more. Even though we're separated and no longer living together, I told him to keep a set for himself. I said that this will always be his house too. But he never lets himself in, he always rings the bell.

I open the front door to my dripping, scowling husband.

"Hi, come in. I didn't know it was raining so hard." I stand back and he walks past me into the hallway. "Shall I take your coat?"

"I'm not staying, Tess. What's this about?" His deep voice booms around the narrow space.

"Shh, keep it down," I say, gesturing towards the kitchen.

"What?" he says, louder than ever. "Why? Is someone in there?"

"Scott, please."

"Okay," he says in an exaggerated whisper.

"Listen," I begin. "I came home from the cemetery this afternoon..."

Scott's face darkens further. He never goes to the graveyard, he says it's too depressing. That he would rather remember them how they were.

"...and when I got home, there was a little boy in our kitchen."

It takes a few seconds for my words to register.

"A little boy?" Scott says, his brow creasing. "What are you talking about? What little boy?"

"That's what I'm trying to tell you," I say, my heart thumping. "He's in there now. His name is Harry."

Scott takes hold of my shoulders and looks into my face as though he's searching for something. "Tessa, what the hell? I hope you haven't gone and done something stupid."

I shrug his hands off and take a step back. "I haven't done anything," I hiss. "I'm telling you what happened. I came home and he was in our house, sitting at the kitchen counter, drawing. And then he asked me if I was his mummy!"

"Christ, Tess. What have you done?" He pushes past me and opens the door to the kitchen, halted in his tracks by the sight of Harry sitting at the table, scooping out milk froth from the bottom of the mug with his forefinger.

I edge past Scott to go and stand with our little visitor, not wanting him to feel intimidated by the sight of an angry stranger. But Harry seems fine. He stares at Scott before switching his gaze to me.

"Harry," I say with forced cheerfulness. "This is Scott, who I was telling you about."

Harry gets to his feet and wipes his sticky fingers on his jeans. He comes around the table and holds his hand out. "Nice to meet you, Scott," he says, his little voice so pure and confident I want to hug him.

Scott's anger towards me has deflated. He stands there with his mouth open before responding to Harry with a dazed handshake. "Hello," he croaks. "Me and Tessa are just going to have a little chat in the hall, okay? We'll be back in a minute."

"Is your name Tessa?" Harry asks me.

I nod.

"But you're my mummy, right?"

I give him a limp smile, unwilling to deny it.

"Okay, Harry," Scott interrupts. "Just give us a couple of minutes."

He grabs me by my upper arm and manoeuvres me out of the kitchen, his eyes narrowed, his lips pressed into a thin line. He closes the door behind us and turns to me, hands opened out like claws.

"Why does he think you're his mum? Where's he from, Tess? Where'd you get him?"

I shake my head. "I told you before. I got home and he was—"

"Yeah, you said, he was just there, sitting at the counter. But that's impossible. A child can't magically appear in your kitchen. Where did you find him, really? Tell me and we can sort it out."

I should have known Scott wouldn't believe me. After all we've been through, he no longer trusts me. He doesn't have my back any more. I'm on my own.

His voice softens. "I know this is hard. I know your heart is broken from what happened, but you can't do stuff like this. You'll get into serious trouble. You could go to prison."

"I didn't find him, or take him, or whatever else you think I've done," I snap, clenching my fists by my sides. "Do you really think I'd take someone else's child after what happened to us? Do you think I'd put another mother through that kind of pain? I'm telling you the God's honest truth. But if you can't believe me, then—"

"It's not a case of not believing you. Maybe you genuinely can't remember what happened. Maybe... Oh, I don't know." Scott's broad shoulders droop and he runs a hand through his dark hair, suddenly looking like a small, tired boy himself.

"We need to call the police, right?" I say.

"Yes. You should have called them before you called me. You should have called them *instead* of calling me."

"I know." I dip my head and chew my lower lip, feeling ashamed. I've put my own inadequacies ahead of Harry, ahead of his parents, and that was wrong of me. What was I thinking? "Can you call them?" I ask Scott. "Please. I don't think I can do it."

He nods and draws his mobile out of his coat pocket. "What shall I say?"

"Tell them the truth," I reply. "That I came home and found him here."

"It sounds so dodgy, Tessa."

"Better than lying."

"Okay. Well, if you're sure."

I nod, unsure of anything, a wave of helplessness surging through me. This little boy delivered by an angel will soon be gone from my life, like everything else.

CHAPTER THREE

It didn't take them long to arrive. Less than ten minutes from Scott's call to their official-sounding ring on the doorbell.

Two officers—a man and a woman whose names I can't remember—are in the kitchen talking to Harry while Scott and I wait in the lounge, an awkward silence filling up the small space. I sit on the sofa in my usual spot, and Scott hovers by the window, staring out into the dark, rain-lashed evening. I listen, hoping to eavesdrop on what's going on through the wall, but they must be speaking quietly as all I can hear is the occasional deep bass note of the male officer's voice. I can't make out any clear words.

What will they think of Harry's story? Will he tell them the same thing he told me? When the police first arrived, I told them exactly what had happened when I got home earlier, and then they asked for mine and Scott's whereabouts this afternoon. Scott had been playing in his usual five-a-side football match, and I was at the cemetery, alone. Aside from asking their questions, neither of the officers passed any comment. They simply wrote down what we said.

"Are you okay?" I ask Scott, who's been awfully quiet since the police went into the kitchen with Harry.

"Hmm?" He turns towards me.

"You all right?"

"Yeah, I suppose so. This wasn't exactly what I had in mind for this evening."

"Me neither."

He grits his teeth and shakes his head. I know he feels like this is my fault. That I've dragged him into something he doesn't want to be a part of. Maybe I shouldn't have called him. I have no real claim on my husband. We're separated, he doesn't owe me anything. But he has always been the one I've turned to. We were always there for one another. It's painful to realise that he now resents my need for him. That he would probably rather be anywhere else than here.

"Thank you," I say.

"For what?"

"For coming when I called. For ringing the police for me."

He gives a sad smile and runs a hand through his damp brown hair. His tall, broad frame usually gives him stature and presence, but this evening he just seems awkward and ill at ease. Too big for the room, like he doesn't fit here any more.

"What do you think will happen to him?" I ask, hugging my knees to my chest.

"I'm sure they'll find his parents."

"I hope they're nice people. Maybe he ran away from them."

"He'll be fine," Scott says dismissively. "The police will sort it out."

I nod, but I'm not convinced.

Scott's eyes widen at the sound of chairs scraping back, of voices getting louder, the kitchen door opening. I jump up from the sofa and follow him into the hallway, where the two officers now stand with Harry between them. He looks forlorn. A little lost, story-book boy.

"We'll be in touch," the female officer says.

My stomach swoops at her words. What does she mean by that exactly?

"Okay," Scott replies.

"Bye-bye, Harry," I say. "It was so lovely to meet you."

But Harry doesn't look at me. Doesn't even respond. I get the feeling he thinks I've let him down. I can't think of anything reassuring to say to him. And in a moment he'll be gone. It will be too late.

"Will you let me know what happens?" I ask the officers, suddenly terrified that I'll never hear from or see this little boy again. That I'll never know what becomes of him.

"I'm afraid we can't really give out that kind of information," the male officer replies.

"But…"

Scott places a warning hand on my arm and I fall silent. I can't take my eyes off Harry's pale, downturned face, his dark curls.

"Did you remember to take your drawing, Harry?" I say. "You don't want to leave that wonderful picture behind."

He doesn't respond. Where is that chatty little boy who was calling me "Mummy" only a short while ago?

"We asked if he wanted to bring the picture with him," the female officer says, "but he said it was for you, Mrs. Markham, didn't you, Harry?"

I can't be sure, but I think Harry gave her a small nod.

"I'll treasure it," I say too brightly. "I'll put it on the fridge where I can see it every day."

Again Harry doesn't reply. But I hope he understands what I'm telling him.

The male officer hands me and Scott a card each. "We'll be in contact, but in the meantime, you can give us a call if you need to," he says. "If you remember anything else that might be helpful."

"Will do," Scott replies. And then, "Take care, Harry. Look after yourself."

The two officers make their way out through the front door onto the wet, slippery path. Harry shuffles next to the woman; her ebony hand wraps around his pale one. Harry's hood is still down and his hair is getting soaked. Why doesn't one of the officers put it up for him? I clench my teeth, then sigh with relief as the woman finally leans down and pulls the hood up, before shaking open an umbrella to shield him from the downpour as they make their way to their car.

I want to believe Harry is going back to a warm, loving family who will cover him in hugs and kisses when he gets home, safe and sound. But my heart is heavy as lead. Scott ushers me away from the door and shuts it behind them.

We stand there for a moment, listening to the drumming rain on the porch roof.

"Well," Scott says, "I'd better be going."

"Have you eaten yet?" I ask. "I can make us both something if—"

"I'd better get back, Tess. I've got food at home for tonight, and it's vile out there…"

"Yes, sure, of course. You go." I catch sight of myself in the hall mirror. My face is blotchy, dark circles ring my eyes, and my hair is a blonde crow's nest topped off with a solid line of greying dark roots—not the edgy, rock-chick kind, but the tired, middle-aged kind that add about ten years. No wonder Scott is keen to escape. He doesn't even want to stay and talk about what happened this evening. To speculate about where Harry is from and how he ended up in my kitchen. Once upon a time, we would have cracked open a bottle of wine and chatted long into the night about something as bizarre as this. Not any more.

"Take care, Tess." He leans in to give me a perfunctory peck on the cheek. The smell of his aftershave blindsides me and I want to put my hands to his face, to keep his cheek next to mine. Keep the warm scent of him in my nostrils. But he's already moving away, pulling open the front door. Escaping. He gives me a last smile and a nod, and pulls the door closed behind him. Gone.

I stare at the closed door and take a breath. I won't allow myself to sink. To wallow. I'll make some supper—something comforting and delicious. Even though I'm not at all hungry.

The kitchen is empty. Quiet and still. Harry's drawing lies on the counter top. I pick it up and examine it: a pretty good likeness of a green steam engine, partly coloured in. To the side, a boy with dark hair and a woman in a flowery dress with a smiley face.

I put my fingers to my hair. Harry said it was a picture of me, but the woman he's drawn has brown hair, and *my* hair is fair. I open the top drawer again to look at the pencils. There's a brown pencil and a yellow one, so he could have made my hair the right colour...

Why am I even thinking this stuff? He's obviously a traumatised little boy. Something has happened to him and he was just pretending that I was his mum to help him get through a tough time. Perhaps he's even colour blind. I'll probably never know.

I'm about to place the picture in the drawer along with the pencils, but something stops me. I told Harry I would put it on my fridge so that I can look at it every day. I can't break my word.

There's another picture already stuck to the fridge with two fruit magnets. It's a drawing of me and Scott and Sam—happy stick figures all holding hands. I remove the bottom magnet and move the picture along to the right. Then I use the magnet to secure Harry's picture to the fridge too. I step back to survey them both. I'll have to buy a couple more magnets to stop the paper flapping around.

I open the fridge. Inside, a small block of cheese and a shrivelled carrot moulder on the middle shelf. Looks like I'll be having beans on toast then. No. I remember there's no bread left. Beans with grated cheese, that'll have to do.

The doorbell rings and I freeze for a moment. Could Scott have changed his mind and decided not to leave me on my own tonight? We'll have to order a takeaway. I run my fingers through my hair uselessly and rush to the front door, pulling it wide open, ready with a smile and a fast-beating heart. But it's not Scott. It's my neighbour, Carly, her chestnut hair pulled up into a high ponytail. She's standing under a black-and-white checked umbrella, and she's smiling her white-toothed smile.

"Hi," I say, disappointment deflating my body. I should have realised it wouldn't be Scott. And Carly is the last person I feel like talking to right now.

"How are you doing, Tess?" she asks, with that confident rasp in her voice.

I try to pull myself together as she raises her beautifully plucked eyebrows, presumably waiting for some kind of response. I wonder what she's doing on my doorstep. Back when Scott and I were still together, Carly and I used to be quite good friends. She lives opposite, moved in around the same time as us. We'd have a natter whenever we saw each other, pop round for cuppas and the occasional barbecue, and even keep an eye on each other's houses when we went away—water the plants, feed her cat, that type of thing.

But then she started getting a bit too pally with Scott. I'd arrive home from work to find her over at our place having a drink with him, or she'd drop things into the conversation that I didn't know about him, like something funny he'd done but hadn't got round to telling me yet. It rankled. She would show up on our doorstep, ask to borrow stuff, then never return it. Scott even gave her a small financial loan once. So I ended up cooling our friendship. Not that Carly is very good at taking hints. She'd still call round and wheedle her way in. Well, until Scott left, that is. After that, I didn't see her quite so often. Funny, that.

"What's up, Carly?" I finally reply.

"I just stopped by to see if you're okay," she says. "I saw the police outside, and a little boy coming out of your house..."

"Oh, right. Thanks. I'm fine. Everything's fine. He was lost, that's all." Call me cynical, but Carly has not dropped round to see how I am, especially not on a foul night like this.

"Lost?" she repeats, her eyes taking on a feverish gleam. "That little boy? Did you find him somewhere?"

I should've known she'd be interested in Harry. Carly used to work for one of the tabloids, but with newspaper sales dwindling because of all the free online news sites, she was recently made redundant. Now she's a freelance reporter and—like so many journalists who've found themselves having to scratch around for work—she's desperate for a story. How can I politely tell her to piss off? It's been a long, hard day, and all I want to do right now is make some food, read a book and forget about the world outside for a few brief hours.

"I'm sorry, Carly," I say. "Is there something specific you wanted? It's just I'm a little busy right now."

"Oh, right. I just thought if something's happened with that little boy, it could make a good story."

Bingo! I was right. "Nothing's happened. There isn't any story," I say. I want to slam the door in her annoying face, but I'm too polite. Besides, I don't want the hassle and embarrassment of any bad feeling between us. It's already awkward enough. "Thanks for coming over, though. It was thoughtful," I add, knowing full well there isn't an ounce of concern in her self-centred, gym-toned little body.

She takes a step forward, places her foot just inside my door. Cheeky cow. "So who was he then?" she whispers conspiratorially, as though we're best mates. "I can do a really nice piece on it, interview you, give you a makeover, get your picture in the paper—or at least online."

"I don't want a makeover, and I really don't want my picture in the paper, and especially not all over the internet. Like I said, there's no story. Honestly, Carly, I'm sorry but I've got things to do." I push the door so she's forced to take a step back. "Thanks for stopping by," I call out so she can't accuse me of being rude. Then I shove the door closed with a satisfying click and stand there fuming, the blood boiling in my veins. The absolute nerve of her.

I lean back against the door and realise my hands are shaking, but whether it's from Carly's unwanted interest, or the shock of finding a little boy in my house, I can't tell. And didn't the police say they would be in touch? Why would they need to speak to me again? I've told them everything that happened. Don't they believe me? My mind feels cloudy, muddled. I try to piece together the events of this evening once more. I came home from the cemetery and found a little boy called Harry in my kitchen. Yes. That's what happened. Isn't it?

CHAPTER FOUR

I haul the stepladder out of the supply shed, happy to be back at work this morning. Yesterday's events with Harry don't feel real. It's like they happened to someone else. But I'm still fuming over Carly's visit. I shake my head at the memory of her as I lean the ladder against a wall with a clang before locking the shed again.

I work at Villa Moretti Garden Centre, just a mile up the road from where I live. My wonderful but pressured career as a landscape architect collapsed two and a half years ago along with the rest of my life, and I guess I'm lucky to have found this job, which just about covers my bills.

Moretti's is a small but perfectly formed slice of Italy, tucked away in English suburbia. Winter isn't its most spectacular season, but the work suits me. I can get lost among the plants, forget about my car crash of a life and concentrate on nurturing seedlings, pruning, cutting, clearing and shaping. It's physical work that tires me out enough to get me to sleep each night. Enough to be able to function again the next day.

The rain has eased this morning, the temperature an almost balmy eight degrees, melting the icy patches and taking the nip out of the air. I swing the ladder sideways under my arm and head over to the outdoor part of the café, its tables and chairs still in storage. We probably won't get them out again until next spring. In the meantime, I need to take advantage of the absence of frost and prune the dormant wisteria covering the pergola. I set up my ladder by one of the posts, climb a couple of steps, and take the secateurs out of my fleece pocket, getting to work on trimming back the shoots.

Normally, this kind of work takes my mind off everything, letting me lose myself in the business of cutting and snipping. Not today. Images of Harry's downcast face keep popping into my head. I replay our conversations about trains and hot chocolate, thinking about the ease of our brief time together. Where is he now? Has he been returned to his family yet, or is he in care somewhere, worried and alone? I have a lump in my throat and a stone in my stomach at the thought of him placed with strangers. Even though I guess I'm technically a stranger, too.

I climb down the ladder and shift it further along the edge of the pergola. I'm about to climb back up when I realise I can't simply carry on and act like nothing's happened. I can't blithely continue with my life and forget about Harry. He came to me for a reason—he called me his mummy, for goodness' sake. I have to at least try to discover what's happened to him.

I peel off my gloves and lay them on one of the ladder's steps, then I pull my phone from my pocket. Damn, I left the police officer's card in my bag in the staffroom. I'll have to go inside for it.

"Morning, Tess."

I turn to see Ben walking towards me with two mugs of coffee in his hands.

"Is one of those for me?" I ask.

"Who else?" He grins and hands me the steaming mug. "One Americano and..." he takes a paper bag out of his coat pocket, "a cinnamon Danish from the café."

"Lifesaver," I say, realising I haven't eaten anything at all this morning. The coffee smells heavenly.

"Can't have my staff keeling over on the job. Not when they're climbing up ladders and wielding sharp implements."

I smile. Ben Moretti is quite possibly the nicest boss on the planet. He took over the family business from his parents, who'd moved over here from Italy in the late sixties. They've recently retired and moved back to their home town just outside Naples. Ben was born and bred here in London. Now in his forties, he looks like an Italian film star, with his jet-black hair and dark eyes. He's a softie, though. Nothing like the suave Italian stereotype everyone thinks he is.

He raises an eyebrow. "You look like hell, if you don't mind me saying."

"Cheers." I twist my lips into a sarcastic smile, but I know he's right. "Didn't get too much sleep last night."

"Everything okay?"

"Long story," I reply. "But this coffee and Danish will fix me up. Thank you."

"I've got time for a chat, if you like?"

"Ah, thanks, but it's nothing really," I reply. I don't have the energy to talk about what's happened. Especially not with my boss. The last thing I need is for him to think I'm some kind of attention-seeker who brings her problems to work. "But thanks for the offer," I add.

"No problem. Well, you know where I am if you ever need an ear."

I smile. "Thanks again for these." I raise the coffee and pastry in his direction.

He returns my smile, then turns away, heading back in the direction of his office.

After wolfing down my unexpected breakfast, I carry on pruning the wisteria. I'm itching to call the police station, but it's already ten o'clock and I still haven't got anything done this morning. I'll finish the pergola, check the tree stakes and ties, then break for lunch at one.

Despite the lack of customers, the next three hours pass by surprisingly quickly. We've only had a handful of shoppers through this morning, but it's to be expected on such a damp Monday. Give it a day or two and the place will be heaving with people buying Christmas decorations and winter plants to adorn their houses before their friends and families descend to celebrate with them. I try not to think about previous Christmases, when I was one of those customers getting excited about making my house beautiful and welcoming. These days, I watch it all going on around me. Detached. Like watching a TV programme about a strange and foreign society that I'm not a part of.

Sitting on a stool in the greenhouse, I'm waiting to be put through to one of the officers who took Harry away last night. The windows have steamed up in here, but through a hazy patch in the glass I can just make out two of my work colleagues eating their sandwiches on a bench at the far end of the nursery. Jez, the head gardener, and Carolyn who runs the shop. They're both pleasant enough, but I haven't really taken the time to get to know them in the nine months I've been working here. I guess I've been keeping myself to myself—I prefer it that way.

"Mrs. Markham?"

My heart thuds at the efficient-sounding female voice on the other end of the phone. "Yes," I reply. "I'm Tessa Markham."

"Hello, this is Detective Sergeant Abi Chibuzo. I came to your house last night after you called us."

"Hi."

"Do you have some more information for us?" she asks.

"Um, no, not really. I'm just calling to find out if Harry has been reunited with his family. You don't have to tell me the specifics, obviously, but I just wanted to—"

"I'm really sorry, but like we said yesterday, we can't give out any information relating to Harry at this time."

I knew deep down that they wouldn't be able to give me any news, but I'm still utterly disappointed.

"But," she continues, "I'm glad you called. We'd like you to come in to go over what happened yesterday. Can you come down to the station? We need to ask you a few more questions."

My heart thuds and my forehead grows hot. "You want me to come to the police station? When?"

"Is now convenient?"

I suppose if I have to speak to them, I'd rather get it out of the way now than have it hanging over me, but the thought fills me with dread. "Now? Um, yes, okay. I'm on my lunch break. How long will it take?"

"We can't say for sure. The station address is on the card we gave you."

The card rests on my knee, but I don't need to look at the address, I already know where it is. Just a short distance if I walk quickly.

I rise to my feet. "Okay. I can be there in ten, fifteen minutes."

"Great. Ask for me at the front desk," she says. "DS Chibuzo."

"Okay, thanks. Bye."

I gather up my bag and phone, and go to find Ben.

Moretti's was constructed around a pair of beautiful seventeenth-century semi-detached red-brick alms houses. Ben lives in one of them, and runs his business out of the other, which consists of a small café and shop downstairs, and his office and storerooms upstairs. I climb the stairs two at a time to find him sitting at his desk, squinting at a sheet of paper, his reading glasses perched on the end of his nose.

"I'm going to have to get a new prescription," he says without looking up. "These numbers are just a blur."

"Good excuse not to pay the bills," I quip.

"Hmm, I wish." He looks up and smiles, tossing the paper back onto his desk. "Everything okay?"

"I need to go out for lunch," I say, unwilling to tell him why. "Thing is, I might be a bit late back. But I can make up the time. Is that okay?"

"Sure, no problem. We're not exactly rushed off our feet."

"Thank you."

"It's fine." He gives me a smile and waves me away. "Go. Eat lunch. Have fun."

If only he knew.

Twenty minutes later, I'm sitting in an interview room with the same two officers who came to my house last night—Detective Sergeant Abi Chibuzo and Detective Constable Tim Marshall. It's all very official and serious, with a table and chairs, and a recording device. There's a plastic cup of water on the table in front of me. My hands are clammy and a pulse throbs behind my right ear.

"Tessa Markham," Chibuzo begins, "you are not under arrest, but you are being interviewed under suspicion of child abduction."

"What!" I cry. "Child abduction? You said you wanted to ask me a few questions, go over what happened yesterday. No one said anything about child abduction!" Am I dreaming? Is this some awful, awful nightmare? My mind has gone spongy and soft. They're both talking, but I can't seem to latch onto their words.

"Ms. Markham? Tessa? Are you okay?" Marshall asks.

I take a couple of deep breaths. "Are you going to arrest me?"

"No," Chibuzo replies. "Like I said, at this stage we're just interviewing you."

"But you said 'child abduction.' You think I took Harry?"

"We're trying to find out what happened," she says. "Are you okay to answer a few questions for us? You have the right to legal advice if you want it."

"Just a few questions?" I ask.

"Yes," Chibuzo replies.

I think about my option to take legal advice. If I say yes, I'll have to wait while they sort out a solicitor. But that will take ages, and I really need to get back to work. If I'm here too long, I'll have to explain to Ben why I'm late back. I've done nothing wrong, so I decide I don't need legal advice. I'll be fine.

"I'll answer your questions," I reply. "I don't want a solicitor."

"You're sure?" Chibuzo asks.

"Yes."

They go over the same questions they asked yesterday. Asking me what happened when I got home, and what Harry and I talked about. I recount the whole episode again, reliving yesterday evening. I hope they'll be finished soon. The clock is ticking; it's almost quarter to two already.

"Back in…" Chibuzo looks down at her notepad. "Back in 2015, on Saturday 24th October, you were found walking through Friary Park, pushing a pram containing three-month-old infant Toby Draper. His mother, Sandra Draper, had reported him missing twenty minutes earlier."

Her statement is like a punch to the gut. Chibuzo looks up. She and her colleague are both now staring directly at me, and I feel my cheeks flaming.

"Yes," I reply, my voice a croak. "Yes, but like I told the police at the time, it was a genuine misunderstanding."

"Would you like to tell us again what happened?" Chibuzo says.

No, I bloody would not like to tell you again what happened. The last thing I want to do right now is rake over all that painful ancient history.

"What do you remember about the incident?" Chibuzo asks.

I take a deep breath. "I was walking through the park and I noticed a pram at the edge of the woods. I left the path and went over to take a look. I saw a baby asleep in the pram. I looked around and couldn't see anyone else, so I thought I'd better take the pram with the baby in to the police station, which is where I was heading when the police car pulled up next to me."

I stop talking, and there's a long pause before anyone speaks.

"Did you have a mobile phone with you at the time?" DC Marshall asks like I knew he would, because this is exactly what the investigating officers asked me last time.

"Yes," I reply. "I did have my phone, but I thought it would be quicker to take the baby to the station myself."

"And did you not think it would have been better to call us anyway, in case someone was worried and looking for the baby?"

"In hindsight, yes, of course that would have been better. But I wasn't really thinking straight."

"Could you elaborate?" Chibuzo asks. "Why were you not thinking straight?"

I know exactly what they're getting at. "In August of that year..." My voice cracks, and so I clear my throat and start again. "In August of that year, my son...my three-year-old son died from acute lymphoblastic leukaemia. I was grieving at the time. I still am," I add.

"I'm very sorry for your loss," Chibuzo says, with a look of sympathy.

But her sympathy hasn't stopped her from bringing it all up again. From making me wade through the pain while they watch and listen. "It wasn't my first loss," I say. "Sam's twin sister Lily died at birth. So now both my babies are gone."

She nods. Marshall looks down at his shoes.

"But you already know all this," I say, staring into her clear brown eyes. "You must have it on your file."

She glances at the papers on the table. "It says here you were suffering from depression. Is that correct?"

"Yes," I reply through gritted teeth. *You'd be suffering from depression too, if your second child had just died.*

"I know this is hard," she persists, "but Mrs. Draper claimed that she turned her back for a second to deal with her toddler, who had run off into the trees. She said that when she turned back around, the pram was gone and she could see you walking quickly down the path with it. She said she yelled after you, but you didn't react. She said there was no way you couldn't have heard her unless you were deaf. She couldn't give chase, because her toddler was refusing to come to her. That's when she rang the police. Did you hear Mrs. Draper calling you?"

"No! I've been over this so many times with you. If I'd heard her calling out, of course I would have stopped and gone back. I wasn't charged with anything then, so why are you asking me about this again?"

"Mrs. Markham," Marshall says in a serious tone, "did you take Harry to your house yesterday?"

"Take him from where? No, I told you he was already in my house when I got home." The air is close in here, my eyes are itching and my body is hot. Too late, I realise I should have waited for a solicitor. "Are you accusing me of something?" I take a sip of water. It's tepid and does nothing to ease the tightness in my throat.

"No," Chibuzo says. "We're just trying to get to the facts. We're trying to determine how Harry ended up in your house last night."

"I've already told you. I'm not lying, if that's what you think. Why would I have called you if I'd taken him? And anyway, where are Harry's parents in all this? Ask them what happened. How did they let their son out of their sight? How did he end up inside my house? There's something strange going on here and it's nothing to do with me!"

"Please try not to get upset, Mrs. Markham... Tessa," Chibuzo says. "We're speaking to everyone involved."

"What about my husband, Scott? Are you talking to him? Or is it only me you've got a problem with?"

"We don't have a problem with you, we just want to find out if there's anything else you can tell us that might assist this investigation. And yes, we spoke to Scott Markham this morning."

My legs and hands are trembling. My breathing is too shallow. I think I'm about to have a panic attack. I remember what the doctor told me: take a deep breath and hold it for five, then exhale slowly. *Nothing will happen to you*, he said. *No matter how bad you feel, you won't die from a panic attack.* It doesn't feel that way at the moment.

"Are you all right, Tessa?" Chibuzo asks, her concerned voice sounding too far away.

I hold my hand out to stop her talking. I wish they would go, leave me to get myself together. "I'll be fine in a minute... panic attack..."

"Interview suspended at... fourteen ten."

CHAPTER FIVE

I probably shouldn't have come back to work, but I didn't want Ben to think I was taking advantage of his good nature. Besides, what would I do at home, other than think? And I really don't want to think about any of it. I aim the hosepipe into the empty plant pot and watch as the water fizzes and splashes, dislodging all the grime and muck.

Thank goodness I didn't succumb to a full-blown panic attack at the station. My breathing quickly came under control and I managed to pull myself together. Chibuzo stopped the interview and Marshall brought me sweet tea and biscuits. They were kind; they told me to go home and rest. Said that I was being "released under investigation" and that they would contact me if they needed to question me further.

Talking about that awful time brought everything boiling to the surface, but I've squashed the memories back down to a light simmer. I can breathe again. Just.

I turn off the hosepipe and stare into the recesses of the plant pot. It's clean enough. But I still have a stack of fifty more to wash out.

"Dodgy prawn sandwich for lunch?"

I glance up to see Ben's concerned face. "Hmm?"

"You look a bit green around the gills."

"You're full of compliments today," I retort.

"Sorry. Just being an observant boss, that's all. I need my staff fit and well." His eyes soften and he tilts his head to the side.

The last thing I need is more sympathy. "Thanks, I'm fine." Even *I* don't believe me.

"If you say so. Look, Tess, I need to talk to you."

God, I hope he's not going to fire me. He doesn't seem cross or annoyed, but you never can tell.

"Don't look so worried," he says. "It's just a business proposition."

I'm staring at him like an idiot. Not sure how to respond.

"Are you free after work this evening?" he continues. "To come for a drink? Nothing funny, I promise. Just something I'd like to talk to you about."

"Um, okay. Straight after work?"

"Yeah. I thought we could go to The Royal Oak, around the corner. I'll even buy you dinner on expenses if you like."

"Oh, that would be great." My stomach gurgles. What with my trip to the police station, I completely forgot to eat lunch. "What's it about, this business proposition?"

"I'd rather talk about it away from here, if that's okay," he replies.

"Uh, yeah, sure." But I wonder what he has to say to me that can't be discussed here at work. I guess I'm going to have to wait to find out.

The rest of the afternoon goes by in a blur. I don't even notice that it's already rolled around to six o'clock. Ben has to come and find me to tell me it's time to stop working. I probably look an absolute mess. Part of me wishes I'd had the chance to go home, shower and change. But then again, it's just Ben, and he sees me looking like crap every day.

I go to the bathroom to wash my hands and splash my face, then I grab my bag and wait while he locks up.

"Okay?" he asks as he slides the keys into his pocket.

I nod, wondering just how awkward this evening will turn out to be. Today has been emotionally draining, and I've never been good at small talk, so I hope he's not expecting witty conversation.

"Do you know The Royal Oak?" he asks as we walk down the road, side by side.

"I've been there a couple of times. It's nice." I remember going there with Scott a few years ago to meet friends for birthday drinks.

"They do a great lasagne," Ben says. "And that's high praise coming from an Italian."

I smile. We manage to chat easily during the short journey, and when we reach the pub, he holds the door open for me.

It's noisy, but the atmosphere is traditional and friendly. Dark-wood panelling lines the walls, and the lighting is warm and soft. Delicious cooking smells mingle with the scent of beer and furniture polish. A typical English pub.

Ben leads me past the bar, where he grabs a menu, and nods at one of the barmen, who greets him by name. We sit at a table by the window and he passes me the menu.

"You recommend the lasagne, right?" I say, without opening it. "I'll have that."

"Good choice. I'll go up and order. What do you want to drink?"

"Orange juice would be good. Thanks."

"No problem. Back in a minute."

While he's up at the bar, I glance around, taking in the mix of people. There are men in suits chatting, a group of women laughing, a few couples, and even some families with young kids, eating burgers or fish and chips with lots of ketchup. I look away quickly, a lump forming in my throat. But then, I think, I'd actually rather be here tonight surrounded by all this life than brooding at home on my own.

Ben soon returns and we clink our glasses and sip our drinks.

"The food will be about twenty minutes," he says.

"Great. I'm actually starving."

"Me too." They're playing some kind of eighties mix over the speakers, but it's not so loud that we can't hear each other.

"So, what was it you wanted to discuss?" I ask.

"Ah, yes. That. Look, I haven't told anyone else yet, and I'll need you to keep this between you and me for now—is that okay?"

"Sure." I shrug, starting to feel a little intrigued.

"Well, I've just had the go-ahead from the bank. Which means I can buy the tyre garage and car park behind Moretti's. I'm going to use the extra land to expand the business. I'll be adding a proper Italian restaurant and café, with an on-site deli. And I'm also going to be increasing the garden areas."

"Wow," I say. "That sounds incredible."

"It actually scares the hell out of me," he says with a smile that makes his eyes crinkle. "But I think I could end up making a success of it." He takes a sip from his pint.

I nod. "You'll do brilliantly, I'm sure."

"Hope so. You know, you're one of my best workers," he adds. "You're nearly always the first to arrive in the morning and the last to leave at night. You do over and above what's expected. I always feel like you're way too good for the job. I'm lucky to have you, Tess."

"Thanks," I say, a warm glow spreading through my chest, relieved that this doesn't sound like a prelude to getting fired. "It's nice to be appreciated. The job's perfect for me, I like the work." I don't tell him that working hard is my way of coping with the grinding emptiness. That if I didn't work to near exhaustion, I would have far too much time to think about my actual life.

"So, that brings me on to my proposal," he says. "Actually, it's *two* proposals."

I raise my eyebrows, waiting for him to elaborate.

"I know from your CV that you used to be a landscape architect."

"Ye-es, but that was quite a while ago."

"Only two and a half years," he says. "I'm sure it's still all up there." He taps his temple.

I chew my lip as my heart begins to pound. That was a different time in my life, a time I try not to dwell on. I was a completely different person back then.

"Thing is," he continues, "with your experience, I'd love to run my landscaping plans by you. Of course, I'd pay you the going rate, but I'd really value your professional opinion."

I nod. In theory, it should be something I'd enjoy. Something that I could do in my sleep. In fact, I really, truly do want to help Ben get the most out of his new venture. I've already had loads of ideas for his current layout. Ideas I've kept to myself, because it's not the place of a gardening assistant to tell her boss how she thinks he could improve his business. But now he's asking for my professional opinion, and I'm not sure I can cope with that kind of responsibility. In practice, my mind is fragile. Anything out of my carefully constructed routine could tip me over the edge, and I don't quite trust myself with this kind of change. I don't know if I ever will.

"You said you had two proposals for me," I say, avoiding an answer. "What's the other one?"

"So," he says, his dark eyes bright with enthusiasm. "Once I get started on the plans, it will take almost a year's worth of project management. Which means my attention's going to be taken away from the day-to-day running of the business. I'll need someone to manage the centre for me." He looks at me pointedly.

"Me? You want me to manage Moretti's?"

He nods. "I can increase your salary. Not quite double it, but almost. I can—"

"Whoa. Hang on, Ben." I take a breath and run a hand over my forehead. "I'm flattered, I really am, but—"

"Don't dismiss it. Not yet. Think about it. Please."

"What about Carolyn?" I say, thinking of my forty-one-year-old colleague who already manages the shop. "Won't she be put out to have me in charge? She's the one you should be asking, surely. And Jez won't want me telling him what to do."

"Jez won't mind as long as he has a free rein to tend the plants. And between you and me, Carolyn's lovely but she's scatty and nervy. Most days she's late. Her lunch hour lasts almost two hours, and she's always got some kind of family crisis going on. I couldn't trust her to run the place while I'm busy with the new plans. I like her, she's excellent with the customers, but I don't think she's up to the job. I don't even think she would want it."

I glance to my right to see a pretty dark-haired waitress hovering at our table.

"Two lasagnes," she says with a smile, putting our food in front of us. "How you doing, Ben?"

"Yeah, good, Molly. You?"

"Oh, you know. The usual."

"This is Tess. Tess, Molly."

Molly gives me the once-over. "Hi," she says with a smile that doesn't reach her eyes.

"Hello," I reply.

"Your mum and dad okay?" she asks Ben. "I miss them coming in."

"They're fine," he replies. "Loving being back in Italy. I'll say hello from you next time they call."

"Yeah, please. Give them my love." Molly stands there for a moment. It looks like she wants to carry on talking but can't think of what else to say.

"Well," Ben says, breaking the awkward silence. "Nice to see you. Take care."

"You too." She twists the bottom of her apron and totters back to the bar on her four-inch heels.

"Does she run the Ben Moretti fan club?" I ask.

"Ha, ha, very funny."

"Ex-girlfriend?"

"No! I used to come in here with my parents quite a lot. She's just being polite."

"Well, I think you're in there."

"And I think I'm changing the subject," he says, his cheeks flushing with embarrassment. "Let's eat."

"This is amazing," I say after my first forkful.

"Told you."

"Bring me here every night and I might just be persuaded to manage Moretti's for you."

"Really?" His eyes light up.

I realise I shouldn't have joked about it. Now he thinks I'm considering it. "Look, Ben, much as I'm flattered..."

His face falls.

"I have a lot of personal stuff going on in my life right now," I explain. "I really don't think I can commit to such a responsibility."

"Tess. I...I heard about what happened to you. To your children. I just want to say how sorry I am."

I put my fork down, suddenly not hungry any more. "How did you know?"

"Carolyn mentioned it quite a while ago."

Great. How does *she* know? She obviously listens to gossip and doesn't have a problem with spreading it, either. I realise I'm hurt by this. I always thought she and I got on pretty well, but then I picture her in the shop at work—she's always talking nineteen-to-the-dozen with the customers. I open my mouth to say something cutting about gossipy colleagues, but Ben continues.

"She meant it kindly, Tess."

"How the hell does she know my business?"

"Apparently she's friendly with your mother-in-law."

I'm pretty sure my mother-in-law thinks I have defective genes. Amanda Markham with her four grown-up healthy children. Scott is the youngest, with three older sisters—the longed-for son.

"Carolyn thought we should know what you'd been through, so we wouldn't say anything inappropriate."

I'm not happy that they all know my business, not happy at all. But I suppose at least it's saved me having to explain stuff.

"So," he says, "I just want you to realise that I know your situation and I'd be understanding if you had ... difficult days."

"Thank you," I mumble.

"I can't pretend to know what you've been through, Tess. The thought of it is, well, it's terrible. I just think it might be good for you, you know, to get stuck into something like this."

I'm touched. Most people can't handle bringing the subject of my children up. Not only is he unafraid to talk about it, he also thinks I'm strong enough to cope with more responsibility.

"I was at the police station today," I blurt out without thinking.

He's just about to take a sip of beer, but stops at my words, shutting his mouth and setting his glass back on the table.

"That's where I was at lunchtime," I continue.

"Why were you there, if you don't mind me asking? I mean, you don't have to tell me, but..."

"No, it's okay. It's a bit of a weird story, though." I give a nervous laugh.

"Go on." He takes a sip from his drink and I take a gulp of mine, wishing I'd had something stronger than orange juice.

I tell him about last night. About Harry. It all comes tumbling out. Not in the stilted way it did at the police station, where my every word was being analysed, but more in an unburdening kind of way. I can tell from Ben's expression that he's surprised and sympathetic and understanding. There's no judgement. No suspicion.

"Wow, Tess. That's..."

"I know, right. It's weird."

"Your head must be spinning. And then I go and add to all your stress with my perfectly timed business proposal." He rolls his eyes.

"You didn't know. And maybe you're right. Maybe it is what I need to take my mind off everything. Just...give me some time to think about it, if you can."

"Sure, of course. Take all the time you need. Well, maybe not *all* the time. I'd probably need to know by the New Year, if that's okay."

I nod, suddenly feeling a lot lighter.

"Now eat," he says.

"Yes, Boss."

We spend another hour or so finishing our meal and chatting about more trivial things like books we've read, funny customers at work and what our worst habits are. Ben is surprisingly good company, easy to talk to. I wonder why I never noticed that before. But soon the events of the past twenty-four hours begin catching up with me. I'm exhausted. Ben insists I take the following day off work. I protest, but he won't take no for an answer, so I finally acquiesce. Hopefully I can just spend the whole day sleeping.

It's not even nine o'clock when I finally stagger through my front door, almost asleep on my feet, but it feels far later. I should really just crawl into bed right now, but there's still one more thing I have to do.

I take my phone with me into the lounge and curl up in the corner of the sofa, tucking my feet beneath me. I'm calling Scott to find out how he got on at the police station this morning. I know I won't sleep until I've spoken to him. Perhaps, by some miracle, he was able to find out what's happened to Harry.

His phone rings three times, but I think I must have pressed the wrong contact button, because a woman answers. I'm so surprised, I don't reply straight away.

"Hello?" she says. "Hello?"

"Hi," I say. "I think I must have called you by mistake. I meant to call Scott. Who's this?"

There's a pause at the other end of the line.

"Hello? Are you still there?" I'm about to hang up and try again, but then she says, "Tessa?"

"Yes. Who's this? Is this Scott's phone?"

"Yes." She sounds hesitant, like she's not sure if it is his phone or not.

"Can you put him on, please?"

"He's...not available at the moment." Her voice is young-sounding.

"Not available? What do you mean? Is he still at work? In a meeting?"

"He's in the shower."

I let her words sink in. A woman has answered Scott's phone

while he's in the shower. I freeze for a moment, feel the blood draining from my face.

"I'm sorry," she says, not sounding sorry at all. "I know this must come as a surprise, but I'm Scott's girlfriend. He really should've told you already."

Scott has a girlfriend. I can still taste the lasagne and orange juice in my mouth. I don't know what to say.

"Tessa? Are you there?"

"Yes. It's okay, I'll speak to him another time."

"The thing is—"

But I don't wait to hear what *the thing is*. I end the call, my thumb pressing down on the icon with a beep. Then I turn off my phone.

CHAPTER SIX

I came home last night ready to crawl into bed, to give myself over to blissful sleep. And then I spoke to *her*.

Scott has a girlfriend. A *girlfriend*. My Scott. The father of our dead children.

I lay in bed last night, my eyes closed, willing myself to sleep. To find oblivion. But my mind refused to be still. Images of them together. Wondering what she's like. How old is she? Is she beautiful? How did they meet? Where? When? Why didn't he tell me about her? I didn't even ask her name. Is she really his girlfriend, or is she just a fling? Do they laugh together? I try to think back to the last time Scott and I laughed. It's not good that I have to think so hard about it; that I can't recall a time in recent years. I know we used to laugh once upon a time. Great belly laughs where we could hardly breathe. Where I had to cry out for him to stop it because I would pee my pants.

How could he do this to me? I know we're not living together any more, I know we're "separated." But it's *Scott*. Me and Scott. I always assumed we'd get back together again. We were together for so long, I can barely remember a life before him. And so I lay in bed, first on one side, then the other, trying to slow my breathing, to clear my mind of all thoughts. I conjured images of empty skies and clear blue lakes; of happy, calm moments in my life. But all those good times were with him. And now they're tainted by the knowledge of *her*.

Every so often, I flicked on the light and checked the time— 1 a.m., 2:20 a.m., 2:35 a.m. I attempted to read my book. I made warm milk. Three a.m. I listened to soothing voices on Radio 4. But here I am in bed at seven bloody thirty, still wide awake, my brain still rattling along like a demented freight train.

What should I do? What *can* I do? No wonder he was annoyed when I called him on Sunday night. I was taking him away from his *floozy*. What kind of a word is that? It sounds like something from the 1970s, not a word I'd ever use. But I can't bring myself to refer to her as his girlfriend. And the word *slut* makes me sound so bitter.

Who am I now? Not a wife? Not a mother? I have no ambition, no place or real purpose. I screw my eyes shut tighter and slide down further underneath the duvet.

The trouble is, after Sam died, so did our marriage. Scott tried to make it work, but I was so consumed by grief, I couldn't acknowledge that he was grieving too. I had no emotional room to think about him or his needs. And then, when he told me he was leaving—not even a year after we lost Sam—I couldn't believe it. I assumed it was temporary. We never made the split official. Even now, a year and a half after he left, I still believe he will come back. Am I wrong? Are we really over?

Dull morning light drifts in from behind the curtains. Car doors slam beyond the window. Children's voices, high and excitable as they walk to school in clusters. I fling back the duvet, giving up the notion of getting any sleep. I have the day off, I should do something.

I go through my morning ablutions on autopilot, slinging on a jersey tracksuit, grabbing a bowl of cornflakes and taking it into the lounge. I hate the sound of other people chewing; it sets my teeth on edge. Makes me gag. I think there's a name for this—it's like a phobia or something. So I'm always careful to eat quietly. But now, sitting alone on the sofa, I chew my cornflakes as loudly as I possibly can. A defiant crunch, crunch, crunch that makes me wonder if I might be losing my mind.

The phone rings, breaking into my rebellious breakfast. It's the landline, which I usually ignore. But what if it's Scott? Or the police? I dump my bowl on the coffee table and scramble into the hall. A glance at the screen tells me it's a withheld number, but I pick it up anyway, prepared to hang up at the first sign of a sales pitch.

"Hello. Is that Tessa Markham?" A woman's voice. Hesitant. A foreign accent. Maybe Spanish.

I'm poised to end the call. This woman could have got my name from anywhere.

"Hello," I bark. "Yes, this is Tessa."

"I'm sorry," she replies. "Sorry, I should not have called."

And then there's nothing but the dial tone. The woman has hung up.

That didn't sound like a telemarketer. Telemarketers don't apologise, and they don't hang up. Even though the call was withheld, I try calling 1471 to see if there's a number I can ring her back on, but it's no good. *Damn*. What if she was something to do with Harry? Maybe she'll call again. I shouldn't have been so abrupt. Shouldn't have snapped at her. I stare at the phone, willing it to ring, but it sits on the hall table stubbornly mute.

I return to my breakfast in the lounge, taking the phone handset with me. Just in case. Less than one minute later, it rings once more. This time I answer it with a gentle "Hello?"

"Tess? Why aren't you answering your mobile?"

It's Scott. I remember I still haven't switched my mobile phone on this morning. My heart hammers in my chest. Does he know I spoke to his floozy last night? Did she tell him about our brief conversation?

"Hi, Scott."

"Sorry to call so early. Are you free tonight?"

Of course I am. I'm free every sodding night. "Um, yeah. I think so."

"Great. Can we meet? Say, seven o'clock at that tapas place near my work?"

"Okay. Why do you want—"

"Sorry, I'm a bit late for work right now. Chat later, yeah?"

"Sure. See you later."

Well, that's something new. Scott never rings me these days. He wants to talk. Talk about what? About *her*? No. This floozy of his can't be serious or he would have told me about her before now. I need to act. Do something about it. Sort myself out. I march out to the hallway and glare at myself in the mirror. I look an absolute state. I mean, I'm thirty-six years old, for Christ's sake. Today I look double that.

If I'm going to meet Scott tonight, I need him to remember the old me. The real me. I'm in here somewhere, aren't I? I haven't quite faded away. Not yet.

Scott and I first met at a friend of a friend's birthday party, and afterwards he told me he'd noticed me straight away. That I was the only one he wanted to speak to that night, but that it took him ages to pluck up the courage to approach me. When we finally did get talking, we hit it off immediately. I can't remember exactly what we spoke about, but I do remember we laughed a lot. He found us a quiet spot in the garden in a dilapidated summer house. We sat on the floor on sun-lounger cushions, drinking beer and eating peanuts. The girl whose party it was had to kick us out in the early hours of the morning. Scott walked me home and we kissed goodnight. After that, we became inseparable. Our friends called us the perfect couple.

If I could just get him to remember what we once had. If he could see that I'm trying to move past our tragedy. Not to forget, of course not. Never to forget. But to… accept? To not waste the rest of my life mourning. To make my days count for something.

That's it, I'm calling Max.

Three hours later, I'm sitting in a comfy swivel chair, cringing before a huge, crystal-clear mirror, spotlights highlighting every crease, splotch and dark circle, every grey root and split end. The image is not pretty.

"Don't mean to be rude, honey," Max says, his hands on his bony hips, "but that hair of yours looks like it's been in a fight with a Brillo pad. We need to lop at least two inches off, preferably more. What would you think about a bob?"

"I'm a gardener, Max. A bob's no good, I need to be able to tie my hair back."

"God!" He grabs my left hand and stares at it in horror.

I glance down to where he's looking, at the red, chapped skin, the split nails.

"What have you been doing?" he cries.

"Told you, I'm a gardener," I reply. "The hands are beyond repair. Concentrate on the hair, if you please. I've missed you, Maxie," I add. I haven't bantered with anyone like this in months.

"I should think so. You *need* me in your life, Tess. This is a disaster area. If you'd left it any later, we'd have needed emergency aid flown in." He turns to one of the juniors. "Bring Ms. Markham a glass of Prosecco."

"What?" I say, my eyes widening. "No. Max, it's only ten thirty, far too early for me."

"Pfft. Normally, I would agree. But in your case, a small pick-me-up is just what you need."

"Go on then, but at least put some orange juice in it."

"Vitamin C, good idea."

Several hours later, I leave the salon with gleaming honey-blonde waves that just skim my shoulders. I feel admiring eyes on me as I step out onto the pavement, and it's not an entirely awful feeling. A woman with dark brown hair catches my eye and I give her a small smile. She instantly lowers her head and scuttles away. I shrug and head towards the Tube station. I'm going into town to buy a new outfit for tonight—none of my old clothes fit me any more.

In Monsoon, I grab a size twelve skirt. I've lost a bit of weight over the past year; all my existing clothes are hanging off me. It's a black pencil skirt with jade-green embroidered flowers. I figure it will look great with black boots and a polo neck. But when I slide it up and over my hips, it's massive. I check the label. Yes, definitely a size twelve. I ask the assistant to grab me a size ten. She looks me up and down and suggests the eight. I haven't been a size eight since my twenties. Sure enough, it fits perfectly, which means I'm about three sizes smaller than I used to be. I guess what with my anxiety, lack of appetite, and skipped meals, I've shed a few pounds without realising.

While I'm queuing to pay, my back tingles with a strange sensation. I turn around to see a woman staring at me. I return the stare and realise it's the same dark-haired woman from outside the hairdresser's earlier. She looks my age, maybe a little older. Did she follow me here?

"Excuse me, are you next?" I turn to see that the shop assistant is speaking to me.

"Sorry, can you hang on a second?" I ask, dumping the skirt on the counter. I turn around again, but the woman has vanished. My eyes roam the shop. She must have left. "I'll be back in five minutes," I call to the assistant, and make my way through the clothes racks, staring left and right. The woman was quite small, and could easily be concealing herself behind one of the rails. I reach the exit and glance up and down the crowded street, my heart pounding. It's no use—I'll never spot her among all these people.

But who is she? I'm certain she's something to do with Harry. She could even be the same person who hung up on me this morning. I pray she gets back in touch. And if she shows up again, I'll make sure I don't let her get away until she explains exactly who she is and why on earth she's so interested in me.

CHAPTER SEVEN

Right on time, I smooth down my new skirt and open the door to the tapas bar where I'm meeting Scott. A wave of warmth, lights and chatter hits me as I walk inside. This is the second night in a row I've been out after work. Not like me at all.

I scan the busy tables, but I don't see him.

A twenty-something waiter in a black T-shirt and dark jeans comes over to where I'm standing. "Would you like a table? There's a one-hour wait at the moment. Or you can sit at the bar…"

"I'm meeting someone," I say. "I think he's booked a table under the name Markham."

He glances down at the clipboard in his hand. "For 7 p.m.?"

"Yep."

"This way." He leads me over to a booth near the back. I catch my breath. Scott is already there, his back to me, a bottle of beer on the table in front of him.

"Can I get you a drink?" the waiter asks.

"Lime and soda, please." I'd love a proper drink, but I want to keep a clear head. This evening is too important for me to screw up. I blow out a breath and then inhale. I can do this, I can win back my husband, I know I can. Images of the two of us holding hands. Him leading us back to our house, his floozy forgotten. Us tumbling onto the bed. Laughing. Crying. So happy to be together again, back where we belong.

"Tess." Scott stands up and does a double-take. "Wow, you look incredible."

I try not to show how insanely pleased I am that he's noticed my makeover.

"I mean, honestly, Tess. You look so beautiful." He leans in to kiss me on the cheek. I kiss him back, savouring the moment, and we sit down facing one another.

"I haven't been here for ages," I say. "Do they still do those garlic mushrooms?"

"Yeah. And those little spicy potatoes you like."

"Yum. Definitely going to have some of those." I don't want to jinx it, but this is already feeling just like old times. The waiter returns with my lime and soda. "Actually, could I have a glass of dry white wine as well?" I suddenly feel like celebrating.

"Sure," the waiter replies, placing my soft drink in front of me.

Scott gives him our food order, already knowing what I want, and the waiter disappears, leaving us alone. Back home, I prepared exactly what I wanted to say. I wasn't going to mention Harry or the police station, this evening was just going to be about the two of us. But now I'm here, I feel a little shy. I'm not sure how to broach the subject of *us*.

"How's work?" Scott asks. "You coping okay?"

"It's good. Actually, my boss offered me a promotion."

"That's brilliant, Tess." He smiles. "I have to say, I was nervous about meeting up with you tonight," he adds.

"Nervous?" My heart flip-flops. Has he been anticipating tonight as much as I have?

"I wasn't sure what frame of mind you'd be in," he explains. "But I can see you've really turned a corner since Sunday. It's like you're back to being the old Tess again. I'm so happy for you."

My heart swells. The waiter has returned with my wine, and

I take a long sip, revelling in the burn at the back of my throat, and the instant head rush.

"Are you going to take the promotion?" Scott asks.

"Not sure yet." I pluck an olive from the terracotta bowl in the centre of the table and pop it in my mouth.

"What does it involve? More money, I hope." He grins.

"Ben wants me to manage Moretti's while he concentrates on expanding the business. Plus, he's asked me to consult on his new landscape designs."

"That's incredible," Scott says, shaking his head. "Surely it's a no-brainer? You've got to do it."

"You think so? It's quite a responsibility. I'm nervous about saying yes in case I cock it up."

"You won't cock it up, you could do that job in your sleep. And anyway, you won't know until you try. Look, Tessa, you deserve something good after all you've been through."

"You too," I say. "You deserve good things too."

"Thank you." He gives me a smile. "Actually, that's sort of why I asked you to come here tonight."

I hold my breath, unable to temper my hopefulness. Trying not to grin at him like a love-struck idiot.

"Ellie told me she spoke to you," he continues. "She said you rang last night while I was in the shower." He shakes his head. "I didn't want you to find out about her like that. I'm sorry. I told her it wasn't her place to speak to you. I wasn't at all happy that she shocked you like that."

So, the floozy's name is Ellie. "Don't worry about it," I say, eager for him to understand that I won't hold a grudge. "It's okay. I don't care about what's gone on in the past, whether you've been seeing someone else. We were separated. I was all over the place, not in any state to give our relationship the attention it deserved. We can move on from all that. You honestly don't have to explain."

"You don't know how good that makes me feel," Scott says, leaning back in his seat, his shoulders relaxing. "Tell you the truth, I've kind of been dreading this evening. Coming here and explaining to you about Ellie, how we feel about one another. I'm really pleased you understand. And I really hope we can be friends."

"Friends?" I repeat, the word lying heavy on my tongue, the shock of realisation creeping through my body. "You mean you and me?"

"Yes, of course." Scott confirms it with a puzzled smile. "It would be a real shame to go our separate ways after everything we've been through. And you'll love Ellie, I promise you. Probably end up really good mates."

His voice fades in and out as I try to process what he's telling me. That Ellie isn't a fling, she's something more. I am to be relegated to Scott's history. An ex. And he wants us to be all cosy and nice about it. He thinks I'm here to give him my blessing, to agree to be friends.

"You and her?" I whisper. "You're actually together? And it's serious?" I give a disbelieving smile that could easily descend into a sneer.

Scott bites his lip and shifts in his seat. He signals to a passing waitress to get him another bottle of beer. "Yes. I thought you realised, I thought you were wishing me well."

My mouth drops open and my chest clenches with a disappointment so crushing I can barely breathe.

"I didn't want to tell you before," he says, "because I didn't want to hurt you. But when Ellie answered my phone last night...well, I felt I had to come and explain. And you're looking so composed and together, I thought you were okay with it."

I'm too stunned to speak, my mind and body growing numb, like I've just been given some kind of paralysis drug.

"We met over a year ago at my office Christmas party," he explains hesitantly. "It didn't start off serious, but...Tessa, I'm sorry, it really is serious now. We're in love."

I think he takes my silence as an indication for him to go on. To continue explaining. But really, I just wish he would stop. I wish he would shut up. I don't want to hear about him and Ellie. About their wonderful relationship and how in love they are. I take a deep gulp of wine, welcoming its ruinous effect on my already screwed-up emotions.

"I came here hoping we would get back together." I manage to speak, but my voice is so quiet that Scott has to lean in closer to hear me. "I was going to ask you to give our marriage another go. I still love you, Scott. Don't you get it?"

But he shakes his head as though he can shake away my words. Words he doesn't want to hear. "There's something else," he says, trying to hold my gaze but ultimately letting it drop, staring instead at his empty beer bottle. "Tessa, I'm sorry," he continues, his eyes still downcast. "Ellie is pregnant."

I reel back in my seat as though I've been stabbed.

"I'm sorry," he repeats, looking up at me now. "I'm so, so sorry. It wasn't planned."

Not by *you*, maybe. The poisonous thought flashes through my mind. He's telling me this thing. He's only sitting a couple of feet away from me, but already he's moving further and further from the man I know. The man I *knew*.

"Are you okay, Tess?"

"No," I say. "No, Scott. I'm pretty fucking far from okay, can't you tell?"

His mouth falls open.

Scott's face, once so familiar, is like a stranger's. His generous mouth, strong nose; the light brown eyes that were once so kind. That gazed at me with love and desire. Now their softness is for someone else. Instead he feels...what? Pity? Frustration? I'm an inconvenience, a loose end. I can see it in his eyes—he can't wait to leave here. To have got this out of the way. Done. Finished. All neatly tied up.

We tried, Scott and I, we tried to have another child. It was something he wanted, but to me it felt like a betrayal. Like I was blotting out our dead children's memory. Replacing them. Scott said it could help us heal, that we could pour all our love into a new family. Make new memories to staunch the wounds. Anyway, for whatever reason, it never happened, and he didn't stick around long enough to see it through.

I can't breathe. Can't be in this place, which is suddenly so loud and cheerful. Raucous laughter and grinning faces everywhere. And worst of all, Scott's unwavering pity. I rise to my feet and glance around for the exit, disorientated, losing my bearings for a moment. Scott is having another child. He is in love with someone else. He's leaving me behind.

I see now that I'm no good any more. It's laughable that I believed a new haircut and a sexy skirt would win him back. I'm damaged. Useless. This isn't self-pity, it's reality. It's true. How can I blame him? I let out a loud sob, then turn and flee.

"Tessa, wait! We need to talk about this!"

But I can't bear to be around him any longer, I need to get out of here. I tug at the throat of my polo neck. It's suffocating. Hot. Itchy. Images of him and the woman on the phone flood my brain. I don't know what she looks like, but I bet she's pretty. Ellie. I already loathe her. For the life she will have. For the life that should have been mine.

I lurch out of the building. Scott won't follow me until he's paid the bill, he's too conscientious like that. Something that makes me so mad right now I could scream. Well, I won't be here waiting for him to apologise again. I won't hang around to give him the chance to ease his conscience. I run down the street, eyes scanning the road for a taxi. It only takes me a few seconds to spot an orange light up ahead. I stick out my hand and plead with my eyes. The cab pulls over and I manage to get myself together enough to give him my address. "Fourteen, Weybridge Road, N11."

He nods and I climb into the back seat.

"Tessa!" Scott calls out from behind me.

But I don't turn around. "Go! Now, please," I beg the driver. "He's coming. I don't want him to..."

The driver puts his foot on the accelerator and pulls away. I hope he won't feel the need to talk to me.

"You okay, love?" he calls out from the front.

I catch his eye in the rear-view mirror, nod and look away. He doesn't press me any further.

Scott and Ellie. Ellie and Scott. Scott and Ellie Markham. They'll get married, won't they? Of course they will. He'll divorce me. I'll have to change my name back. It'll be like the four of us never existed. Erased from his life. They'll be married and have a beautiful little family, and everyone will say how lovely it is for Scott. That after everything he's been through, he's managed to find a second chance at happiness. And then they'll whisper: but it's such a shame about his ex—what was her name? Tessa, yes, that's it. Such a shame. She still lives on her own, never got over it. You don't get over these things, do you?

I can't lose it. Not yet, not here in this stranger's taxi. I press my fist to my mouth. I must keep it all inside until I get home. Look out of the window. Look at the shopfronts, at the bars and restaurants, at all the happy people. Don't think. Don't think about Scott. About Scott and Ellie and their beautiful new baby.

It's a twenty-minute cab ride. I can't afford it—especially

after that ridiculous waste of money on my hair and new clothes—but there's no way I could have handled being on the bus with other people, and it would have taken me at least two hours to walk it.

I try to let my mind go blank. To dampen down the crushing disappointment. The sense of betrayal and humiliation. My mind is spinning. I can't switch it off. The rational part of my brain reminds me that we split up over a year ago. Scott has no duty to look out for me any more. But why keep the news about Ellie from me for so long? All this time, when I was calling him and chatting with him—thinking we were still in it together—all this time and he was already pulling away from me, humouring me. Poor, stupid, annoying Tessa.

"Nearly there now, love. Weybridge Road, right?"

"Yes, please," I call back, my voice not sounding like my own.

He turns off the main street into my road, and my heart sinks a little further, if that's even possible. I wish I could run away—I don't want to be here, I don't want to face my thoughts alone.

"What's all this?" the cab driver says. He slows down, but we're still a few houses away from my own.

"It's a bit further along."

"I know, love. But take a look at that lot. You got One Direction playing in your house tonight? Is Her Majesty paying you a visit?"

I lean forward and stare through the windscreen to see a crowd of people up ahead, spilling out across the pavement and into the road itself. "What's going on?" I ask.

"No idea."

We cruise down the road at a snail's pace, getting closer and closer to the hold-up. There must be at least thirty people crowded outside my house. As we approach, I start to get a very bad feeling. The throng have turned to stare at the taxi. There are lights in the road. Cameras. Microphones.

"Journalists," my driver says. "You haven't killed anyone, have you?"

"Shit," I mutter.

"Are they here for you, love?"

We've pulled up outside my house now, and the taxi is attracting journalists like iron filings to a magnet. Faces peer through the glass at me, cameras fire off rounds, and I try to shield my tear-streaked face with my bag.

"Got anywhere else you can go?" the driver asks. "I wouldn't recommend getting out."

Muted voices fly at me through the glass.

"Tessa! Can you tell us about the boy?"

"Did you abduct him?"

"Tessa, do you want to tell us your side of the story?"

They must be talking about Harry. But how do they know? Why are they here? There's nowhere else I can go. Scott's place is obviously out of the question. Work will be locked up, and anyway, I can't burden Ben with all of this. My parents passed away years ago, and I have no siblings, no close friends—I pushed them all away after I lost Sam. I can't show up on any of their doorsteps now with yet more troubles.

"How much do I owe you?" I ask the cabbie.

"Twenty-seven pounds, love."

I try not to flinch at the expense and hand him a twenty and a ten. "Keep the change," I say recklessly.

"Cheers. I don't think you should go out there, they look like a pack of wolves."

"I'll be fine," I say, not believing it.

"Suit yourself. I'll wait here, make sure you get through your front door okay."

"Thanks." I nod, square my shoulders and open the cab door. But I'm not prepared for the sheer force of humanity around me. The noise, the lights...It's overwhelming, and it's all I can do to stop my knees buckling. They're so close I can almost feel their breath on my face as I try desperately to avoid eye contact.

I keep moving straight ahead, and open my gate with shaking hands. Thank God they don't follow me into my front garden. Instead they bark out their questions and take photos of my back while I rush along the short path to the door.

I should have got my keys out when I was safely in the taxi. Now, I'm having to stand on the doorstep and fumble around in my bag while listening to their staccato shouts and cries from the pavement. After what seems like an eternity, but can only be a few seconds, I pull out my keys, slot the right one into the lock and almost fall into the hall, slamming the door behind me, my heart thumping with fear and confusion.

What the hell just happened?

CHAPTER EIGHT

My mind is still reeling with Scott's revelation, but how can I even process it with all those people outside my house? My brain can't cope with everything that's being thrown at it. This fresh crisis has sent my pulse into overdrive and my guts swirling. I don't dare switch on any of the lights in case the press outside can see in.

The answerphone flashes on the hall table, its angry red light a warning of danger. I press the message button and it informs me I have forty-one messages. *Forty-one.* I take a deep breath and press to listen. The first one is from a national newspaper journalist asking me to call her. The next message is from another paper. After that it's a call from the local TV news. I listen to two more similar messages and then press the stop button. The answerphone still flashes. I place my finger over the light so I can't see it. Just knowing about all those messages— all those people trying to pressure me to speak to them—makes my head swim. Most of them are probably from the journalists who are at this moment standing right outside my house. How long are they going to stay there? All night? Surely not.

The landline rings. I ignore it. Then I have a better idea—I crouch down, scrabble about at the back of the hall table until I find the phone line, and yank it out of the wall. The ringing stops. Good.

I straighten up and try not to think about all those people out there. Circling. Waiting. Even inside my house, I feel exposed, vulnerable, no longer safe. I hitch my skirt up, drop to my knees and crawl into the lounge towards the window—the street lamp outside giving me enough light to see by. I pull each of the shutter cords until the blinds close up as tight as they will go. I crawl into the dining room/office—a stale and musty room I never use any more—and close the blinds in here, too. Lastly, I straighten up, get to my feet and head into the kitchen at the back of the house, taking care of the last of the downstairs blinds. There are still small gaps in the slats, though. I wish I had heavy curtains instead. Even with the windows covered, there's no way I'll feel secure enough to put the lights on.

In the dark, I collapse onto a chair at the kitchen table, afraid to go back into the sitting room at the front of the house. Should I call the police? Would they even do anything? It's quiet. Only the hum of the fridge and the sound of my ragged breathing. I cower in my seat like a cornered fox in a hole, waiting to be torn apart by the hounds. At least they can't get in.

With violently shaking hands, I turn on my mobile. I realise my default reaction is to call Scott. But I can't do it. Not after what he told me this evening. His devastating revelation seems like days ago. No, right now I need to find out exactly what the media are saying about me. They've obviously found out about Harry, but why is it such a big story? What have they been told, and who told them?

I open Google on my phone and type in my own name. As the search results begin to populate, my body goes cold. My name is showing up in a list of headlines that fill the whole screen. They even have a photo of me, taken before my new haircut but still recent. It must have been taken yesterday, because I'm wearing my new work fleece. This is unreal. I can't

believe I'm in all the newspapers. I tap the result at the top of
the list and wait for the page to open.

I scan the story. They're saying I abducted a five-year-old boy.
Okay, they're not actually saying I did it, but they're asking the
question: "Did Tessa Markham abduct a five-year-old boy?"

No, I bloody did not.

Again I wonder how they found out about Harry. Could
someone at the police station have said something? No...Of
course, it's so obvious. I suddenly realise who it was.

Carly.

My snooping neighbour. It had to be. Who else saw Harry?
No one. But how did she find out about the rest? Well, I hope
she got a nice juicy payout on the back of my misery. What a
bitch.

I click on another image. This time it's of a journalist with a
microphone. The video starts up. She's standing on my street!
Pointing to my front door, asking if the woman who lives
here is a serial child abductor. Oh God, she's talking about
when I found the baby in the pram. They're interviewing the
child's mother. She's there with the reporter, outside my house,
damning me. Saying how it was a travesty that I wasn't found
guilty back then. They're making me sound so terrible, like I'm
guilty of these heinous things. But I'm not. I'm not. Am I?

"*It's been two days, and the child has not yet been reunited with
his family. No one knows where he came from or how he ended up
with Tessa Markham. Perhaps there are more questions that need
to be asked.*"

I click on another image, of a local newsreader in a studio.
He's talking about my past, about my dead children. Saying
that soon after Sam died, I was suspected of child abduction,
but no charges were ever brought. Why haven't they mentioned
that it was me and Scott who called the police on Sunday? I

mean, would I have called the authorities if I'd abducted Harry, if I meant to keep him?

I can't bear to watch any more. To have it all raked over yet again. To have them speculate over the worst thing that can happen to a mother. Why am I being forced to confront all this again? Won't my past ever leave me alone?

My mobile judders in my hand, making me almost lose my grip on it. Don't tell me the press have got hold of this phone number too. But now I see it's Moretti's number. It must be Ben calling, he must have seen the news. He's probably calling to fire me. I guess I can kiss goodbye to that promotion, whether I wanted it or not. I can't face talking to him. Not now.

Ten seconds later, my phone pings, telling me I have a voice message. I sigh. May as well see if I still have a job to go to tomorrow.

"Tessa, it's Ben. Please call me when you get this message. Look, I've seen the news. I'm worried about you. The press are being a bunch of jerks. Try and ignore them if you can. I can come over if you need some moral support."

My throat tightens at his kindness. I can't believe he's seen all that crap on the news and still thinks I'm a decent human being. My phone rings again: it's Ben calling back. This time I answer.

"Hello." My voice sounds small, pathetic.

"Tessa, I just left you a message. Are you okay?"

"Not really."

"Shall I come round?"

"Better not." I manage a grim laugh. "I've got half of Fleet Street outside my house."

"Shit. I can still come over, though. I don't care about that lot."

"I really appreciate you calling, Ben. I can't tell you how

much I…" My voice breaks and I take a breath. "You didn't have to do that."

"Of course I did. I wanted to check you were all right. I need you to know that I'm on your side, okay?"

Now he's done it. I wish he would stop being quite so lovely. I don't think I'm going to be able to answer him without crying.

"Tess? You still there?"

"Yes," I squeak.

"That's it, I'm coming over."

"No!" I take a breath. "No, no, I'm fine, honestly. I should probably just go to bed and hope they've lost interest by tomorrow."

"You don't have to come to work, take as much time off as you need."

"Thank you, but at this point, work is all I have." It comes out sounding bitter, so I add a fake laugh. "I will come in, if that's okay."

"Of course. But only if you're sure."

"Hundred per cent," I reply, hot tears sliding down my cheeks.

"Okay, I'll see you tomorrow. But call me if you need anything. I mean it."

"I will. Thank you, it means a lot…to know someone's on my side. They've twisted everything, you know."

"I can imagine," he says softly.

"Okay, well, see you, Ben."

"Bye, Tess."

I end the call reluctantly. For a brief few moments I don't feel quite as hopeless. But I have to face the fact that, despite Ben's kind words, I am truly alone in this. Dreading the night ahead, I shuffle over to the sink, pour myself a glass of water and climb the stairs.

Will this nightmare never end?

CHAPTER NINE

I wake before my alarm clock. Somehow I slept all the way through last night. How, I have no idea. I dreamt of whimpering babies and screaming journalists and—oddly— people with sharks' faces. But at least I slept. And now the memory of yesterday comes crashing into my head. Scott, Ellie, their baby, the media...Are the police going to want to speak to me again? Surely after everything the press are saying, they will be under pressure to find out who Harry is, where he came from. And, most importantly, how he ended up in my kitchen.

The alarm clock goes off, derailing my thoughts. Probably a good thing. There's no point speculating. I decide the best thing for me right now is to get up, get dressed, go to work and try not to think too much. I know that's wishful thinking, but I can try. At least Ben's on my side. I wonder if Scott has seen the news, if there are any journalists camped outside *his* flat. Nice of him to call and see how I'm doing.

I slide out of bed and tiptoe over to the window. Twitch back a corner of the curtain and peer down into the damp, dark morning. My whole body gives a little jolt of fear when I see the journalists are still out there, laughing, chatting. Uncaring about how their lust for gossip impacts on my life. Did they stay out there all night, or have they regrouped this morning?

My stomach lurches at the thought of going outside and

having to face them. I've done nothing wrong, so why should I let them intimidate me? But it's not just them, is it? They've been taking pictures, filming, writing stuff about me, so now everyone in the country knows about my past and will start drawing conclusions about what I have or haven't done. Old friends and colleagues will be shaking their heads, pitying me or hating me for what they think I've become. Assuming I'm guilty before I've had a chance to prove my innocence.

I shower and dress and tiptoe down the stairs, my heart pounding. I'm not hungry, but I shake a few cornflakes into a bowl. There's no milk, so I'm faced with the choice of eating them dry or with water. I opt for water and they're actually not that bad. Not great, but not too disgusting. I chew and swallow, chew and swallow without tasting. I'm still not allowing myself to think about Scott. If I do, I know I'll never make it into work, I'll just lie on my bed and give in to my sadness. I picture myself sobbing, howling, smashing things. But the reality is, I'm here, eating my breakfast with a calm exterior, going about my daily routine.

I rinse out my empty bowl, throw on my fleece, hat and gloves and grab my phone and bag. If only there was a back way out of my house. But I live in a row of terraces; our little houses are all joined together, our gardens separated by high fences and bushes. There's no way out. Unless I pole-vault over twenty garden fences, the front door is basically it.

I take a breath. They can't hurt me, they won't touch me. I just need to ignore them. Be purposeful. Don't respond and don't break down. So why are my knees going soft and my palms sweating?

Stop thinking, do it quickly.

I bow my head and open the front door. Immediately, there's the flash of lights and the click, click, click of cameras. They're clustered around my front gate, spread out along my wall, calling my name from the pavement. Throwing out provocative questions that I try and fail to block out. A car drives past and beeps its horn several times, whether at me or the journalists, I can't tell.

I walk carefully down the path and open my gate.

"Are you going to talk to us, Tessa? Tell us why you took him?"

Outside the gate, I turn left, but they're blocking my way. I try to walk around them, stepping down into the road, but they move with me. It's no good; if I want to get by, I'm going to have to force my way through. I shoulder past two youngish guys, casually dressed in jeans and parkas. They cast a quick grin at one another, like this is all some hilarious game. Then I shove my way through the rest of the pack and start walking quickly.

"Can you look up at the camera, Tessa? Let us get a good photo?"

I keep my head down. Keep moving, one foot in front of the other. Don't think about the neighbours and what they must be thinking. Take deep breaths. Don't let them see I'm scared.

"Where did the boy come from?"

"Did you take him?"

Their questions bring Harry's sweet face to my mind, and an unexpected tear drips down my cheek. But I don't want to wipe it away, to draw attention to the fact they've made me cry. I'm more angry than sad right now. I want to yell at them to piss off and leave me alone, but they'd probably love that, so I keep walking. Marching along the pavement, dodging other pedestrians, who must be wondering what the hell is going on—unless, of course, they recognise me from the news.

Is this circus going to follow me all the way to work?

Fine, I think. *Fine. Follow me, see if I care.* I square my shoulders, run a gloved hand over my tear-streaked cheek and begin to jog.

"You can't run from the truth, Tessa!" a journalist calls out.

"You wouldn't know the truth if it punched you in the face!" I yell back, instantly biting my lip. Bang goes my resolution to maintain a dignified silence. My response has released a torrent of new questions.

"So give us your side of the story!"

"Tell us what happened, Tessa."

"Did you take the boy?"

"How did he get into your house?"

"Were you acting alone?"

Shut up, shut up, shut up!

The whine of a motorbike approaching from behind. More bloody press trying to pap me. It cruises by my side, a guy on the back taking photos, calling out my name, asking the same questions as the others. I stop in my tracks, letting it coast ahead before jogging across the road to put some distance between me and the bike—not that it will make any difference, they'll still be able to get their shots from the other side of the street with their long lenses. The rest of the media troop behind me, following me across the road, still shouting, still clicking their cameras.

I'm not used to jogging. I haven't run like this for months and I'm in bad shape. Sweating, out of breath. My increased pace hasn't put these guys off one bit. In fact, they look like they're enjoying it, revelling in my added discomfort. I'm not even halfway to work. How will I keep this up? I slow to a fast walk, sweat clinging to my back, my chest tight, sharp pains shooting up my shins. I should have stayed home. How did I ever think I would have the mental and physical stamina for this?

Don't stop. Don't cry.

A shiny truck pulls up on the kerb ahead. Probably more of them come to harass me. The passenger door opens in my path and I hear someone yelling my name. I'll have to alter course to avoid the door.

I stop for a second. I know that truck.

"Tessa, get in!"

Oh, thank God. It's Ben.

I sprint to the vehicle and throw myself into the passenger seat, slamming the door behind me and sliding down low in the seat. Ben pulls away into the traffic, and in the wing mirror I see the gaggle of press on the pavement where I left them, like stranded passengers on a runway.

"Thank you!" I pant, my heart pumping so furiously I'm worried it's about to explode.

"They're outside Moretti's too," he says, grim-faced.

"I'm so sorry, Ben."

"You don't have to apologise. I just didn't want you to have to deal with them on your way in, but I see you've already been mobbed."

"I don't know what I would've done if you hadn't..." I don't trust myself to say any more without breaking down.

"Hey, hey, it's okay. You're safe from them in here. Bunch of bastards."

I take a breath. "They can't get into the gardens, can they?"

"Not legally, no. I've told them they're not allowed on the premises. Some of them offered to pay their way in, but I told them to keep their money."

"Thank you." I shake my head, still bewildered at how things have come to this.

"A couple of them tried to get me to talk about you. Asked what you're like and...well, if I thought you took the boy. Don't worry, I didn't say a word."

"Ben, I really am sorry. I hope it won't affect your business. Look, I totally understand if you don't want me to come to work at the moment."

"Are you kidding? I'm getting free advertising here." But his smile doesn't look natural, and I notice tense worry lines around his eyes. He's putting on a brave face. Having your business associated with a suspected child abductor is not the image anyone wants to portray. I don't know how long he'll be able to keep this up before he's forced to let me go. And I wouldn't blame him.

Within minutes, we reach Moretti's, and my heart starts pounding once more when I see the crowd outside the gates. Journalists and onlookers stare in our direction, hungry for yet more juicy titbits to add to their fabrications.

"I'd get down if I were you, Tess," Ben says. "Don't give them the opportunity for any more photos."

I don't wait to be asked twice, unclipping my seat belt and sliding into the footwell.

I hold my breath as we cruise through the gates, my skin prickling as they rap on the glass and call out my name, sensing their eyes peering down at the top of my head.

"Cheeky gits," Ben mutters. "It's okay, Tessa, we're in. I'll park round the corner so they can't see you getting out."

Ten minutes later, as I'm opening up the storage shed, Jez comes over.

"Morning," he says, his ruddy face inscrutable.

"Morning," I reply, wondering what he makes of the rabble outside the gates. Whether he's seen the news. If he's going to mention it.

"The beans, caulis and tomato seeds arrived yesterday," he

says with a sniff, "so if you could start sowing them into pots this morning…"

"Yes, sure. Are they in here?" I ask, tilting my head towards the interior of the shed.

"In the far greenhouse. You'll find everything you need over there."

"Great," I reply, eager to get to work.

He clears his throat. "Hope you're okay," he adds, looking down at his boots.

"I'm fine," I say, nodding. "Thanks."

"Good." He nods too, and heads into the recesses of the shed.

I breathe a little easier and head over to the greenhouse area, keen to get involved in the task ahead. But as I walk, a leaden lump begins to form in my stomach, a growing sense of dread. I'm here now, safe at work. But what happens when I leave this evening? Maybe I should go out there and speak to the press, give them my side of the story. But the thought of facing them…and what if they twist my words?

Since I left home this morning, the sky has lightened a few shades from charcoal to gunmetal. I slouch along the rows of plants, wondering if I shouldn't just sell the house and move abroad. Start again. There's nothing to keep me here. Scott has moved on, I have no real friends any more, no family. I could go somewhere warm, reinvent myself. And then I think about Sam and Lily, their graves becoming neglected and overgrown. How could I ever leave them? How could I enjoy a new life knowing that they were lying abandoned with no one to tend to them?

I pass by the greenhouses, their infant plants lined up in uniform rows, protected from the sharp British frosts and any number of greedy bugs. Finally, I reach the one at the end, open the door and step inside, inhaling the moist, loamy air. I spy the crate Jez has left out for me and get to work.

Hours pass as I press the tiny seeds into rich, dark compost, stick labels on the pots and line them up neatly, a sense of satisfaction growing as one row becomes two, and then three. As I work, I make out the bumbling shapes of customers browsing the plants at the other end of the garden centre. Back here, I'm invisible.

I'm not sure what time it is when Carolyn rushes into the greenhouse, her eyes bright, her cheeks pink. I instantly think something terrible has happened. That the police have come for me, or the media are here inside the garden centre. "Can you come and help out in the shop?" she pants, disrupting the fleetingly calm environment. "I've got to give Janet a hand in the café. Ben's covering for me at the moment, but it's manic out there. Everyone's decided to do their Christmas shopping today for some reason."

"Sure," I reply, slipping off my gloves and wiping my hands on my jeans. "Why is it so busy?"

"No idea, but we need to hurry back. There's a queue out the door and Janet's run off her feet."

I follow Carolyn back past the greenhouses, her wiry body radiating panic at the sudden influx of customers. I think back to what Ben said about why he wasn't offering her the management of Moretti's and I can see why. If she flies into a tizzy at the appearance of a few customers, he probably wouldn't feel comfortable handing over the running of the place. But am I really any better qualified?

Ben lifts his hand as I weave my way towards him, past the queue of customers. Carolyn has already flitted over to the café.

"That's five pounds twenty change," he says to an elderly lady clutching a pair of gardening gloves and a packet of Christmas cards. "Would you like a bag?"

"No thanks, I'll pop them in my handbag."

Ben turns to me. "You okay here if I go and get some more change? We're running a bit low."

"Course, you go."

He lowers his voice and turns away from the queue of people. "Just thought I'd let you know that the press are still out there, I'm afraid. So it's probably not a good idea to go out for your lunch."

I feel the blood drain from my face, ashamed to have brought this awful mess to work with me. "I'm so sorry," I whisper.

"Hey, you don't need to apologise," he murmurs. "I'm just giving you a heads-up."

The next woman in the queue clears her throat pointedly.

Ben leaves me to it and I get to work, ringing the cash register, thoughts of journalists turning me into a slow, fumbling idiot.

"I gave you a twenty-pound note," my latest customer says, folding his arms across his chest.

"Um." I look at the till display, which is showing an amount of change corresponding to ten pounds. "I'm sure it was a ten-pound note you gave me," I say.

"You calling me a liar?"

I feel my face heat up. "No, of course not."

"Hey, don't I know you?" A middle-aged woman standing behind Mr. Aggressive tilts her head and narrows her eyes at me.

"I...I don't think so."

"Yes. Yes, I do. You're that woman on the news, the one who took the kid."

A ripple of recognition weaves its way back along the queue.

"What about my change?" the man barks at me.

"I...I'm not sure..."

"I gave you a twenty, so you need to give me another tenner."

I snatch up a ten-pound note from the till, convinced the

man is pulling a fast one. I know I've been distracted today, but I could've sworn he gave me a ten-pound note. I don't have the energy to argue with him, though, and decide that if the till is short at the end of the day, I'll put my own money in to make up the difference. "Here you go," I say sharply, thrusting the note at him.

"Should think so too," he snaps. "Trying to rip me off."

But I don't respond—I can't think what to say. Everyone in the queue is staring at me like I've got two heads. The man stuffs the note in his pocket and is about to walk away when the woman pipes up once more:

"Those journalists outside," she says. "They're waiting for *you*, aren't they?" Then she turns around and says in a voice so loud that practically everyone north of the river could hear. "It's her! She's that child abductor off the news. Took that little kiddy, she did."

I stare at her, mute with horror, my insides turning to slush. What can I do? Anything I say will only make me sound guilty. I shouldn't have come to work, I'm not prepared for any of this. I don't know what to do.

How did my life come to this?

CHAPTER TEN

"Everything okay here?" Ben strides through the shop towards me. I'm so pleased to see him. "Tessa? You all right?"

"Tessa Markham, that's her name," the woman cries. She holds out her phone and takes my picture.

I gasp at her cheek.

"Excuse me, I'd like you to leave," Ben says to her.

"What!" The woman's face turns scarlet with outrage.

"Right now, please," he adds firmly, pointing to the exit.

"Suppose you're in on it too," she snarls at him. "I was about to buy two fig trees," she adds, pointing to her trolley. "But you can effin' well forget it now."

"With you looking after them, Madam, they'd probably wither and die."

"I...What did you just say?"

"Actually," Ben continues, "before you go..." He takes the phone off her and presses a couple of buttons. "There, I've deleted the photo of my colleague. I'm sure we can all do without another social-media vulture sharing someone else's misery."

To my surprise, a few customers in the queue clap and nod. I want to applaud him too.

"Goodbye," he says calmly, handing the woman's phone back. "Don't let the door hit your arse on the way out."

Her mouth drops open and she turns to leave. "I can tell you now," she says, "I won't be coming back here again."

"Pleased to hear it," Ben replies.

I'm rooted to the spot, trembling. Everyone is staring at me like I'm some kind of rare zoo exhibit. A few stares soften into genuine smiles as I catch their eyes.

"Tess," Ben takes my hand, "come with me."

"What about your customers?"

"They can wait," he says gently. "I'm going to get Carolyn to come back and man the shop, but first…" He leads me past the gawping customers, out of the shop and round the back of the building, through a gate and into a private walled garden.

My mind is racing with everything that's just happened, but I can't help staring around at these fragrant surroundings. I've never been in here before. Even in winter, with everything dormant, it's perfect. An arched stone pergola sits in front of the house with a weathered wooden table and chairs beneath it. Ornate terracotta pots gush with evergreens and winter berries. Low walls and hedges border gravel and stone pathways that take the eye away into the hidden distance.

"Is this your garden?" I ask, everything else forgotten for a brief moment.

"Yes," he says. "It's still a work in progress. I'm doing it gradually."

"It looks pretty finished to me." An image flashes into my mind of my own neglected front garden. I make a mental note never to invite Ben over. Well, at least not until I've attempted to get it back into some kind of order.

I realise he's still holding my hand, his fingers cool against my skin. As he leads me towards the house, we pass a plucky robin perched on a stone bird table, pecking at some scattered seed. Ben opens a glazed arched door and we enter a warm, rustic, farmhouse-style kitchen, messy in a homely way. He directs me to a knotty oak table, where I sit, dazed, on a long, low bench.

"Stay there," he says, opening an old-fashioned cream refrigerator, pulling out a pan and setting it on a dark-green range cooker. Then he takes a ciabatta loaf from a bread bin, slicing off two chunks. "The soup will take about five minutes to heat," he continues. "Finish it all off. There's butter in the fridge if you want some with your bread. I'll go back to the shop for a while."

"But I can't let you—"

"It's one thirty now," he interrupts. "I don't want you coming back to work until at least half two." And with that, he leaves.

I glance around the inviting space, my heart still racing from the encounter with that acidic woman. I would love to have a nose around Ben's house—it looks like an incredibly calm and inviting place to live—but I respect his privacy and remain in the kitchen. After eating a steaming bowl of home-made minestrone soup, I feel a little more refreshed, much less shaky, and ready to return to work.

That afternoon, the garden centre is quieter and I'm able to go back to my seeds and the blissful silence of the greenhouse. When Jez comes in to see how I'm getting on, he confirms that there are still a few journalists hanging around outside the gates. I wish I could stay in this peaceful place forever. At 4 p.m., dusk sweeps across the gardens and I have to switch on the halogen lamp to see what I'm doing. All too soon, it's time for Moretti's to close and for me to go home.

My pulse begins to race in anticipation of the walk home. Maybe I should call a cab, but I can't afford to shell out for any more taxis—it defeats the object of going to work in the first place. I can't ask Ben for a lift; he's already done so much for me that I feel I'm becoming a burden. But I needn't have worried. He's leaning against his truck, and when he sees me, he waves me over.

"Hop in, I'm taking you home."

The polite part of me wants to decline, but the terrified part heaves a sigh of relief and gets in.

"Thank you, Ben." I pull down my seat belt and clip it in place.

"As if I'd let you walk out on your own and face that lot."

"They're all still there, then? I haven't dared look."

"I'm afraid so." He starts up the engine, turns on the headlamps and cruises towards the gates.

"Which means they'll probably be outside my house, too."

"I can come in with you," he offers.

"No, no, I'll be fine. If you could just drop me outside, that would be amazing."

"Let's see when we get there. Just a thought, but you might want to undo your belt and scooch down again."

"Good point." I do as he suggests and brace myself for rapping on the window and shouted questions.

"Get ready," Ben says.

The engine growls as he accelerates hard through the gates and out onto the road. I hear the screech of tyres and use the heels of my hands to steady myself against the front of the footwell. I hear shouts from outside, and bright camera flashes briefly illuminate the truck's interior.

"Well, that was fun," Ben says. "Haven't driven like that since I was seventeen and trying to impress Marie Philips. You can come out now."

I straighten up and sit back in the passenger seat. "Marie Philips?"

"A girl from school."

"Did it work? Was she impressed?"

"No. She fell for a twenty-two-year-old car mechanic from Finchley. I didn't stand a chance."

We drive the rest of the way in companionable silence. I peer in the wing mirror every so often to check if anyone is following us. The traffic is quite heavy now, so maybe we are being followed, maybe we aren't. I can't tell.

As we turn into my road, my body tenses. No surprises: the cluster of journalists is still there, gathered by my front gate. I don't know what they're expecting. I'm not going to talk to them, so they should just bugger off home.

Ben slows the truck. "You can kip at my place if you want. The spare bed is really comfy."

"I'll be okay," I say. "Thanks, though."

"Thing is, I won't be able to pick you up tomorrow. I've got a meeting with the bank first thing."

"It's okay, Ben. I don't expect lifts from you. You've been an absolute godsend today, but I've put up with them once, so I'm sure I'll be able to handle them okay tomorrow." This is a blatant lie. The thought of walking to work with them following me scares me senseless.

"Stay home if you can't deal with them, we can cope." He catches my eye, letting me know he means what he says.

"Thanks, but I want to work." We're right outside my house now and the press are gathering around Ben's truck like zombies hungry for flesh. "Here goes," I say, sounding braver than I feel. I take a breath to steel myself.

"Good luck, Tess."

"Thanks, Ben. I mean it, you've been so kind. And good luck with your meeting tomorrow." I open the car door and barge my way through the throng.

"Who was that in the car, Tessa? Was that your boss?"

"Are you two together, Tessa?"

"Is he your boyfriend?"

"Did he help you abduct that boy?"

Finally, I'm through my front door. Home. I should probably eat something, but I still haven't managed to do any food shopping. I climb the stairs, pull on my pyjamas and fall into bed, too tired to deal with any more crap. Too tired to think. My eyes close.

I must have fallen asleep immediately. But now I'm awake, staring wide-eyed at the curtains, an almighty smash of breaking glass ringing in my ears, a dull pain in my leg. What the hell? Loud footsteps running away. I turn on my bedside light without thinking about who might be able to see in.

There's something red on the covers next to my leg. A brick. *A brick!* I swing my legs out of bed and stand up, crying out as a sharp pain shoots through my foot. I glance down. Glass— glass everywhere. As I gradually recover my senses, I realise that someone has chucked a brick through my bedroom window.

A glance at my alarm clock shows it's almost 4 a.m. Heedless of the glass strewn across the carpet, I peer out through the jagged hole in the window, the icy air making me catch my breath and shiver. The journalists are still out there, staring up at me. Some are pointing down the road. Did they see who did it? They must have. But I don't dare go out to ask them.

House lights start coming on across the street. Bleary faces appear at bedroom windows. They must have heard the crash of glass. I wonder if any of the neighbours will come to see if I'm okay. Somehow I doubt it.

I stare down at my left foot. There's blood on the carpet.

My whole body shakes; my teeth begin to chatter. It's just the cold, I tell myself, from the night air streaming in. And then I do something I know I shouldn't: I blame it on the shock, on the fact that I'm still half-asleep. I grab my mobile from the nightstand and call Scott.

His voice is thick with sleep. "Tessa?"

"They threw a brick through my window," I say. "Please, can you come over?"

"Who did? A brick? It's probably just some idiot who's seen the news," he says sleepily. "They'll have run away by now. You need to call the police."

"Can't *you* come over, Scott? Please," I beg. "Our bedroom window's smashed. There's glass everywhere. It's freezing." I can't control the tremor in my voice. "I . . . I don't know what to do."

"Just call the police, Tessa. They'll sort you out. I'm sorry, but Ellie needs me here. We've had the press outside our house all day too. The stress isn't good for her and the baby. Actually, it's been bloody awful. I couldn't even go in to work today."

I shake my head and end the call without saying another word. Suddenly wide awake, I realise Scott will no longer be there for me. Not any more. I should never have called him.

My initial fear and confusion morph into something harder as I dial 999.

CHAPTER ELEVEN

While I'm waiting for the police to arrive, I sit in the kitchen picking fragments of broken glass from my foot. Once I'm sure I have all the tiny pieces out, I wash and bandage it up, barely registering the pain. In fact, it's almost a welcome distraction. Why would someone throw a brick through my window? Why is all this crap happening to me? I know why. This is trial by media: I'm guilty until proven innocent. To the general public I'm a child snatcher, regardless of what I have or haven't done.

The doorbell rings. Is it my imagination, or does it sound louder than usual? The echoing chime reverberates through my body, setting my teeth on edge. I limp down the hallway to the front door, hesitating. What if it's not the police?

"Hello?" A male voice from outside. "Tessa Markham? It's the police. You called us earlier."

I open the door to two uniformed officers. I thought they might have sent Chibuzo and Marshall. I don't recognise these guys. They're young. Younger than me. Behind them, on the pavement, the press are almost well-behaved. There are fewer of them at this time of night, or should I say, morning. No jostling and shouting out to me while the police are here. A few flashes from their cameras and that's it.

"Thanks for coming," I say to the officers, pulling my dressing gown more tightly around my body. "Come in."

They step inside and I lead them to the kitchen, where they take my statement. Once they've heard what happened, they ask to see the bedroom window, so we go upstairs.

"The journalists out there," I say. "Did they see anything?"

The dark-haired officer replies. "According to them, a person on a motorbike rode past, slowed down and threw the brick, then sped up and rode off."

"Did they get a licence number?"

The officer shakes his head. "Sounds like the plates were purposely smeared with dirt. A couple of the photographers got off some shots, but they were all out of focus. Too busy watching your house."

Typical—a bunch of press hounds camped outside, hoping to get a shot of an innocent woman, and when the real crime happens, they're too slow to react.

"We've got an alert out for the vehicle," he continues. "And we'll take full statements from everyone out there after we've made sure you're okay."

Stepping into the chilly room with its flapping curtains, glass everywhere and that cold red brick on the bed, I feel violated, even worse than when it actually happened. Maybe because I was half-asleep before. Maybe because I've now had time for it to properly sink in.

"Do you have any idea who it might have been?" the fair-haired officer asks.

"No."

"Anyone you've been in an argument with recently? Or someone who might have a grudge against you?"

The other officer nudges his colleague, but the fair-haired officer doesn't seem to know who I am. Maybe he doesn't watch the news.

"The media have decided I'm some kind of child

abductor," I say. "Whoever sent this brick obviously agrees with them."

The fair-haired officer flushes. "Ah, yes, of course. Sorry."

So he *has* heard of me then. "It's all a load of made-up nonsense," I say. "Your lot don't seem to think I'm guilty, but since when has the truth mattered when there's a story to sell?"

"You'll want to get that boarded up," the dark-haired officer advises. "You on your own here?"

I nod and chew the inside of my lip. "Yes, I'm on my own."

"Got any chipboard?" he asks.

"I...er, I don't know. If there is any, it'll be in the garden shed."

"Right, come on, show me the shed. I'm sure we can find something and I'll board it up for you. Won't take five minutes. My old man's a chippy, taught me everything I know." He gives me a wink, and I'm pathetically grateful. "I'm PC Dave Cavendish, by the way," he says. "And this useless article is PC James Lewis."

PC Lewis flushes once again. I give him an encouraging smile.

Downstairs, I slip on a pair of old Crocs, and Dave and I head out across the soaking grass to the dilapidated shed at the bottom of the garden while his colleague waits in the kitchen. I unlock the shed and it takes him around twenty seconds to find what he needs—an old kitchen cabinet with chipboard backing, and a staple gun.

Ten minutes later, my bedroom window is boarded up, the glass all swept away and my bed stripped and changed.

"This can't be part of your job description," I say. "Won't you get in trouble?"

"It's a quiet night," he says with a smile. "You'll need a glazier to fix it properly, but this will do as a temporary measure."

"Thank you so much," I reply.

"Your foot..." he continues.

"I stupidly stood on some of that smashed glass."

"You wanna get that looked at properly. Don't want it getting infected."

"Thanks," I say, knowing I probably won't do anything about it. "Do you think you'll catch whoever did it?"

"Truthfully, it's doubtful. But if it's any consolation, I don't think they'll come back. Probably just some idiot who thinks they know better than the police. Call us if you have any more problems." He jerks his head towards the street. "That lot out there giving you much grief?"

I shrug—I don't have the energy to tell him they're making my life a misery.

"We'll have a word on our way out, warn them to behave themselves."

Once the officers have gone, I hobble back up to my bedroom. It all looks fairly normal in here now. With the curtains drawn, I can't even see the board across the window. But the air is cold and damp. Tainted. I know I won't be able to climb back into bed and close my eyes as though nothing has happened. How can I fall asleep in here knowing there's someone out there who hates me enough to do something like this?

I scoop up my alarm clock and duvet and leave the bedroom, closing the door behind me. It hardly seems worth going to bed just for an hour and a half, but what else am I going to do? I realise I don't like spending time in my house any more, even without all the press hanging around. Actually, I haven't enjoyed being here since Scott left. It's a house of memories. Lifeless. I'm not sure if it has given up entirely, or if it's waiting for something.

I wander along the short landing to the back bedroom: Sam's

bedroom. I step inside and inhale the stale air, foolishly hoping to catch a remnant of his scent. But there's no trace of my little boy. I place my alarm clock on his low nightstand and lie down on the bare mattress of his toddler bed, curling up in the foetal position and pulling my king-size duvet around me. It's only when I huddle under the covers that I realise how cold I am. My duvet is still freezing to the touch and I wish I had a hot-water bottle or an electric blanket...a warm body to spoon with, to press my icy toes against.

Eventually, I manage to fall into an uneasy slumber shortly before my alarm goes off. I wake disorientated, and then I remember last night. Right on cue, my foot starts to throb. I ignore it and uncurl myself, stretch out the kinks in my back and stand up. After throwing on my work clothes, I hobble downstairs and peer through the lounge blinds into the dim, cloudy morning. Oh joy. My fan club is back in force. There are more of them here than ever. Word must have spread about the brick thrower—I'll need to order a taxi to work.

As I munch on cornflakes and water again, I berate myself for calling Scott last night. It's humiliating to remember how I pleaded with him to come over. He's already made it crystal clear that he has more important things to worry about now. He's hardened his heart towards me. This Ellie woman is going to be a permanent fixture. I can just about deal with her, but I'm not sure how I'll be able to handle the rest of it—Scott having a new family. Even thinking about it twists my guts and leaves me short of breath. In my mind I see this faceless woman bending over her newborn while Scott looks on adoringly. *Stop thinking about it.*

I gaze at Sam's and Harry's drawings stuck to my fridge, the sweet, childish images lifting my heart a little.

I should probably check the news to see what lies they're

spreading about me this morning, but I can't face it, and besides, I don't have time. A car horn sounds out the front: my taxi's here. I dump my cereal bowl in the sink, snatch up my handbag and head towards the front door with not quite as much terror as I felt yesterday.

I run the gauntlet once again. Bulbs flash and questions are hurled. Same as yesterday. Thankfully, I only have to endure it for a few seconds, limping down the path and elbowing my way across the pavement until I enter the blissful calm of the taxi.

Work is my sanctuary. A haven. Even with the occasional gawping customer, I feel safe here, I have a purpose. The morning passes at a steady pace. I begin by sweeping the pathways, then continue with my veg planting in the greenhouse. I haven't caught sight of Ben yet. He must still be at the bank. I hope his meeting goes well. I realise that I'm coming round to his proposal more and more. Maybe this extra responsibility is what I need to pull me out of my half-life and into something more real. But I can't decide anything while I have all this stuff going on. If only the police would solve the mystery of who Harry is and where he belongs. When they clear my name once and for all, maybe things can start getting back to normal.

"Tessa." I glance up from my seed packets to see Carolyn standing at the greenhouse door, fluffing out her short mousy hair with her fingertips. "You've got a visitor."

No. Go away. I don't want a visitor. "Hi, Carolyn." I manage a smile. "A visitor?"

"She says she's a friend."

"Who is it? Do you know?" I put down my trowel and wipe my hands on my apron. "It might be one of the press pretending to be a friend."

"Sorry, I didn't ask."

In my head, I curse her for being so dumb, although I guess that's unfair of me. It's not her fault.

"She's in the café," Carolyn adds. "I'd better get back to the shop."

"Okay, thanks. I'll be there in a mo."

Carolyn turns and walks briskly back the way she came. I sigh and leave the greenhouse, limping behind her. I don't have a good feeling about whoever is out there waiting for me.

CHAPTER TWELVE

The café is already half full, even though it's only 11:30. I wave to Janet, who's serving behind the counter, and she smiles and points to a table in the corner where a woman sits with her back to me. The woman in question has shiny brown hair with sunglasses pushed up onto the top of her head. I haven't witnessed the sun in north London since September, so I'm guessing it's a fashion thing. I walk around the table, nervous to see who it is and what she wants.

Carly. My whole body tenses at the sight of her.

"Tessa!" she gushes, standing up and leaning in for a kiss on each cheek. Awkward doesn't cover it.

I step away from her, my mind whirring.

"Hope you don't mind me coming to meet you at work like this," she says, her gravelly voice irritating me already. "This place is gorgeous, isn't it? I can't believe I've never been here before." She sits back down and takes a sip of her coffee.

"Was it you?" I demand.

"Me?" She tilts her head.

"Yes, you. Did you sell that story about me to the newspapers?"

She sighs. "You're being quite aggressive, Tessa."

"You told my colleague you were a friend," I say, "but you're not here as a friend, are you?"

"Well," she shrugs, "whatever the reason I'm here, we are still friends, aren't we?" She gives me what I'm sure she hopes is a winning smile, but I'm not falling for it.

"My boss has barred the press from coming in," I say, my hands resting on my hips. "So I'm afraid you've had a wasted journey. You'll have to leave."

Her eyes harden for a split second, but she reattaches her smile straight away. "Yes, but I'm not here in my capacity as press. I'm here to have a chat as a friend and a neighbour. I saw the board across your upstairs window this morning. I was worried."

"That's bollocks," I say, a little too loudly, drawing the attention of an elderly couple at the next table. They tut and angle their bodies away from me. I sit down opposite Carly and lower my voice. "This is my workplace. I'm here to work, not chat with my neighbours."

"So why don't I come to yours after work?" she pushes. "I can bring a bottle of something sparkling and we can have a natter. Be like old times."

She's persistent, I'll give her that. "I'm busy after work," I say.

"Okay, how about I take you out for something to eat? What time's your lunch break?"

"Listen, Carly, I'm not going to have lunch with you, or have a drink with you, and actually, I think you've got a nerve coming into my workplace and badgering me like this after what you did."

"Did you have a break-in last night?" she asks. "An accident? I heard someone might have thrown something through your window. Were you hurt?" She takes another sip of her coffee.

"You know very well what happened. And right now, you need to leave," I say through clenched teeth. "I'm not talking to you any more."

"Fine," she says airily, rising to her feet. "I came here to be friendly, hoping you might want to give me your side of the story.

Everything in the papers is speculation, because you refuse to confirm or deny what actually happened with that poor boy."

"But why should I?" I cry. "I've done nothing wrong."

"So tell me the truth." She stares at me like I'm an idiot for not doing as she asks. "I can stop all this speculation and write the facts. Then you can get on with your life. It's a win-win."

She's good. Trying to get an exclusive story out of me by making out she wants to help me. "I'm going to ask you again," I say. "Was it you who sold the story to the press about Ha— about the boy turning up at my house?"

She purses her lips and pulls the ends of her hair with her fingertips.

"It *was* you, wasn't it? You put two and two together and came up with thirteen. Well, thanks for screwing up my life, you self-centred cow." I realise my voice is way above the acceptable levels for a genteel garden-centre café, and all the customers are now openly staring at us.

She gives a short laugh. "Calling me a cow isn't going to help, Tessa."

"What's going on?"

I turn to see Ben standing behind me, and he doesn't look particularly happy.

"I'm sorry, Ben," I say, my face heating up. "This is Carly. She's a journalist and she's harassing me." I turn to glare at her.

"I'm actually Tessa's neighbour." She holds out a beautifully manicured hand. "Carly Dean," she says to Ben. "Nice to meet you..." She raises an enquiring eyebrow.

"Ben," he says, taking her hand and giving it a brief shake. "Moretti."

"Hi, Ben." She smiles. "I came to see if Tessa's okay after last night."

"What happened last night?"

"Didn't you hear?" Carly says, putting a hand to her chest as though she's shocked on my behalf. "Someone smashed Tessa's window." She gathers up her phone and handbag, and begins rooting around in her purse.

Ben turns to me, concern creasing his face. "Is that true, Tessa? God, are you okay? You should've called me."

"It's fine," I reply. "I'm fine. The police came, they boarded it up for me."

"The window breakage is already on the news websites," Carly adds. "The press are really interested in this story. No one knows where the boy came from and how he found himself in Tessa's house. And now this attack on her property. It's awful. And it's also a mystery." She deposits a two-pound coin on the table—a tip. "I don't suppose you know anything about the boy, do you, Ben? His name? Where he's from?"

"I think that's enough questions," he replies, trying to cut her off. "I'd like you to leave now, Ms. Dean."

"Please, call me Carly. Is this your place?" she asks, her face softening, going into full-on flirt mode.

"Yes," he says, ignoring her smile and her hair flick.

"I could do you a lovely write-up. It's divine here. Are you Italian? You look Italian." She gives a throaty laugh.

I'm not a violent person, but I really want to slap her hard right now.

"Look, Carly, I'm afraid I'm going to have to insist you leave," Ben says. "I can't have you pestering my staff."

"No problem," she trills. "But I hardly think neighbourly concern can be construed as pestering." She hands him a card. "Call me about that write-up. I have a national interiors magazine in mind that would lap this place up."

He takes the card and slides it into the back pocket of his jeans. I feel a stab of something. Anger? Jealousy?

Carly tosses her hair one last time and sashays out of the café. Ben's eyes darken as he watches her leave. Then he turns his gaze on me.

"You okay?" he asks.

"I'm so sorry, Ben. I didn't know she'd turn up here. I was trying to get rid of her when you came in."

"I was talking about last night," he says. "That must have been terrifying."

"It wasn't the best night I've ever had." I try to laugh, but it comes out as a strangled squawk.

"It's your day off tomorrow, isn't it?"

"Yeah, but I can come into work if you need me."

"No. Take the chance to chill out, relax."

I want to tell him that the only place where I can even remotely relax is here at work, but I guess that would make me sound too sad. "How did your meeting go at the bank?"

"Yeah, it was fine. Pretty straightforward. Anyway, as long as you're okay, I need to go and catch up on some paperwork."

"Yes, sure. I'll get back to my planting," I reply.

We go our separate ways and my heart feels heavy in my chest. Is it my imagination, or is Ben not quite as warm towards me as before? I don't suppose I can blame him. Yesterday I was in an altercation with a stroppy customer, and today I've disrupted the calm of the café by shouting at my neighbour. He must wonder why the hell he's employing me. I wish he hadn't walked in just as all that was going on. I could throttle Carly for coming here. Ben has been more than patient with me so far, but I can't see him putting up with this drama for much longer, and losing my job is the last thing I need.

CHAPTER THIRTEEN

After we've closed up Moretti's for the day, I nip into the staffroom to collect my handbag and call a taxi to drop me home. As I sit on the worn leather sofa and pull my phone out of my bag, Carolyn comes into the room. I look up and smile, even though I can't help being a little annoyed at her for letting Carly in to harass me earlier.

"Tessa, can I have a quick word?" she asks. She's standing awkwardly, shifting from foot to foot, not meeting my eye.

"Sure." I put my phone down on the arm of the sofa. "What's up?"

"Janet told me what happened in the café today," she says hesitantly, "with that journalist woman. And I just wanted to say how sorry I am. I should've checked who she was before coming to get you."

"Oh, thanks. But it's not your fault, Carolyn," I say, feeling guilty that I was blaming her only a moment ago. "How were you to know who she was? She's a good liar."

"I've been feeling awful about it all afternoon." Carolyn looks as if she's about to cry.

I stand up and give her arm a squeeze. "Please don't feel awful. I'm over it already." I force out a smile.

"Anyway," she says. "I wondered if I could give you a ride home tonight?"

"Really?" My heart lifts. "That would be brilliant."

"It's the least I can do."

"Actually, would you mind dropping me at my local super-market instead? The one by that new pizza place on Friern Barnet Road. I've got no food at home and it's tricky to get to the shops, what with the whole media-circus thing."

"Of course. No trouble at all." She relaxes her shoulders.

Suddenly the dark evening doesn't feel quite so oppressive. I shove my phone back in my bag and walk with Carolyn out to the yard. Even my foot isn't hurting as much any more. When I see her VW Passat Estate, it dawns on me that the press will easily spot me if I sit in the passenger seat. I think Carolyn realises this too, as she stops and stares at the vehicle, her lips pursed.

"What about if I lie down in the boot?" I suggest. "It looks like there's loads of room."

"Would that be okay?" she asks, her voice unnaturally high. "Otherwise they'll probably follow us, won't they?" I can sense the panic radiating off her. I bet she's regretting her offer of a lift.

"I think it would be perfect," I reply. "That way, I'll be hidden and they won't know I've left work. I might even get to do my shopping in peace."

"Great, okay." Carolyn opens up the capacious boot and I crawl in, positioning myself against the left side like a Mafia victim.

"If you use that blanket to cover me..." I suggest.

"It's the dog's blanket," Carolyn says. "It's not very clean."

"I don't mind, it won't be for long. Then you can shove that bag of wellington boots right next to me."

Carolyn catches my eye and I let out a giggle. She stifles a smile.

"That's the first time I've laughed in months," I say. "I think I must be cracking up."

"Well, it's not every day you get to travel in this much style," she replies.

At this, we laugh so hard I think I might do myself some permanent damage. Tears stream down our faces, and our cackles fill the night air. I'm still snorting as Carolyn spends the next minute arranging the back of her car.

"There," she says finally. "You'd never know anyone was under all that lot."

"Are you sure you're still okay with this?" I ask from beneath the blanket, the whiff of old dog filling my nostrils.

"Yes," she says. "Just don't move for the next few minutes. I'll tell you when it's safe to come out."

Soon we're driving slowly out through the gates, and I can hear the shouted questions the media are firing at poor Carolyn.

"Is Tessa still at work?"

"What time's she due to leave?"

"Are you friendly with her? Want to give us an interview?"

I hadn't thought about how all this must be impacting on my work colleagues. I'm surprised they're not annoyed at me for adding all this extra hassle to their lives. I hope none of them will be tempted to speak to the press although I do keep myself to myself at work, so at least there would be nothing much for them to talk about.

Carolyn drops me off outside the supermarket without incident. She looks almost drunk with relief that it's all over. A quick glance around the pavement tells me that no one is paying me any attention at all. What a luxury to be able to shop without being hassled.

I take my woollen hat from my fleece pocket, jam it on my head, pull it down over my ears and step into the brightly lit supermarket, praying no one recognises me. Basket in hand, I make my way up the busy aisle and start choosing goodies. My stomach growls at the sight of freshly prepared fruit salad, pre-cooked arrabiata pasta, sliced cheese, milk for my cornflakes, two chocolate eclairs in cardboard packaging. It's all I can do to stop myself ripping open the box and stuffing both pastries in my mouth. I'm becoming almost dizzy with hunger. I restrain myself, and decide that I have enough in my basket for now—I'll grab some bread and go to pay.

Rounding the corner, I get the familiar uneasy sensation that I'm being watched. I glance to my left and right, but all the other customers appear to be engrossed in their shopping. No one looks my way. Sweat prickles on my upper lip. The bread can wait, I want to get out of here.

I head down towards the row of tills. They're all busy, even the self-service ones. I make my way to the back of the shortest queue, but there are still at least half a dozen people ahead of me. As I toss a glance over my shoulder, I lock eyes with her. That short, brown-haired woman, the one who's been following me. Who is she? I leave the queue and make my way back up the aisle towards her. How did she know I was here? She can't have followed me from work.

She's turned away now, half-walking, half-running towards the back of the store. My basket bashes against someone's arm.

"Watch where you're going, idiot!" he cries, a look of outrage on his face.

"Sorry," I gasp.

I finally reach the back wall, but the woman is nowhere to be seen.

There! She's making her way back down to the exit. I dump

my shopping basket on the floor and follow her, but someone grabs my arm to stop me.

"Hey!" I cry. "Get off. I'm trying to—"

"Tessa?"

I turn to glare at whoever it is. She has my sleeve in her hand. I don't recognise her. She's small, with an angelic face, blonde curls and wide blue eyes.

"Do I know you?" I snap, turning away again to see if I can spot the other woman. But she's gone—I'll never catch her now.

"You *are* Tessa, aren't you?" she says.

"What paper are you from?" I say, my shoulders drooping.

"I'm not a journalist," she says. "My name's Eleanor Treadworth."

"Sorry, who?" And then it dawns on me. I look her up and down, note her flawless skin, her immaculate designer boots and jeans, the navy Puffa jacket that would make most people look like they were wearing a sleeping bag but on her comes off as stylish and chic. I also notice the way she has one hand resting on her jacket, over her belly.

It's Ellie. Scott's Ellie.

And here I am, dressed like a tramp, reeking of dog, barging my way down the aisle of a supermarket like a demented woman. I have no idea what to say to her. This woman who has taken away my last chance at happiness with the man I love...loved?

"Are you okay?" she asks. Her voice is high and childish. Affected. "It's just, you seem a bit—"

"What do you want?" I ask. *Besides my husband.*

"Look, I wasn't going to contact you, but I'm glad I've run into you like this. Because...Well, the thing is, Tessa, I know you've had a rough time in the past, but you have to understand... all this stuff in the media about you and Harry is really stressing Scott out."

"How do you know Harry's name?" I snap, knowing the media still don't have this piece of information.

Her cheeks turn pink. "Scott told me."

I scan her features, trying to work out if she's lying, but she carries on talking.

"Like I was saying, all this media attention, it's not good for Scott. He can't sleep, he's so worried about it all. And you know I'm pregnant. I need to stay calm for the baby."

I stare at this cherubic creature in front of me and I'm not sure whether to laugh at her insensitivity or shove her into the ready-meal chiller cabinet. Of course, I do neither.

She takes my silence as her cue to carry on talking. "You calling him up at all hours of the day and night isn't going to help anyone, least of all you. It's selfish, can't you see that? Look, Tessa, you have to try to let go of the past, move on with your life and let Scott go." Her expression is all fake concern, like she understands what I'm going through. But from the look of her, she can't be more than twelve.

"How old are you?" She still has her hand on my sleeve and I shake it off.

"I beg your pardon?" she says.

"You know. Your *age*—what is it?"

"Twenty-six, but I don't see what that's got to do with any-thing."

So she's ten years younger than me. This embryonic creature is giving me advice on how to move on with my life. I don't think I can trust myself to reply. If I open my mouth, I'm not sure what I'll say, what I'll do. Submerged rage bubbles up from my gut, but the last thing I need is to be arrested for GBH so instead, I simply stare at her.

Silence hangs in the air like thunder about to break. She chews her lip, less sure of herself now. Good. More words trickle from her mouth, but I don't hear them. Don't respond. She touches my arm again in that condescending way. I shake it off once more. Then I turn away. Retrace my steps and retrieve my abandoned shopping basket from further up the aisle. I don't look back to see what she's doing, I just pray she doesn't try to follow me. If she does, I'm not sure I can be held responsible for my actions.

CHAPTER FOURTEEN

I hardly remember queuing up to pay for my shopping or the short walk home from the supermarket. My head is still full of Ellie and her condescending speech. Did Scott really tell her Harry's name? She seemed flustered when I asked her how she knew it. But mainly I'm furious that she thinks she has the right to tell me how to react, how to feel. Yes, Scott and I are over, but how dare she warn me off?

Once I reach my house, I storm through the bulb flashes, clicks and cries from my welcoming committee. I'm so mad, their intrusive behaviour barely registers. I stomp up the garden path, open the door and flip on the hall light. I'm sick of skulking in my own house, of creeping about in the dark. I carry my shopping bags through to the kitchen and bang my way around, stuffing food in the fridge and cupboards without concentrating on where each thing actually goes. I take a knife from the cutlery drawer and punch holes in the top of the arrabiata carton before shoving it in the microwave. While I'm waiting for it to heat up, I shove half a chocolate eclair in my mouth. I really don't care that I'm having my pudding first, I think I'm entitled to eat what I like after the crappy week I've had.

The gooey chocolate and cream tastes like heaven, and I sit down at the table, sliding the rest of it in my mouth before I've even swallowed the first half. But even while I'm enjoying the confectionery, my body is still tense with anger. I lean my forehead on the table and give a cry of rage. Ellie might be a patronising cow, but she's so pretty. So perfect. No wonder Scott has fallen for her. And she's having a baby. *His* baby— a half-brother or sister to our twins. I lift my head off the table and bring it down again with a bang. Once...twice. Not enough to do any damage, just enough to make a noise, to shake the fury from my body.

Then I turn my head and press my cheek to the tabletop, carry on chewing my eclair through choking sobs. Imagine if anyone I knew could see me now. They would have me taken away in a straitjacket. I give one last frustrated growl before pushing myself upright again, my palms flat on the table.

The microwave pings. I pour myself a glass of water, dump the arrabiata into a bowl and grab a fork from the drawer. I could carry on sitting here in a simmering rage, or I could try to take my mind off *her*. I decide to go and watch some TV, though not the news.

I head into the living room and turn on the side lights. I thought I was too angry to worry about the press, but there are slight gaps in the blinds that a long lens could see through, so I turn them off again, annoyed that I care. In the semi-darkness I place my water and pasta on the arm of the sofa, snatch up the remote and flick on the TV.

Thursday night...I try to think what's on the telly on Thursdays, what I could watch to distract me from my life. The screen lights up and I freeze. There, on the TV, is a picture of Harry. With trembling fingers, I press pause. A head-and-shoulders shot of him wearing his school uniform—a striped private-school-type blazer and tie. He's smiling, his sweet face so open and happy, his brown curls gleaming.

So they've discovered his identity.

I gaze at the image for a moment, scared to unpause the television in case they say something bad. Something I won't be able to handle.

My thumb hovers over the play button. I press it. A news presenter is speaking:

"*The mystery child, whose name we now know is Harry Fisher, has finally been reunited with his father in Dorset. The boy first came to our attention earlier this week when he was discovered in the home of Tessa Markham, a gardener who lives and works in the London Borough of Barnet.*"

Harry's picture is replaced by that awful image taken of me earlier in the week. I'm coming out of my house in my work clothes and I look grumpy, disorientated and pale—exactly how you'd imagine a mad child abductor to look.

"*Ms. Markham has previously been under investigation for snatching a three-month-old infant, but no charges were ever brought.*"

I clench my jaw at their selective description of me. My photo disappears from the screen, thank goodness, and is replaced by footage of a news reporter speaking from outside what looks like a Georgian farmhouse set on a country road. Maybe that's the house where Harry lives. Dorset, though— that's miles away, isn't it? I think I went there once on a family holiday when I was younger.

"*Harry's family have declined to be interviewed at this stage, but in a statement to the press, his father, Dr. James Fisher, commented: 'As you can imagine, it's been a very stressful time. I'm relieved and happy to have Harry safely back home where he belongs.'*"

A black-and-white newspaper cutting fills the screen. It shows a man in a dinner jacket at some kind of black-tie event. He looks as though he's in his forties. He has a beard and is wearing glasses. I'm guessing this is Harry's father. For a second or two I'm sure he looks familiar. But he's Harry's father, so there's bound to be some resemblance.

"*Sadly, Harry's mother died in October 2017 from an aggressive form of stomach cancer, which makes the five-year-old's return home to his widowed father doubly special. It's remarkable to have a happy ending to this mystery that has had the nation gripped for so many days.*"

The story ends and they move on to a piece about a local school closure. I know I said to myself that I didn't want to watch the news, but I'm desperate to see if there's any further information about Harry. I flip through the channels while absent-mindedly eating forkfuls of pasta, chewing without tasting. Finally, I reach another news channel, but they're discussing politics. I keep going until I've checked out every station. There's nothing more on the story, I'll have to wait until the nine o'clock news. I turn off the television, knowing I'll be unable to concentrate on watching anything else, and finish up my pasta.

That news report was frustratingly low on facts. There's so much that still doesn't make sense. How did Fisher's son end up here in London? How and why did he get to my house? Why did it take so long to reunite them?

I jerk my head up as a car door slams out the front. Then another. Engines slow down and speed up again. The babble and chatter from the press seems to have grown in the last few minutes. I sidle over to the edge of the window and peer out: there are loads of them out there. Now that Harry is back with his father, I foolishly thought the media might leave me alone, but it looks like they're more interested in me than ever.

I creep back to the sofa and sit in the unlit room, sipping from my glass of water. There's something still nagging at me about the boy's father, but I can't think what. That picture of him...He really did look familiar. How can that be? I don't know anyone in Dorset, do I? I do a mental scroll-through of everyone I know—friends, work colleagues, family—but I can't think of any ties to the county.

A chill sweeps across my shoulders and down my spine as another unwelcome thought comes to me. One I've been trying to push away all week. But it keeps coming back, tapping on my forehead and pushing at my chest. Because there really is only one explanation that makes any sense, even if I don't want to acknowledge it.

What if the reason I recognise Fisher is because I've seen him before? What if I'm actually losing my mind? What if I did abduct Harry?

CHAPTER FIFTEEN

I dismiss the thought almost as soon as I think it. I couldn't have taken Harry—I don't have a car, I haven't been to Dorset in years. I was working last Saturday and I visited the cemetery on Sunday. If I had somehow subconsciously snatched a child, why would I go all the way to Dorset to do it? And Harry himself said that "the angel" had brought him here. Whoever the angel was, he certainly didn't think it was me.

None of it makes any sense.

My whole body is suddenly heavy with exhaustion. I wasn't looking forward to my day off tomorrow, but right now I think I'm going to need it. After my earlier shopping trip, I now have everything I need for a day at home. I'm going to get an early night and lie in until midday. I'll make myself breakfast and take it back to bed with a book.

And then I remember that the window in my bedroom is boarded up. That there's still a draught whistling through it. That it feels damp and strange and unwelcome up there. I could sleep in Sam's room again, I suppose, but the bed is too small, the memories too raw. The sofa in here is pretty comfy, but how could I sleep so close to the rabble outside? I wouldn't be able to relax. I have this house to myself, but nowhere in it feels like home, apart from maybe the kitchen, but I can hardly sleep in there. I tug my boots off, pull my legs up under myself and close my eyes.

Next thing I know, I'm woken by the doorbell. I force my eyes open. Light streams in through the slats in the blinds. The sun is shining out there. How long have I been asleep? I uncurl and stretch. The doorbell chimes again. I could ignore it, but what if it's Scott, or someone else I know? My mouth tastes stale. I run my tongue over my teeth and drain last night's glass of icy water.

Rubbing my scratchy eyes, I get to my feet and inch over to the window, peering through to the front doorstep. My hackles rise when I see who it is. Ugh. She's the last person I feel like talking to. Maybe if I ignore her, she'll go away.

The bell rings again and there's a sharp rapping on the door. This is harassment. I would call the police, but I've seen enough of them lately. I stride into the hall, crouch down and open the letter box.

"Piss off, Carly," I call out as the sharp morning air flows inwards, making me shiver.

"Tessa, can you open the door?"

Too late, I realise I should have pretended not to be in. Now she and the rest of them will know I'm holed up in here. "Go away," I cry. Aside from anything else, I must look and smell a total fright. I fell asleep in my work clothes last night. I need a shower. I can't let the immaculate Carly see me looking like this.

She bends down to the letter box so that we're now eye to eye. "Tessa, I know I overstepped the mark, but I've got some information. Something that could clear your name once and for all."

Overstepped the mark? That's an understatement. I snort. It has to be a trick, a ruse to get my attention.

"Look," she says. "I get it, you're annoyed with me. That's fine. But this time, I really think you need to hear me out."

"I don't *need* to do anything, Carly. It's my day off, I just want to be left alone."

"I've got something to tell you . . . about the case."

I weaken. If she's telling the truth, I'd be stupid not to hear her out. "This had better not be some trick to worm your way inside and harass me. I'm not giving you a story so you can twist it."

"I promise you, Tessa. You'll want to hear what I've got to say."

I hesitate. Can I trust her? Probably not. But if the worst comes to the worst, I can always kick her out.

"Look," she says, "do you want to find out what's really going on? Do you want to clear your name with the public?"

I straighten up, wipe the sleep from my eyes and run my fingers through my tangled hair. Positioning myself behind the door so the rest of the press can't see me, I open it a crack, shivering as a chilly breeze gusts into the hall. "Come in quickly, then."

The whirr of cameras goes off behind her as they catch sight of me letting her in. She squeezes through the gap in the door and I slam it closed behind her, muffling the shouts from outside. Carly glances around before landing her gaze on me. I see her take in my dishevelled appearance, but to her credit she doesn't pass comment. She's beautifully turned out, as usual, in a navy wool dress, knee-length boots and a smart brown leather jacket.

"I need coffee," I say. "We'll go in the kitchen."

She follows me down the hall and takes a seat at the kitchen table without being asked.

My one luxury is our Nespresso machine. I suppose I'd better offer her a drink, too, but it irks me to do so. She definitely doesn't deserve one. "Coffee? Tea?"

"A black coffee would be great," she says, rubbing her hands together to warm them.

I turn my back to her and make our drinks; the noise of the machine is too loud for us to have a conversation without raising our voices, so we wait. Once the coffees are ready, I turn back around and join her at the table.

"This is like old times," she says. "Haven't been over here in ages."

"So?" I say, plonking her drink in front of her and taking a sip from mine. "What's this information you've got?"

"Well," she says, tilting her head and eyeing me over the top of her cup. "The thing is, there's more to this story than I originally thought."

"For Christ's sake, Carly, it's not a 'story.' It's people's lives, *my* life."

"Sure. Yeah, of course."

I glare at her, trying to suppress the quivering anger suffusing my body. This self-important cow has contributed to one of the most terrifying and stressful weeks of my life, and she has the nerve to sit at my kitchen table all calm and composed like I'm making a big deal over nothing.

"You know what I mean," she adds.

"But do you know what *I* mean, Carly?" I say, banging my mug down on the table, slopping hot coffee over my hand. "You obviously sold a story to the press that had nothing to do with facts, and everything to do with making a name for yourself. You implied that I was guilty of taking Harry purely because I was accused of doing a similar thing after my son died. But the thing is, I'm not guilty of anything. The police didn't charge me. And yet you, in your ambitious, tawdry little world, you thought it was perfectly okay to sling mud, knowing it would stick and stink. Knowing my life would be made unbearable. But you didn't care, you didn't give a damn. You still don't." My voice is quivering with anger.

Carly sips her coffee, unruffled, waiting for me to finish. This makes me want to yell at her even more, to elicit an apology, or even an acknowledgement, but she's not biting.

"Well?" I say.

"Look," she replies. "It's just my job, Tessa. It's not personal."

"That's not an excuse! You're a human being, aren't you? You live across the road from me. You can see what your 'job' has resulted in. Me being persecuted. Me almost losing my job. Not to mention the fact that Scott's life is also being turned upside down by the press."

"He's with someone else now, isn't he?" she says.

An image of Ellie's doll-like face flashes up in my mind. In my head I'm screaming, but in reality I simply sigh, too exhausted to shout any more. "Just tell me what it is you want to say, and then I'd like you to leave."

"Okay." Carly steeples her fingers together, and I notice she's wearing some really nice silver stacking rings. They look like the kind of jewellery I'd have worn if my life had turned out differently. "Like I said," she continues, "I think there's more to this...situation than I thought."

"Like what?"

"I'm not exactly sure what's going on yet, but I don't trust James Fisher."

"Harry's father? Why not?"

"I've got a friend who works on the local police switchboard," she says, "and he heard from someone on the Dorset switchboard that Fisher took four days to report his son's disappearance. Four days. Don't you think that's odd?"

A friend on the inside? So that's how Harry's story was leaked. I should bloody well report Carly to someone.

Her face becomes more animated now. "Fisher's reasons for not coming forward sooner are really shaky. I went down to

Cranborne yesterday—that place is in the back of beyond. I thought I'd been teleported back in time fifty years."

"Cranborne?" I interrupt. "Is that in Dorset?"

"Yeah. It's where Fisher and his son live," she says.

"You went there? Why?"

"I tried to talk to him, but he wouldn't speak to me. Wouldn't even open the door. He won't talk to any of the papers. He's locked himself up in his house with Harry."

"Well," I say. "You can't really blame him for that. It's pretty intimidating having a load of press camped out on your doorstep."

"Point taken. But it still doesn't explain why he left it so long to go to the police. I mean, think about it—your five-year-old son goes missing. You can't find him. You search for maybe twenty minutes and then you start really freaking out and so you call the police. At a stretch, maybe it takes you an hour or two to call them. It certainly doesn't take four days."

I find myself nodding. "That is strange."

"I know, right? So, I managed to track down his old housekeeper. She lives here in London. But she wouldn't speak to me either."

"What's she got to do with anything?"

"Well, for one thing, she worked for the Fishers for years, so she knows them. She might be able to give me the low-down. And also, Fisher sacked her after his wife died. Maybe she has a grudge against the family. Maybe she knows something interesting. It would be worth talking to her, don't you think?"

"I suppose."

"No suppose about it. I think the woman's hiding something."

"But if she won't talk to you, how are you going to find out?" I ask.

"We-ell..." Carly drums her navy-painted nails on the table-top. "She won't speak to *me*, but maybe she'll speak to you."

CHAPTER SIXTEEN

"Me?" I say. "What makes you think she'll talk to *me*? My face is plastered all over the papers. If Fisher's ex-housekeeper believes half of what's been written, she probably thinks I'm the devil."

"I disagree," Carly says.

"Of course you do."

"No, I just mean she might know what's really going on here."

"So you admit that your story is a complete fabrication," I say.

"I didn't say that," Carly replies, sitting up straighter in her seat. "I meant that if she knows what's going on, she won't be worried about what's in the papers."

"You don't know that," I say, crossing my arms grumpily. "And anyway, I thought you said she'd left her job. She'll be out of the loop, won't she?"

"Well, we won't know unless we ask," Carly says. "Nothing to lose, and all that."

She's got a point, but I'm reluctant to be guided by my sneaky neighbour. Not after what she's just put me through.

"Look, what's the worst that can happen?" Carly adds airily. "She sends you away, refuses to talk to you. You've wasted a couple of hours. What else have you got going on in your life?"

"Cheers," I say.

To her credit, her face colours. "I didn't mean it like that. I just meant—"

"Relax, it's fine. I know my life is a pathetic void."

"Now you're just feeling sorry for yourself."

"You think?"

"So, are you going to go and see her?" Carly asks, draining her coffee and putting her cup back down with a clunk on the table.

"Not sure. How would I get past that lot out there? They'd follow me."

"Leave that to me," she says with a half-smile.

One hour later, I'm washed, dressed and breakfasted, and feel almost like a new person. Or if not new, then at least not like the unsavoury hobo I was impersonating earlier. I have my phone, my keys and my handbag. I'm loitering in the hallway, pretty much ready to go. A quick glance at my wristwatch tells me Carly should be ready by now. I send her a text to say I'll be walking out the front door in exactly sixty seconds.

My heart clatters against my ribcage. Why am I doing this? I tell myself not to be a wimp. Those journalists out there are just people. They won't hurt me, will they? I check my watch—thirty seconds to go. Carly had better not let me down.

Twenty seconds.

Ten.

I turn the knob on the front door, tensing up as I ease it open a crack. I peer further up the road, but it's empty. I'll give it another ten seconds, just to be on the safe side. Then I spy the glint of her red car. It gives me the boost of confidence I need to yank open the door, step out into the lemony sunshine and stride down the frosty path towards the mob.

"Tessa!"

"Tessa, love!"

"Are you going to work?"

"Do you know James Fisher? Did he contact you after what happened? Is he pressing charges?"

"Give us a couple of minutes of your time, Tessa!"

I keep my head down, open the gate and barge through them, their collective breath hovering about me like a shroud in the icy air. I listen for the sound of the car engine coming closer. But there are so many journalists surrounding me, in my face, yelling, clamouring for me to look up, to speak, to give them what they want, that I can't see or hear anything from the road behind them.

A car horn honks, long and loud. The press turn as one for the briefest of moments, giving me time to slip between their warmly wrapped bodies, under arms and around cameras until I reach the bright red Fiat idling in the middle of the road. I dart around to the passenger side just as Carly flings open the door. I slide in, slam the door and tug down on the seat belt.

Carly presses on the accelerator and floors it down the road. We're both panting and, to my surprise, laughing.

"That was insane," she cries, throwing the car into second as we screech round the corner. "Check behind us. Is anyone following? Any cars or motorbikes?"

"Nothing yet," I say, still out of breath.

"Ha!" she crows. "That lot will hate me now."

"Because you've driven off with me?" I ask.

"Yeah. Sorry, bit of professional rivalry there," she says.

"That isn't why you're doing this, is it? You didn't lie about—"

"No, no. Don't worry, their jealousy is just a bonus."

I shake my head. She really is something else. What must it be like to be that devoted to your career? To be so snarled up in it you don't know where you end and it begins? I glance sideways at her. My strange neighbour. She's humming something, but I can't make out the tune. Such a striking face— high cheekbones, cat-like eyes—but somehow the whole effect is harsh, like a brittle veneer is covering her skin. I give my head a shake; it must be the lack of a proper night's sleep making me have these odd thoughts.

"Sorry I can't drop you at her place," she says, "but I've got a meeting with an editor in an hour."

"It's fine," I say, wondering if her meeting is about me. "Now that I'm away from the rest of the press, I can relax a bit. Just drop me at the Tube station."

"Let me know how you get on," she says. "And Tessa, don't be meek and mild. If that woman knows something, she should damn well give you answers. Guilt-trip her into it if you need to."

I raise my eyebrows. That's easy for her to say—she asks questions for a living. "I'm not guilt-tripping anyone," I retort.

"You've got an opportunity to get some answers," she says. "Don't blow it."

"God, you're relentless," I say.

She grins. "Yep, you know me." She puts on her left blinker. "Okay, I'm not supposed to stop here, so jump out quickly. I don't want a ticket."

I do as she asks, stepping out onto the busy pavement outside the Tube station. I bend down to push the door closed.

"Be forceful, Tessa," she calls out. "And don't forget to text me afterwards."

"Right." I slam the car door and watch her motor away, merging with the rolling traffic, the sunlight glinting off the cars, making me squint and turn away.

* * *

It's already 10:15 as I alight from the Tube onto the platform at Turnpike Lane, clutching the folded piece of paper that Carly handed me earlier. On it is written an address and a name. Even Carly's handwriting looks like a newspaper headline. Black ink. Thick block capitals. Definite. Unequivocal. No room for error. Exactly the sort of handwriting I'd expect from someone like Carly Dean. But maybe she's furnished me with a lifeline here. Maybe this housekeeper woman will give me some answers about Harry and how he ended up at my house. Maybe she'll tell me something that will remove all suspicion from my name. I can only hope.

I step out of the station onto a wide expanse of pavement that looks as though the planners started out with the grand idea of making it into a piazza, but gave up halfway through. A couple of leafless trees stand off to the side next to a lone bench, a black-and-gold bin, some electricity boxes and a few bike racks. I stand for a moment to get my bearings, unfolding the scrap of paper and checking the address again, even though I've already googled and memorised it. I stare around at the criss-crossing roads and pavements, at the sweep and rumble of four-lane Friday traffic, and set off across an impossibly wide road towards a parade of shops.

A short while later, I'm standing in front of a peeling orange door set back between a sandwich bar and a betting shop. There are two buzzers—one with the name S. Lewis, the other with no name. I press the blank one and wait. Ten seconds later, a woman's voice comes through the intercom.

"Hello?"

"Hi," I say. "Is that Merida Flores?"

"Who is this?" Her voice sounds faintly accented.

"My name is Tessa Markham. I was wondering…can I have a quick word?"

The static through the intercom disappears.

"Hello?" I say, knowing she's taken her finger off the button and can't hear me any longer. "Hello?" I press the buzzer again and wait for a few moments. Then I step back and crane my neck to peer up at the bay window of the flat above the betting shop. I catch my breath as the curtain inches back and a woman stares down at me. Our eyes lock.

My hand flies to my mouth as I realise I know her: it's the same woman I've been seeing everywhere. She immediately twitches the curtain closed again. Why has Fisher's ex-housekeeper been following me? There must be something she wants to talk about. Why else would she be interested in me? Maybe she's scared. How can I get her to let me into her flat?

I step back up to the door and press the buzzer once more. There's no response. I think back to what Carly told me—to be forceful and not to blow it—but I can't stand here harassing the woman. Having been subjected to that myself, I know how awful it feels. Still, I now get the feeling that Merida Flores knows what's going on. That she wants to talk to me but something is preventing her. Only question is—what? Or who?

An idea comes to me and I press the buzzer one more time.

No response.

I press it again.

"Yes?" It's her.

I catch my breath. "Hello. Look, I'm going to go to the café down the road. The Costa opposite the Tube station. I'll wait there for one hour. Please come and meet me there. Please."

She doesn't reply. The static over the intercom disappears. Did she hear what I said? Is she going to come and speak to me?

CHAPTER SEVENTEEN

I make my way back along the pavement to the café, the chill December wind barrelling me down the street and sweeping me across the road. It's liberating to walk without having to look over my shoulder, although I'm not quite confident enough to risk being out in public without my woolly hat pulled down low by way of disguise. If I can keep from being recognised, it will be a novelty to sit and relax in a place without feeling under siege from the media. Will Fisher's ex-housekeeper come to meet me? I hope so. Maybe she'll feel more comfortable on neutral ground.

I push open the door to the coffee shop and step inside, enjoying the smells of cinnamon and coffee, the warmth from the hot air vents, the chatter of strangers. After queuing for a few minutes, I order an Americano, recklessly add an almond croissant, and find a seat away from the window. The croissant is warm and sweet. I lick icing sugar off my lips and take a sip of the scalding coffee, allowing my mind to go blank for a few blissful minutes. Enjoying this moment of respite. Willing my thoughts to keep away. But I can't stop myself from glancing up every time the door opens. From peering through the window to see if Merida Flores will walk past. With a jolt, I wonder if there's another Costa on another road, opposite a different Tube exit. I quickly google my location, but this appears to be the only one in the vicinity.

Half an hour goes by. I order another coffee. Too soon, an hour has passed. It's clear she isn't coming.

My phone buzzes in my bag. I wipe my hands on a napkin and fish out my mobile. It's a text from Carly.

Well?

I sigh and tap in a reply.

No good. She wouldn't talk to me.

Go back and try again.

There's no point.

Well, that was a giant waste of time.

I don't reply. What can I say? I hate to admit it, but Carly was right—there's a lot more going on here than I first thought. I wonder why Fisher's ex-housekeeper would follow me around but refuse to talk. Is she keeping an eye on me for some reason? Maybe she's still secretly employed by him. But why? And where do I fit into all of this?

What else can I do? I really don't believe there's any point in returning to the woman's flat. The expression in her eyes was one of genuine fear—I don't want to be the cause of that.

I ponder it all for a few moments, reluctant to give up and go home. What would I do back there except mope around and worry? Much as I still dislike Carly, she has given me the kick up the backside I need to be proactive. To find out if there really is something else going on behind the scenes.

I realise there is something I could do...but it's so outrageous that even the thought of it gets my pulse racing and my fingers tingling. The sounds of the café swell and recede. Can I really be contemplating this?

I navigate my way along icy country lanes in a little Toyota, in what's turning out to be a freaking blizzard. The weak afternoon light is a dim consolation. It's been snowing since I hit Winchester. Perhaps I should've checked the forecast before I set off. Too late now. After I left the café, I dusted off mine and Scott's joint credit card and used it to hire a car. Guilt needles me. I promised myself I would never use this card—I probably should have cut it up to avoid the temptation. But I tell myself it's in a good cause. With hindsight, I probably should have started my journey a lot earlier in the day, but by the time I'd found a cheap hire-car place and filled out all the paperwork, it was past midday when I left London.

After following diversion signs due to an accident, I reach the quaint town of Wimborne, the lights of its bay-windowed shops and cafés attempting to lure me from my car. But I ignore their call and drive straight through until I'm back out into the Dorset countryside, my fingers gripping the steering wheel, my eyes darting from the satnav screen to the road ahead, spinning snowflakes dive-bombing the windscreen.

The road curves this way and that, with high snow-covered hedges on either side. Every time a car approaches from the opposite direction, I press the brakes, unfamiliar with the bends, paranoid about crashing. Road signs point down dark, narrow lanes to villages with strange names like Witchampton, Gussage All Saints, Monkton Up Wimborne and Sixpenny Handley.

And then, suddenly, there it is—the sign telling me I've reached Cranborne. The dashboard clock shows 2:50 p.m. already. I've been driving for almost three hours, which may not sound a lot, but the last time I got behind the wheel of a car was over a year ago, when I drove Scott's BMW back from a friend's barbecue in Surrey. A day I'd rather forget. Scott and I argued terribly on the way home—I guess that day was the beginning of the end for us.

I must be crazy for doing this; for going to Fisher's house. But I really have nothing left to lose. Even if they lock me up, could it be any worse than the way I'm living now? A prisoner in my own home. A home I no longer love. I need to be brave. To demand answers. To confront this man and ask him if he has any clue why I'm embroiled in this drama. Plus, if I'm honest, Carly's revelation about James Fisher taking four days to report Harry missing has made me worry about the boy. And I can't help myself: I need to see that he's okay.

I pass a garden centre on my left and it reminds me of work. Of how I'll have to drive back home this evening if I'm to make it in for tomorrow. Weekends are our busiest times. I wonder how Ben is doing; if his offer of a promotion still stands. If my job still even exists after all the hassle I've caused him this week.

The hedgerows give way to a high red-brick wall. I briefly wonder what lies beyond, and then suddenly I'm in the heart of the village. I slow down, taking it all in. A couple of houses, a bookshop on the corner, an old inn, and now a row of terraced houses lines the street. A fire station, a thatched cottage, and here's another long red-brick wall to my right. Everything is topped with snow—buildings, verges, trees—though the gritted road is thankfully clear.

The satnav tells me to turn off down a narrow lane. All the houses down here are pretty cottages sitting close to the road. Halfway along, my stomach flips and my heart begins to race as the satnav tells me: "*You have reached your destination.*"

Immediately up ahead stands an impressive double-fronted Georgian house, set back from the pavement, with a snow-covered front garden and a cherry-red front door. I worked out Fisher's address before I left, using a combination of Google Maps and the news-report footage taken outside his home.

Now that I'm here in person, I recognise the house instantly. And, even better, the lights are on: he must be home.

Just as I'm about to pull up outside, I'm devastated to see a small crowd huddled together on the opposite side of the road. Not any old crowd—the press. My gut reaction is to slam on the brakes, do a seven-point turn and get out of here. But that would alert them to my presence. Instead, I wind my scarf around my mouth, sink down into my seat and drive past them as fast as I dare without arousing suspicion.

Damn. I should have known they'd still be here, still staking out his place. Their presence has scuppered my unsophisticated plan to go up to Fisher's front door and ring the bell. The media would love it if they found out I was in Cranborne. Goodness knows what tomorrow's headlines would be: "Child Abductor Back to Try Again!"

This is possibly the worst idea I've ever had. What am I doing here? I'm not a reporter or an investigator, I'm a gardener. I don't do this kind of stuff. Whatever possessed me to think I could do it on my own?

After speeding on down the road, I find myself back out in open countryside once again. I park in a shallow lay-by, turn off the engine and kill the lights. Silence. Flakes of snow melt against the windscreen as the inky dusk gathers outside. What now? Daylight will have disappeared within an hour, tops. I don't fancy wandering around these empty lanes in the dark. If I'm going to do anything, I'll have to do it now, before the light goes.

I adjust my scarf until it completely covers the lower part of my face, and pull on my woollen hat so only my eyes and the bridge of my nose are showing. If I can't go up to the front door and ring the bell, I'll simply have to find a way around the back.

Before I have the chance to think myself out of it, I get out of the car and begin marching up the road, my feet leaving light prints in the snow. I have to press myself into the hedgerow every time a car whizzes past, spraying grit and slush. The only other person mad enough to be out here walking in this weather is an old boy with a grizzled sheepdog at his side. He says good evening and touches his cap as he passes by. I nod and murmur something that isn't even a word before continuing on my way back towards the village.

Just before I reach the first house on Fisher's side of the road, I notice an almost-concealed path winding off to my right. I can't see where it leads, as it bends around the corner. There are no "Private Property" or "Keep Out" signs. Okay, nothing to lose.

With a brick wall on my left and overhanging trees to my right, I trudge along the narrow path, the soles of my boots squeaking against the snow. I'm reassured to notice other recent footprints, so hopefully I'm on a public right of way and won't meet an angry farmer brandishing a shotgun.

After a couple of minutes, I reach the end of the boundary wall. The pathway opens up into lush countryside. I stand there for a moment, taken aback by the glorious winter scene—a rolling snow-covered meadow bisected by an avenue of trees. In the far distance, at the end of the trees, sits a huge stately home, like a mirage in the pale light. Ordinarily, I'd love to explore further, but my attention is taken elsewhere, for to my left is exactly what I was hoping to see—a neat row of back gardens. And one of them belongs to James Fisher.

CHAPTER EIGHTEEN

I quicken my pace and jog down the sloping meadow, past all the other gardens, until I reach the one I want. The largest of the lot. It's hidden from view by a high wall, but a wrought-iron gate set into it enables me to see through to shivering fruit trees, their branches creaking in the wintry breeze. Beyond that, a snow-covered expanse of garden stretches away up to the house itself. I press the gate latch and push, then pull, but of course it's locked. The windows at the rear of the house are dark, but through the back door I spy an open interior door leading through to a brightly lit hallway. From this distance, it's like looking at a perfectly proportioned doll's house.

I'm confident I can scale this wall. It's almost shoulder height, and if my arms are strong enough, I might just manage it. I glance around, but can't see a soul. If I wasn't so focused on doing this, I'd be completely creeped out being here all alone in the thickening gloom. As it is, I don't have the luxury of feeling scared. I've got to get over this wall.

I pause. What the hell am I doing? My conscience nags me. I'm about to trespass on private property, to break the law. What if the press snap me climbing over the wall? Imagine. They'd have an absolute field day. Brand me a stalker as well as a suspected child abductor. But my desire for answers overwhelms my fears.

I roll my shoulders back and forth and take a breath. Then I press my right toe against the wall, grab on with both hands and heave myself up so that I'm draped inelegantly across the top. I slide my legs down the other side and drop to the ground with a dull thud, remembering to bend my knees so I don't jar my joints.

My heart pounds. I'm now on private property. *Don't think about it.* Through the bare-limbed fruit trees, I stare down the long garden, clenching and unclenching my fists, trying not to dwell on the fact that I now need to pee. Somehow I move my legs, propel myself towards the house, across the white lawn, my footprints stark and incriminating.

Reaching a slightly raised patio, I slow my pace and come to a standstill, wondering what to do. Can I really be about to rap on this stranger's back door? I creep up to the right-hand window and peer into a dark room, creating blinkers with my hands to block out next door's security light, which has suddenly clicked on, making me even more nervous. I'm looking into the kitchen. The decor is dated, with a battered-looking Aga and 1960s units. The room is an absolute tip, with dirty plates piled high at the sink, old boots and shoes strewn around the floor and all kinds of unidentifiable paraphernalia covering the worktops and the table at the far end.

I cross the terrace to the other window. The curtains are drawn, but there's a gap where they don't quite meet in the middle, enabling me to see in. A massive oval table dominates what I assume to be the dining room. On it sits an ancient computer, stacks of lever-arch files and piles of paperwork. I wonder if Fisher and Harry are even at home. Just as I'm pondering this, the door to the dining room swings open and the overhead chandelier floods the room with light. It's Fisher, tall and very real.

I freeze as he stops and stares right at me. *Holy hell.* My insides turn to water as he takes a step in my direction. How am I not yelping in shock right now? I shrink back from the gap in the curtains, heart hammering, sweat breaking out under my hat and scarf. Did he see me? How could he not have?

With jelly legs and trembling hands, I step forward once more and peer around the curtains, see him take a seat at the computer, not casting a single glance my way. I exhale a long, relieved breath. Seeing him like this, up close, bearded and bespectacled, so stern and serious, I wonder how I'll find the courage to confront him. But if I don't, what then? Turn around and go home, this whole expedition a complete waste of time, money and energy? No. And annoyingly, a part of me wants to tell Carly: look, I'm not a complete wimp. I can do this stuff, I can clear my name myself. I don't need to resort to your underhand methods. I push away the fact that technically I'm breaking the law right now.

I watch Fisher for a moment, getting my breathing back under control, calming my mind, trying to figure out exactly what I want to say to this man. How I'm going to persuade him to talk to me. But my brain won't behave the way I want it to. It's a jumbled mess. Either I stay here rooted to the spot, or I take the few steps required to carry me to the back door and get this over with.

After a few more moments' dithering, I find myself standing at the kitchen door, my raised fist ready to rap on the glass. I bring it down three times. Knock, knock, knock. Dull thuds on the thick pane, rattling its wooden frame. To my ears, the sound is obscenely loud, but will Fisher be able to hear it in the dining room next door?

"Daddy!"

It's him. Harry. He's here. His small blurred shape crosses the hall.

"Daddy! Did you hear that?" he cries, his thin, high voice excited. "Someone's at the door!"

What will Harry do when he sees me? Will he call me his mummy again? Will he be the open, friendly boy from my kitchen? Or will he freeze up and act like I'm a stranger?

I hear the low rumble of Fisher's voice, but I can't tell what he's saying. Harry appears in the hall once more. This time he moves more slowly, his head down. He disappears back the way he originally came. I move to the edge of the door to get a better view, and catch sight of his hand on the banister. He's going upstairs. Maybe Fisher sent him up there, out of the way. I realise—with a thud of disappointment—that I probably won't get to speak to him after all.

Then Fisher walks into the hall, his back to me, filling the space with his large frame. He opens the front door a crack. Peeks through. He doesn't realise that the knocking came from the back door. He's probably worried it's someone from the press. I know the drill.

Once he's closed the front door, I rap again on the glass. Harder this time. Fisher's head snaps up and he squints in my direction. It's dark out here now, so I'm not sure he can even see me. "You're on private property!" he calls out, striding through to the kitchen. "Get out of my garden! If you're another damn reporter, you'd better bugger off before I call the police. I've told you, I've nothing to say to you lot."

"Dr. Fisher?" I call out. "My name's Tessa Markham . . . You've probably heard of me."

Silence. He reaches out and clicks on a switch, flooding me with light. He stays rooted to the spot, and for a long moment we stare at one another through the glass.

"Dr. Fisher?" I say warily. I can't make out his expression. Right now, he's the one in semi-darkness and I'm the one on display.

Finally, he crosses the rest of the kitchen to get to the back door. I step back as he pushes it open, a waft of warmth and old cooking smells flooding outwards. Seeing him up close like this, I get that feeling again that I've seen him before. I give a tentative smile, even though my heart is clattering against my ribs like a freight train.

"Tessa Markham," he says, as though stating a fact.

"Hi. I'm really sorry for showing up like this. I couldn't ring your front doorbell because of the press. I didn't want them to see me. I just…I just wanted you to know that I didn't take your son." I'm gabbling now, but I don't seem to be able to stop. "I wondered if we could talk for a moment. If maybe I could come in."

Fisher just stares at me like I'm deranged.

"I'm sorry," I add, "but do we know each other from some-where? I'm sure I recognise you. Not from the papers, from somewhere else."

"No," he says. "I don't know you."

"Are you sure?"

"Don't come here and question me!" he snarls.

I take a step backwards, shocked by his twisted facial expression.

"You took my boy!" he booms. "What the hell are you doing here in my garden? I'll bloody well have you arrested. You've caused me and Harry so much pain. Do you have any idea…?"

"I'm sorry," I say with a shocked sob. "I didn't mean to upset you, I just needed to explain. And to find out what Harry was doing in my—"

"Don't you dare talk to me about my son! My wife has just died," he cries, "and then you…you took him. Get out of here and don't ever come back!"

I don't wait to be told twice. I turn and stagger back up

the garden, shocked at Fisher's switch from calm confusion to blistering anger. It takes me four attempts to claw and heave myself to the top of the wall. As I'm hauling myself upwards, I'm terrified he's going to come after me, tear me down and begin yelling at me again. Or worse.

I can't imagine why I thought this would be a good idea. Of course this man whose child went missing wouldn't want to speak to me—the only suspect. I must have been crazy to believe he would entertain the idea of letting me into his house. *Am* I crazy? Is that it? Right now, I understand that coming here was not the action of an entirely sane person. I was already under suspicion of taking Harry. Now... now what must Fisher think of me, creeping up to his back door like a thief or a murderer? I should never have come. Am I losing my mind? Is the reason I recognise him because I've seen him before with Harry? Did I do something bad? If I did, why can't I remember?

I'm still clinging to the top of the wall. My legs are shaking, and I think I'm in shock. Fisher's anger has pierced my body like a physical wound. I somehow manage to drop down from the wall back into the dark meadow, and run up the hill until my lungs give out. It takes me a few minutes of lurching back and forth to locate the pathway onto the road.

Back at my hire car I fumble for the keys, wrench open the door and fall inside. My breathing is louder in here, ragged and harsh. I wipe the tears from my cheeks and lay my head on the steering wheel as shock and fear work their way through me.

Some time later, I don't know when, I start up the car and begin the long drive back to London in a state of exhausted numbness. Again I wonder what possessed me to come here. Bloody Carly, getting my hopes up. Making me believe I could find answers. I should never have listened to her. Now I've gone and made things ten times worse.

I reach the outskirts of London at around 7:30, but it feels far, far later. When I finally get to Barnet, my stomach begins to knot at the thought of running the gauntlet again. What if the press have somehow found out I've been to Cranborne? No. How would they know? They couldn't. Not unless Fisher told them, and I get the feeling that he is as likely to speak to the press as he is to invite me to stay for a long weekend.

Nosing the car into my road, I try to mentally prepare myself for the familiar sight of journalists, but I still can't stop my stomach giving an almighty lurch when I see them in the street—more of them than ever, milling about, leaning against walls, smoking, chatting. And worse than that, parked right outside my house is a car with blue-and-white flashing headlights.

The police are here.

CHAPTER NINETEEN

I park up about a hundred yards from my house and sit for a moment gathering my limited energy for whatever lies ahead, wishing I could just curl up and fall asleep in the car. It's a tempting thought, but the police are there, waiting. If I don't come out now, they'll catch up with me eventually. And if one of the journalists were to spot me sleeping, I'd be surrounded in no time. No, I'll just have to be brave.

I hold my breath and open the door, stepping out onto the icy pavement and heading towards my dark, sad-looking house with its overgrown garden and boarded-up first-floor window. It's only a few seconds before one of the journalists notices me and strides my way, a hungry look on his face. Almost as one, the rest of them turn like a pack of wolves and begin eagerly filming me and snapping away on their cameras.

As I come nearer to the house, two officers get out of the police car. I recognise them: it's Chibuzo and Marshall. Marshall starts speaking to the press. I don't hear what he's saying, until he raises his voice. "Okay, move back," he commands.

Of course, they listen to *him*. Reluctantly, they step down off the pavement to let me through—a small mercy—but it still doesn't stop them yelling out their questions.

As usual, I don't respond. Just keep my eyes aimed at

the frosty ground, only occasionally glancing up to get my bearings.

"Evening, Tessa," Chibuzo says as I draw closer. "We'd like you to come down to the station for a chat."

The cold creeps through my coat and settles on my chest. "A chat?" I say, my voice wobbly and high. "I'm really quite tired. Is there any chance I could come tomorrow instead?"

"We'd rather you came now," she says firmly.

"Am I under arrest?"

"Not at the moment," she says, but I can detect a warning note in her voice.

"Okay," I say, not feeling like I have much choice.

"We can drive you there if you like," she says, gesturing to the silver BMW parked outside, its silent lights still flashing.

I consider how that might look to the press. Me getting into an unmarked police vehicle, being driven away. "I'll meet you there," I say.

Chibuzo nods.

Less than twenty minutes later, I'm back in an interview room, the chill in my body spreading outwards to my fingers and toes, despite the stifling, musty heat of the room. Marshall fires up the recording equipment and Chibuzo runs through the time, date, who's in the room and all that official stuff that makes everything feel ten times worse.

"Mind telling us where you've been today, Tessa?" she says, her voice distinctly less friendly than the last time I spoke to her at the station, her brown-eyed gaze unwavering.

I'm sure they know. Why else would they have been waiting outside my house? Fisher must have called them after I left. I decide I have no alternative but to tell them the truth.

"I'm sorry," I say in a small voice. "I went to Cranborne. To see Dr. Fisher. To explain. After everything that's been in the news, I needed him to know that I didn't take his son."

"James Fisher claims you trespassed on his property," Chibuzo says.

"I didn't want to," I begin.

"So you admit to trespassing?" she says.

I huff at her interruption. "I told you I didn't want to. I would much rather have gone up to his front door and rung the bell, but as you probably know, the media are camped outside his place, too. If they saw me at Fisher's front door, they'd have drawn all the wrong conclusions and I'd never have heard the end of it. So I went round the back and knocked on that door instead."

"I see," Chibuzo says.

"I'm sorry," I say, hearing the petulant tone in my voice.

"Did you realise at the time that you were trespassing on private land?" she says. "I have to warn you that if you attempt something like that again, you could be arrested for harassment."

"I'm sorry!" I cry, this time really meaning it.

"For now," Chibuzo says, "we're issuing you with a harassment warning. It's called a police information notice, or PIN for short." She hands me a document.

I stare at it, the words a blur on the paper, as she carries on talking.

"It states that you have been accused of trespassing and harassment. It lists the points of law and warns you that if your conduct continues, you could find yourself arrested."

"What?" I say stupidly, not understanding what she's telling me. "I didn't harass him!"

"Don't worry about the letter too much," Chibuzo says

kindly. "These PINs aren't actually covered by legislation. They don't constitute any kind of formal legal action, they're more like a warning of wrongdoing. Telling you not to do it again."

I suppose I should be grateful they didn't arrest me outright. But I'm still shaken up by the formality of the document.

"Why did you really go there today, Tessa?" Chibuzo asks.

"I already told you. I wanted Fisher to know that the stuff in the media is all lies."

"Don't you think that going to his house could've been seen as an aggressive act?" she says.

"Aggressive?" I stutter. "No, not at all. If you must know, I wanted to ask him why it took him so long to report Harry missing."

Chibuzo's eyes narrow and Marshall stops writing for a moment to look up at me. I notice the quick glance that passes between them.

"How do you know about that, Tessa?" Chibuzo asks.

Shit. I can't tell her that someone from inside the force leaked it to Carly. That might make things worse for me. I think quickly. "One of the reporters outside my house told me."

"Which one?" Chibuzo asks.

"I don't know. One of them shouted it out, they're always yelling things like that."

Her shoulders relax; she seems to buy this. "Well, you more than anyone should know how much credence to place on those tabloid stories."

"But Harry was with social services for days before his dad came forward," I persist. "Why did Fisher leave it so long to report him missing? He was—"

Chibuzo cuts me off. "We strongly advise against playing amateur detective. We have the facts, and if anything seems amiss we'll follow up on it. You taking matters into your own hands isn't helping anyone, least of all yourself."

"It's my reputation that's being dragged through the mud," I counter.

"Tessa," Marshall says. "Did you take Harry last Sunday and bring him to your house?"

"What!" My chest tightens. I can't believe they're going over all this again. "No, I didn't take him. How many times do I have to tell you before you'll believe me? I never set eyes on him until I found him in my house."

"The thing is," Chibuzo says, "you going all the way to Dorset today, it doesn't look good, no matter what your reasons."

"Okay," I agree. "I know, I messed up. I shouldn't have gone. But I'm under a lot of stress with all those journalists camped outside my house. I just wanted to try to clear my name. But I get it, I made a mistake."

"Look," Chibuzo says, her tone softening once more. "Like I said, we're just warning you that it's in everyone's best interests if you stay away from Dr. Fisher and his family. Leave the man in peace, okay? Can you do that for me, Tessa? I don't want to have to turn up at your house to arrest you."

"Fine," I say quietly, already feeling like a criminal.

"Good." She ends the interview and gets to her feet.

Marshall stands to join her, and tells me I'm free to go.

I cannot wait to get home, despite the chaos outside my house. Today has seemed to last forever. I drive back on autopilot, cursing the police for showing up like that. Because of them, the press will now recognise my hire car. They'll see me coming. Sure enough, as I head towards the house, the pack turns towards me. With a grim smile, I flick the headlights to full beam to blind them as a little "fuck you." My small triumph doesn't last very long, as they soon crowd around the car. I fling the door open, hoping it will hit one of them in the face or, even better, the nuts. But they're wise to it, and move back out of the way just in time.

"What did the police want, Tessa?"

"Are you in trouble?"

"Can you tell us where you've been all day?"

I stride past, head down, trying to block out their cries. Surely they'll give up soon and go and pester someone else. Can't they tell this story is dead? Over. Finished. I have the feeling that this really could be the end of it all. That I'll never know why Harry was brought to my house. That it will be one of those mysteries I'll simply have to live with.

I walk through my gate and up to the front door, desperate to get inside. To sit down and organise my thoughts. At last, I close the door behind me and lean back against it for a moment, listening to the blood whooshing inside my head. The house is damp, cold as an ice box, the hall light no comfort. I must have left it on this morning. I walk through to the kitchen. It seems like weeks since I was last here. I can hardly believe it was just this morning. In fact, time has been playing strange tricks on me all week. It's only been five days since Harry showed up at my house and turned my life sideways yet it feels like months ago.

I freeze as I hear a soft thump from upstairs. What the hell was that? I strain my ears. Voices upstairs...burglars? It can't be. No one would be crazy enough to break into my house with all that lot outside. My heart judders as I hear the creak of a door, then footsteps on the landing.

Whoever it is, they're about to come down the stairs.

CHAPTER TWENTY

Maybe it's Scott. But then who's he talking to? Not Ellie, surely. He better bloody not have brought her into my house. Just in case it's an intruder, I gingerly slide open the cutlery drawer and pull out a carving knife. It's pretty blunt, but it could still do some damage.

"Hello?" a woman's voice calls out from the stairs. *My* stairs. "Tessa, is that you?"

I recognise that rasp. But she can't have let herself into my home without permission. Surely not. She wouldn't dare. "Carly?" I call out, striding into the hallway to see her staring down the staircase at me.

"Hi, Tessa," she says with a smile, bold as brass.

"What the hell are you doing in my house?" I cry.

"Don't be mad, Tessa. It's a surprise." She takes a few more steps until she's halfway down the stairs. I'm still at the bottom, staring up at her.

"I've had enough surprises to last a lifetime," I retort. "And answer my question. What are you doing here? And who were you talking to? I heard voices."

"Just trust me," she says. "You'll be pleased, I promise."

I'm so angry right now I want to push her down the staircase and kick her out onto the street. I begin marching up the stairs towards her.

"Is that a knife?" Carly takes a step back.

I realise I'm still gripping the carving knife, brandishing it in her direction. "I thought you were a burglar." I drop my hand to hold it loosely at my side.

"Oh, right." She backs up to the landing. "Well, I'm not a burglar, as you can see."

"Hmph," I reply. "How did you get in?"

"I wanted to do something nice for you."

"Answer the question, Carly. How did you get in?"

She mutters something under her breath.

"What?"

"The key under the plant pot," she mumbles.

"How dare you!" I cry. Scott stupidly told Carly about that key back when we were friendlier and she agreed to come over and water the plants in the garden while we were on holiday. And I—even more stupidly—didn't think to remove it after Scott moved out. In fact, I'd forgotten it was even there. "Is it back under the pot now?" I ask.

She gives me a sheepish look, so I hold out my hand.

"You sure?" she asks, raising her eyebrows and tilting her head. "It might be handy for me to hang onto it in case you ever get locked out."

I give her my best scowl and push my outstretched hand up close to her face.

"Fine, okay." She draws the key from her pocket and drops it into my palm.

"Look, Carly, I'm sorry, but I'm not in the mood for what-ever it is you want to surprise me with. I've had another shit day in a long line of shit days, and I'm having an even shittier evening. I just want to go to bed and read my book with a cup of tea, if that's not too much to ask. So please, take your surprise and get out. You're bloody lucky I don't call the police."

"That's a bit overdramatic," she says. "Just trust me. You'll like this."

Trust her? Ha. That's a joke. It takes all my willpower not to scream at her. How can she have such a thick skin? She hasn't even apologised for being here. Can't she see how completely out of order she is?

"So," she says, "my brother, Vince, he's a builder. I asked him to come over and fix your window. Ta-da..." She pushes open my bedroom door to reveal a scruffy guy in his early twenties next to my bed, standing on a stained and paint-splattered blanket, rummaging around in a large tool bag. He looks up and nods my way. I glare at him, noticing he's already removed the sheet of chipboard from the window and propped it up against the wall. The curtains billow as freezing air sweeps into the room.

I'm so taken aback, I can't actually think of anything to say. I'm furious at Carly for presuming it would be okay to let herself and her brother into my house while I'm out. But I can't yell at her like I want to because she's here to supposedly do me a favour although I'm highly suspicious of her motives. She'd better not have been snooping around. I narrow my eyes, wondering what she's up to. I don't believe she's doing this to be nice.

"There's no catch," she says, reading my mind. "I just want to help."

"You should have asked," I say.

"I was going to, but you were out," she says. "And this is the only time Vince is free to do it. I saw you come back, speak to the police and go out again. Look, after all the crap you've had to deal with, I figured you could use a break."

If I kick her out now, I'll look like an ungrateful cow. "I haven't even had any quotes yet," I say. "How much is this going to cost?"

"Vince doesn't want any payment."

With my current financial situation, an offer like this is not to be sniffed at. On the other hand, I could really do without more people disrupting my evening. "How long is it going to take?"

"Vince?" Carly says.

"Half an hour, tops," he replies without looking round.

"Okay then," I say. "Thank you, I suppose." This doesn't mean I trust her, but at least once her brother's fixed the window it'll keep out the arctic draught and I'll be able to sleep in my bedroom again.

I take a couple of steps across the landing to the airing cupboard, press the central-heating switch and wait for the rumble and swoosh of the boiler to fire up. It'll take ages for the house to warm up, so I shuffle back into my bedroom—where Vince is now pulling out shards of glass from the window frame—and grab a fleecy sweater from the chest of drawers. I slide off my coat, pull the sweater over my three existing layers of clothing and shrug my coat back over the top. Not for the first time, I wonder why I can't be left alone. Just for one day.

"Don't suppose I could have a cup of tea?" Vince says hopefully.

I roll my eyes.

"I can make it," Carly offers.

I ignore her. "Okay, how do you take it?"

"Milk, two sugars."

I stomp back down the stairs and into the kitchen. Carly follows me. What's she still doing here? Is she planning on staying until her brother's finished? I'm not sure why she needs to be here too, but it would be churlish to ask her to leave. After all, she is doing me a favour. Although if I was being picky about things, this whole press debacle was her fault in the first place, so really, fixing my window is the least she could do.

"Sorry my text was a bit abrupt this morning," she says as I switch on the kettle. "It's just, I was really banking on you speaking to Flores. Finding out what she knows."

"Yeah, well, I did try, but short of breaking down her door, there wasn't much else I could do."

"Sure, I get that," she says.

"And it's *my* life we're talking about here." I'm a little indignant that she secretly thinks I've somehow failed. "It's not like I didn't want to speak to the woman. I mean, if there's anyone who wants to know what's going on, it's me."

There's a long pause.

I reach into the cupboard and draw out the last three clean mugs. "Tea?" I ask, hoping she'll say no and leave.

"Please. Black, no sugar." She doesn't say anything else for a while, which must take incredible self-control for someone as pushy as Carly. This must be her new strategy—to be nice and non-journalisty. I doubt it will last long.

I finish making the tea, take Vince's up to him and come back down to the kitchen.

"Hope you didn't get into any trouble because you visited Flores," Carly says as I walk back in.

"No, why should I? Oh, you mean the police car outside."

"I thought Flores might have reported you," Carly adds.

"No, the police wanted to talk to me about something else. Just a trivial follow-up thing." I can't tell her I went to see Fisher. If I do, it'll probably end up all over the news.

"What follow-up thing?" Carly asks.

"Nothing. They were just…er…clarifying something in my last statement." I take a sip of tea and rack my brains to think of a way to change the subject.

"Why have you gone so quiet?" Carly asks. "Is it something to do with Fisher?" She fixes me with a stare, so I look down into my mug, hoping she can't read minds. "Did you..." I squirm in my seat. I've never had a good poker face. "You did, didn't you!"

"Sorry, I don't know what you're—"

"Did you go and see him? Is that where you've been? Oh, just admit it, Tessa. That's the reason for the hire car. You went to see Fisher, didn't you?" She grins and leans forward, her green cat-eyes gleaming.

I don't reply. My cheeks heat up and I shift in my seat. She's guessed. *No.* She doesn't know for sure. I just need to keep my mouth shut and not tell her where I've been. Not if I don't want this media hell to blow up even more. The kitchen is silent save for a few scrapes and bangs coming from upstairs. "You know what, Carly, I really am tired. How much longer is your brother going to take up there?"

"Not too long," she says. "But come on, Tessa, if you spoke to Fisher, what did he say?"

My face must be flaming scarlet by now, the warmth from my cheeks enough to give the central heating a run for its money.

"Okay, how about you tell me off the record?" she tries.

I honestly don't believe anything is "off the record" with Carly Dean. I clamp my lips together, refusing to reply. If I tell her, she'll sell me out again and then I can wave goodbye to any chance of the press leaving me alone. It'll be even worse than it is now. This girl is relentless, how am I going to get her off my back?

CHAPTER TWENTY-ONE

"Look," Carly says, growing serious, "just tell me. Did you go to see Fisher today? I swear I won't write anything until we have proof of what he's up to, but you have to talk to me otherwise I can't help you."

Is she right? Can she help me? I've had no luck getting information myself. Maybe, instead of being an adversary, she could be my ally. Maybe.

"Okay." She nods, as if having come to some internal agreement. "How about you tell me what you know, but I won't write anything until we have the full story?"

Could I ever bring myself to trust her? Probably not.

She sighs. "How about if I let you see what I've written before it's printed?"

"How much would you get paid for a story like this?" I ask, suddenly curious.

She smirks, and I'm instantly irritated. "I can pay you a percentage, if that's what you're holding out for," she says.

"I don't want money!" I spit, rising to my feet.

She loses the smirk and holds the palms of her hands out, trying and failing to placate me. I turn away from her, gripping the counter top while I count to ten. How does this woman manage to rile me every single time I lay eyes on her?

"Sorry," she says. "I'm sorry. I realise this isn't about the money for you, Tessa. And you might not believe it, but money isn't the only driver for me either. Well, okay, it probably is the main one—I'll lose the house if I don't land a good story soon—but I also want to help you get answers. I just wanted you to know that if I do make anything out of this, you'll get your share."

"You might lose the house?" I say, turning back to face her.

"Yeah, well, that's the joy of being freelance. The ups and the downs."

"I'm sorry to hear that, Carly. I obviously don't want you to lose your home. It's just…I wish you didn't have to be quite so…" I trail off, not wanting to finish the sentence as the only words in my head are "cut-throat," "mercenary" and "ruthless."

"I know I can come across like a bull in a china shop," she says. "That's just the way I am, it's what makes me good at my job. My mum says I'm determined."

"That's one way of putting it," I say with a reluctant smile.

"Okay, Tessa, how about this…?"

I shake my head at her continued perseverance. "I'm sorry, but it's no good, Carly. I've had enough. I need to go to bed and you need to leave."

"Please come and sit back down. Listen to my final offer. If you don't like it, I'll leave you alone and never bother you again. Not even to borrow a pint of milk when I've run out."

"Is that a promise?" I murmur.

"Yes, it's a cross-my-heart-and-hope-to-die promise." She gestures to the empty chair and I gingerly sit back down. "So," she begins, "the way I see it, Fisher's hiding something. If you did speak to him, you probably know more than I do. But I can help you dig deeper and find out how his son ended up at your house. If we work on this together, we've got a better chance of discovering the truth. True, I'm doing this for my career, but...I also like you—despite what you might think—plus I can't stand it when someone gets away with something. And I think Fisher is getting away with something, and I think you do too."

She leans back in her chair and laces her fingers together. "So how about this: we tell each other everything we find out. I promise not to sell the story until we've discovered all there is to know. You can read what I write, plus you get to veto anything you don't like. But I have exclusivity so you can't tell anyone else."

I absorb her words, turning them over in my mind like coins to be weighed and measured. If I don't go for her terms, then I'm back to where I was before. Stuck. Knowing nothing. Accepting that I'll never find out what really happened with Harry. If I do accept her deal, then I'm putting my fate in her hands, hoping she'll be true to her word and that she won't sell me out the minute I've confirmed I went to see Fisher.

I realise that coming here to fix my window was a ruse to get in and have me confide in her. Either that, or an opportunity to snoop while I was out. But how else am I going to get answers? Sod it, I may as well tell her. Ultimately, I need her help. "Okay," I say. "But I want you to put it in writing."

She gives me a quizzical look.

"Your proposition, what you just told me. Put it in writing and sign it." I walk over to the odds-and-ends drawer and pull out an old sketchbook and a biro, sliding them across the table towards her.

"Not sure it's legal if it hasn't been witnessed," she says.

"Just write it out and sign and print your name with the date," I say. "That will be good enough for me."

I pace the kitchen while she writes out the deal and signs

her name. I take the proffered sketchbook from her, read through what she's written and then sign my name underneath hers.

"So," she says. "Are we good?"

I nod and sit back down as Carly takes a small notebook and pencil out of her handbag.

"You're right," I say. "I went to see James Fisher."

"I'm impressed." She exhales. "You have got balls after all." I can almost hear the cogs whirring in her brain. *Does she have a story for me? Is this going to be great for my career? Am I going to make a mint?* "So, you went to see him," she continues. "And he spoke to you."

"More like he yelled at me and I almost got arrested," I say, twisting my lips into a scowl at the memory.

"Tell me exactly what happened," she says.

I describe my trip to Cranborne. How I went around the back of Fisher's house and knocked on his door. I tell her what I said to him and how he yelled at me. I don't mention seeing Harry in the hallway. It's not relevant to anything and I somehow feel uncomfortable about it.

She nods and makes uh-huh noises as I recount the day's events, rounding off with the police visit. With them issuing me a PIN warning me to stay away from Cranborne unless I want to be arrested.

Her forehead furrows.

"Something wrong?" I ask.

"Uh, is that it?" she says.

"What do you mean?"

"Well, you've basically just told me that you went onto Fisher's private property and he told you to get lost."

I nod. "Yes, because that's what happened."

"I thought you'd had an actual conversation with him, that

he'd told you something interesting. We're no further along than we were before."

"But it shows he has something to hide, doesn't it? Him being so aggressive towards me."

"No, Tessa. He did what anyone would do if a stranger suspected of abducting their child showed up at night in their back garden, banging on the door."

"Fine," I snap. "You wanted to know what happened, so I told you."

"Thanks for nothing," she murmurs, stuffing her notebook and pencil back in her bag and rising to her feet.

God, I want to slap her. "You're the one who came round here uninvited, Carly. You're the one demanding I share my life with you. So don't go getting all stroppy when I don't tell you what you want to hear."

She rolls her eyes and turns to leave.

But even as I'm clinging to my anger and indignation, I remember something else. Something I really should share with Carly. "Hang on a minute, hang on. There's something I forgot to tell you."

She turns back to face me, her face resigned to the possibility that what I'm about to say will prove equally disappointing.

"I didn't mention it before," I begin, "but...well...someone has been following me."

Carly's eyes narrow and she takes out her notebook once more.

"Not a journalist or anything like that," I add. "A woman. I spotted her a few times watching me in the street while I was out shopping or walking. I didn't know who she was, and every time I tried to confront her, she gave me the slip. She looked like she was scared of me. Anyway, when I went to see Fisher's housekeeper this morning, I caught her looking down at me from the window of her flat. And, well, it's her."

"Fisher's housekeeper has been following you?"

I nod.

"Okay, this is more like it, Tess. Tell me when and where you've seen her before."

I detail the times and places I've seen the woman. "She could have been following me on other occasions, too, but those were the only times I actually saw her. Do you have any theories why?"

"No." Carly chews the end of her pencil. "Maybe we need to ask *him*—Fisher."

"Already tried that," I say. "It didn't work out too well."

She doesn't reply.

"So what happens next?" I ask, nervous about what her response might be.

"I'm tied up this weekend, which is bloody annoying," she says, "but first thing Monday morning, I'm going to confront Flores, see if I can get her to talk. I seriously doubt she will. Sounds like she's scared of something. If I don't have any luck there, I'll head to Cranborne to confront Fisher. My gut is telling me the housekeeper's scared of him. I'm going to be asking him some serious questions."

"You'll be lucky," I say. "He's not answering the door to journalists."

"Don't worry about that, I'll get him to talk to me."

"How?"

"I'll work out the details," she says, her mouth set in a determined line.

CHAPTER TWENTY-TWO

It's 10:30 by the time Carly and her brother leave. I offer Vince a cheque for twenty pounds, feeling guilty that his sister has roped him into helping me out. But Carly tells me to keep it. Cynically, I guess that's because she's hoping I'll make her a nice chunk of cash from my car-crash life. I still don't trust her, but at least she's signed a document saying she won't print anything without my permission. Actually, I'm exhausted by the whole thing, and despite being bone-weary, I'm looking forward to going to work tomorrow, back to a bit of normality. Some respite from this crazy alternate universe I'm inhabiting. My day off was hardly the break I was hoping for. Maybe a good night's sleep will sort me out.

As I get changed into a pair of fleecy pink pyjamas, I'm cheered by the fact that my room feels so much nicer now. Warmer, and less like the boarded-up student squat of a few hours ago. I crawl under the covers, set my alarm and switch off my bedside lamp. Lying on my side, I close my eyes.

It's quiet. Just the beating of my heart in my ears, and my uneven breath. In. Out. In. Out. An occasional hiss and gurgle from the radiator. A distant car engine. I will myself to fall asleep, but my brain is like chewing gum, a sticky mess. Too many thoughts racing around with nowhere to go: the house-keeper, Carly, the police... But the one battling for supremacy in my mind is the question of Dr. Fisher and where I recognise him from. Do I know him? Or is it just that I've seen his picture so many times in the paper and on the news that I merely *think* I know him?

I'm never going to fall asleep, am I? I push the covers away and fumble for the lamp switch, clicking it on and screwing my face up against the sudden brightness. Scrabbling about for my phone, I plump up the pillows behind my head and open up Google. I tap in the name *Dr. James Fisher* and then *Cranborne*.

The results begin filling up the screen. All the posts are from this week. And all are regarding his son's recent disappearance. My name is mentioned in most of the pieces—most of them uncomplimentary. I grit my teeth and keep scrolling through, knowing it isn't good for me to be reading such awful things: *child snatcher…abductor…mental health issues…two dead children.* I take a breath and look away from the screen for a moment. These lurid stories aren't the type of thing I'm looking for, I'm interested in Fisher's past. Where he used to live and work.

I delete the word *Cranborne* and try the search again. Once more I'm forced to scroll down past all the current stories. Eventually I come to a newspaper article from 2012. James Fisher is one of several doctors to be quoted—but is it *my* James Fisher? There's no photo. The piece is about the rising cost of insurance for private obstetricians. I skim the article until I reach the bit about him:

Dr. James Fisher, one of the most experienced obstetricians in the country, said the rise in insurance premiums had forced him to almost double his charges to £7,000 over the past three years.

"If the insurance goes up, the charges go up," explained

Dr. Fisher, who sees around 120 private patients a year. "In fact, this could very well put a stop to private births in the UK. Unfortunately, there's nothing I can do about the rising premiums. Instead, I'll be setting up a new practice away from London to cut down on overhead costs and hopefully pass these savings on to my clients."

I read through the rest of the article, but there's no further mention of Fisher or the name of the hospital where he works.

I spend the next ten minutes or so scrolling through the other results. There's nothing that definitively suggests Harry's father is the same doctor as the one from that first article. One of them brings up a "Meet the Team" page for a maternity clinic in Wimborne, Dorset, along with a photo of the man I met in Cranborne. This must be where he currently works. His photograph—a corporate headshot—sits at the top of the page to the left of a short biography. *Qualified in 1992, with over ten years' experience as a gynaecologist, and now a consultant obstetrician and gynaecologist in Wimborne…*

So now I know that the James Fisher in London and the one in Wimborne are both gynaecologists. That's too much of a coincidence; surely they are one and the same man? I continue scanning the results. Just as my eyes are beginning to grow heavy, a name jumps out at me from one of the articles— a hospital monthly newsletter: *Having previously worked at Parkfield Hospital, consultant James Fisher is now leaving the team here at the Balmoral Clinic to set up his own practice in Dorset.*

There it is! The connection: the Balmoral Clinic. A chill sweeps over my body. That must be why I recognise him. My heart begins to twang painfully, like a string being plucked. James Fisher practised at the clinic where I gave birth to my children.

After my parents died, I was left a small inheritance. Most of this went on the deposit for our house, but Scott persuaded me to use the rest to have our twins in a private hospital, rather than use the NHS. Apparently, his favourite footballer and his wife were having their child at the Balmoral, a swanky private birth clinic here in London so Scott thought I should do the same. Granted, the midwives were lovely and the place was like a boutique hotel, but I really didn't see the point of wasting all that money when I could have had my children for free in a perfectly good hospital. And ultimately, despite the five-star treatment, that posh clinic couldn't prevent my daughter's death.

I had a natural birth, delivering Sam first and then Lily. Sam was fine, but Lily died only half an hour after being born. I didn't even get to hold her while she was alive. The report said it was due to umbilical cord compression resulting in a lack of oxygen and blood flow. Apparently this type of cord compression is common when carrying twins, but only a small number of babies die because of it.

I always wondered if we should have questioned the hospital staff further—asked for an autopsy or an inquiry. But at the time, Scott and I were all over the place, not thinking straight. Relieved at Sam's safe arrival, but devastated by the loss of Lily.

I remember holding Sam in my arms when they told me Lily hadn't made it. A boy and a girl, I kept saying to myself over and over like a chant. A boy and a girl. We hadn't wanted to know the sexes beforehand, we wanted it to be a surprise. Sam had dark hair like Scott, and Lily was fair like me. I can see her in my mind's eye. Picture her perfect little body with her ten pink fingers and ten pink toes, tiny shell-like ears and almost translucent skin. And her utter, utter stillness.

I blink, shaking away the image as my mind begins to race,

synapses firing, lights flashing on, my body quivering. What does this new information actually mean? Surely it has to mean something. Something big…?

What if…what if Fisher was the consultant who delivered my babies? Our assigned consultant—Dr. Friedland—couldn't attend the birth as he was ill at the time with gastric flu. I can't remember the name of the doctor on duty when Sam and Lily were born. He was briefly at the delivery, but disappeared soon after, leaving Scott and me in the care of the midwives. Could it have been Fisher?

I sigh with frustration. Why can't I remember? There is one way to find out. I recall Sam's red book—the health record that detailed his developmental milestones. Surely the name of the medical staff who attended the birth would have been recorded in it?

I jump out of bed, slip my feet into my ancient, ratty slippers, and head downstairs, still clutching my phone, my mind whirling with all this might mean. Then I pad through the hall and into the dining room, which used to double as my office. I switch on the overhead chandelier—an extravagant purchase from back when I used to care about stuff like interior design. The light in here is dim and shadowy. I look up and notice that only one of the five bulbs still works.

I stride across the room towards my desk—a dusty white slab of wood—and crouch down to pull open the bottom drawer of the filing cabinet tucked beneath it. Sam has his own file, a slim folder containing all his paperwork and achievements. A file I expected to grow fatter over the years, but which instead has remained the same sad width. Lily's file is even slimmer.

Walking my fingers across the tops of the alphabetised files, I scan from P to R to S. But to my irritation, Sam's file isn't here. Perhaps it's been put back incorrectly. My knees ache from crouching, so I sit on the draughty wooden floor and cross my legs as I painstakingly search through first the bottom drawer and then the top drawer of the filing cabinet. Still no sign of Sam's file, or Lily's. I check again. Nothing. I begin opening desk drawers, checking bookshelves. I heave out the filing cabinet from underneath the desk. There are various dusty papers squashed behind it, but nothing about Sam. No red book.

Maybe Scott moved it. He wouldn't have taken it with him, would he? It's not the sort of thing that would be on his radar. Paperwork has never been his forte. I pull up his number on my phone and call him. After six rings, it goes to voicemail. I call again. Voicemail again. I check the time: it's 11:40. Late, but not hideously late. Okay, maybe it is. But damn it, this is important. I call again.

"This had better be good, Tessa." His voice is croaky, like I just woke him up.

"Sorry, Scott. I know it's late."

No reply, just the weight of his annoyance across the airwaves.

"Do you know where Sam's red book is?" I ask.

"His what?"

"You know the one. The red book, his health record."

"I don't know. Couldn't this have waited until tomorrow morning?"

"It should be in the filing cabinet with all his other stuff," I say.

There's silence on the other end of the line.

"Scott? You still there?"

"Look, Tessa, don't get mad, but I took Sam and Lily's files."

"You did *what?*" I shift around onto my knees and sit on my heels. "Why did you take them? They're just as much mine as they are yours."

"I know that, but I was worried about you. After we lost

Sam, you became obsessed with their pictures and records. You used to spend hours going through everything, looking at their charts, talking to yourself."

"I wasn't that bad. And anyway, it comforted me to read about them."

"Don't you remember?" he says. "Your therapist had to help wean you off looking at them."

I push away the memory. It was a dark time, I don't want to remember it.

"Once you were able to put them away," he continues, "I thought it'd be best to hide them just in case you went back to them. It's not healthy to dwell on all that stuff. You don't need those files, Tessa. Forget them."

"Where are they now? Did you put them in the attic? In the wardrobe?"

"No, I brought them with me when I moved out."

"You took them!" The thought of my children's records not being here in the house throws my pulse into overdrive. I may not spend time poring through them any longer, but I always assumed they were here with me in case I ever needed to look at them. Like an ex-smoker who keeps one cigarette in a drawer for emergencies.

I take a breath to calm down. Yelling at Scott isn't going to help my cause. I've worked myself up into such a state, I've almost forgotten why I wanted the files in the first place. "I'm coming round to get them."

"It's too late to come over, it's almost midnight. And anyway, you're not having them. You don't need them."

"I *do* need them."

"I'm hanging up now, going back to bed. You should go to bed too."

"Don't hang up, Scott. Just listen. If you won't give them to me, then do me a favour. Go and have a look in Sam's red book and see if it says the name of the doctor who delivered him."

"What? What's all this about? Why do you need to know that? Have you been drinking, Tessa? You sound a bit manic."

"Just find the name of the doctor for me. Please."

"Tessa, you need to drop this. I'm going to end the call now, and I think you should make an appointment to go back and see your therapist."

"Scott! Don't you dare hang up on me!"

"Tell you what, I'll make a deal with you. I'll give you the files back after you've been to see a therapist."

"No, I don't need to see anyone." I debate whether to tell him about my discovery—that Dr. Fisher used to practise in the clinic where the twins were born—but it's all just coincidence at the moment. Scott would probably think I was delusional, seeing conspiracy theories where there aren't any, giving him more fuel to add to his argument about me seeing a therapist. Plus, I don't trust him not to tell the police—or Ellie. And if they thought I was digging into Fisher's past, they'd call me back into the station. I need more concrete evidence before I tell anyone.

"That's my deal," he says wearily. "Take it or leave it. Believe it or not, I still care about you, Tessa. I want you to be happy."

"Fine," I snap. "I'll see a therapist. And then you have to give me back the files."

"Okay."

"Promise?"

"I promise."

I stab the phone screen and end the call. Looks like I have little choice but to do what he asks. But can I trust him to do as he's promised? Since Scott got together with Ellie, it's like he's a completely different person. It's like she's twisted him into someone else.

CHAPTER TWENTY-THREE

My alarm wakes me on Saturday morning and last night's discovery hits me once more. What could it mean? There are so many thoughts swirling through my mind. But I can't let my imagination run away until I know for sure whether or not Fisher actually was my doctor the night my babies were born. Bloody Scott, taking the twins' files and trying to make me see a therapist. How dare he hold me to ransom like that!

I fling the bedclothes back and get out of bed, automatically heading to the window and peering through the curtains to see how many press are out there this morning. It's dark outside, the street lights still glowing. I can't see anyone. Perhaps they're in their cars, getting a last bit of shut-eye before making my life hell again.

As I shower and dress, I decide that I'm not going to allow Scott to dictate to me. I don't believe he wants me to see a therapist out of concern for my well-being. If he was really worried about me, he would have phoned when he first saw my name splashed across the headlines. He would have come over when he discovered the press were harassing me. He would have been there for me when I told him someone had lobbed a brick through my window. No, the only thing Scott is concerned about is keeping me away from him and his perfect new family-in-waiting. I pull my jeans on and stomp over to the chest of drawers to get a pair of socks. It's the last clean pair—I'll have to do some washing tonight.

I think the only reason Scott wants me to see a therapist is so he can palm me off onto someone else. He's trying to get rid of me. I sit heavily on the edge of the bed and pull on my socks. I don't suppose I can blame him, but it still hurts to be cast aside like an old handbag with a broken strap. *Stop it, Tessa. Don't get maudlin.* I know what I'll do, I'll call the hospital. They'll have records of who delivered whose baby. Surely.

I have my hire car for seven days, so I decide I'll drive to work to keep the press at bay. Forty minutes later, I pull open the front door, preparing to do battle with the horde. But the pavement outside is empty. Silent. A puddle of morning light spreads out behind the houses opposite. Do I dare to even hope? I step out onto the frosty path and glance up and down the road: they're not here, the press have finally gone. I exhale and experience a momentary feeling of lightness.

No need for the hire car today, then. I walk to work with a nervous sense of freedom, trying to stop myself from holding my breath every time someone walks towards me, or past me, or when a car drives too close to the pavement, or I hear laughter, or someone talking louder than a whisper. Rolling my shoulders back and forth, I tell myself to calm down and enjoy it. They've gone, they've actually gone. I think I had convinced myself they would be with me forever. But I guess with no new elements to the story, no new angles to dissect, they've lost interest. My story is finally today's fish-and-chip wrapper.

I reach work fifteen minutes early, and the pavement outside is as blissfully clear of journalists as the road outside my house was. Despite everything else on my mind, I almost skip through the gates. I didn't realise quite how much the media presence was dragging me down. I wonder if they've left Cranborne, too.

"Morning, Tessa." Ben crosses the front yard and walks towards me.

It feels like weeks since I last saw him. Time playing tricks again.

"Good day off?" he asks, doing his crinkly-eyed smile thing.

I smile back, relieved that he seems pleased to see me. I'd made myself believe he was mad at me because of all the disruption my life has brought to Moretti's.

"It was...different," I reply. "But at least the press have gone."

"Sounds like something that needs to be discussed over dinner and a drink," he says. "You up for it after work? My treat. To celebrate the media finally leaving you alone."

I pause. Ben is great company, but I need to call the maternity clinic at lunchtime to see if I can find out any information about Fisher. And, depending on what they say, I may need to keep this evening free.

He must have noticed my hesitation. "No worries if you're busy," he says. "We can always catch up another time."

"Do you mind? I've got a few things to sort out."

"Sure, no problem. I might need you to help out in the shop this afternoon," he says, switching to boss mode. "Now the sun's out, I've a feeling it's going to get busy today."

"Of course," I reply.

"And with the press gone," he adds, "you shouldn't get any more hassle from the customers."

"I can live in hope," I say.

The morning passes quickly. Most of my time is spent helping customers and netting Christmas trees. Ben was right, it is busy. Usually I prefer to work in the background, with the plants, away from actual people, but I don't mind the demands on my time today—it takes my mind off everything else.

At one o'clock, I grab a cheese roll from the café and take it to my favourite spot in the far greenhouse. The place where I'm least likely to be bothered by anyone. I only take a half-hour lunch on Saturdays, so I'd better make this quick. I call the Balmoral Clinic, the number still stored in my phone from before. A woman answers almost straight away.

"Hi," I say. "I have a query. I wonder if you can help."

"I'll try my best," the woman replies.

"Thanks. A few years ago, I gave birth to twins at your clinic and I was wondering if you could give me the name of the doctor who was on duty at the time."

"A few years ago?" the woman echoes.

"Yes."

"Well, yes, I suppose we would have that information on our database."

"Oh, that's great news," I say. "The date was the third of March—"

"But we can't give that kind of information out over the phone," she interrupts. "You'd have to put your request in writing."

My heart sinks. That will take ages. "How about if I email you?"

"No, I'm afraid we would need a signed letter from you."

That could take days! I can't wait around that long. "I really need the information today," I say, trying my best to sound like a nice person she might take pity on.

"Even if we could answer your enquiry, there's no one from admin here at the weekend," she says. "If you're local, you could always visit in person. You'll need to bring two forms of ID, though—something with your address, like a utility bill."

"Brilliant. Today?"

"No. Like I said, our admin staff don't work weekends. Pop in on Monday between nine and five thirty."

"Okay," I reply, deflated. "Thanks."

"No problem."

This is so frustrating—I'll have to wait a whole two days to find out what I need to know. How will I be able to wait that long?

I split the rest of my day between the shop and the garden, with barely two seconds to breathe, let alone think about James Fisher. By the time six o'clock rolls around, Carolyn, Janet, Ben and I are all on an exhausted high.

"Great day, everyone," Ben says, cashing up at the café till. "Thanks for all your hard work."

"No problem," Janet says as she heads to the door. "See you tomorrow."

"Bye," we all call.

"I'm off, too," Carolyn adds with a wave, walking across the café.

"Oh, Carolyn," I call out, catching her up. "Can I ask a quick favour?"

"Need another lift?" she asks. "You know those newspaper people have gone now?"

"Yeah, thank God. And thanks for the offer, but I don't need a lift. No, I was wondering if you're able to swap a half-day. I've got an appointment next week, so I was hoping I could work Sunday morning for you if you'll do Monday morning for me."

"You want to work tomorrow morning?" she asks.

"If that's okay?"

"It's more than okay. My feet are killing me, I'd love a lie-in tomorrow. You're on, if it's okay with the boss." She raises her voice so Ben can hear that last part.

"If what's okay with the boss?" he calls back over the chink of coins being poured into banking bags.

"Me and Tess are swapping. She's in tomorrow morning, I'm doing Monday."

"As long as someone's here, that's fine by me," he replies.

On the walk back home, I text Carly. If she's going to see Fisher on Monday, I need to keep her up to date with everything I've discovered.

Hope you're having a good weekend. I've got some pretty big news about Fisher.

???

I found out he used to work at the same maternity clinic where I gave birth.

No. Fucking. Way.

I know. It's pretty mental.

Which clinic? Was he your consultant?

The Balmoral. Don't know if he was on duty that night or not. Am going to the clinic on Monday morning to find out.

Cool. You go to clinic. I'll go to Cranborne. Let me know if you find out anything else. Something "fishy" going on here— geddit? Sorry, crap joke.

I smile grimly at the phone screen. Yeah, something fishy is definitely going on here. Something that's making my stomach feel like there's a writhing worm in it, slithering about, cold and uncomfortable. And I suspect this feeling will stay with me until I've worked out exactly what it is.

CHAPTER TWENTY-FOUR

I stop at the supermarket on my way home to pick up some essentials, my whole body brimming with nervous energy. I should run it off or something, but I know I won't do that. I'll probably go home and read instead. Try to distract myself until Monday, when I can go to the clinic and hopefully find answers. I'll work Carolyn's shift tomorrow morning and then, in the afternoon, I'll go to the cemetery.

Back home, I dump my shopping on the table. Stare around the silent kitchen. Am I really going to spend another long, miserable night alone when my perfectly nice boss has asked me out? I shove the food in the fridge and pull my phone out of my bag. He answers it after two rings.

"Tess?"

"Hi, Ben." My mouth is dry. I swallow. "I was wondering if that offer of dinner and a drink still stands."

"Yes. Sure it does."

"Great. Shall we meet at the Oak?"

"It'll be a nightmare in there on a Saturday evening. How about I cook us something instead?"

"You cook?"

"Of course I cook. I'm Italian, remember? Two things in Italy we take very seriously, cooking and football, but I'm not much of a football fan." I hear the smile in his voice and find myself smiling back, even though he can't see. "Give me an hour," he says. "Don't use the work gates, come round the front of the house and ring the bell."

"Okay," I reply. "Want me to bring anything?"

"Just you."

I shower and change, deciding not to go overboard, opting for jeans, a pale blue wool jumper and a pair of navy suede ankle boots with spike heels—my one concession to the fact that it's a Saturday night. *Is this a date?* I wonder.

There's no way I'm walking over there in these heels, so I decide to make use of the hire car. I check myself in the hall mirror—my hair's still a bit damp, but it'll be fine. My face could do with a bit of help, though. I root around in my bag for a lipstick, find one rolling around the bottom and take off the lid. Pale pink, that'll do. I smear it on lightly and press my lips together. Okay. I'm ready, I think. No, I am. One last glance in the mirror, and I leave the house and walk down the pathway onto the gloriously empty pavement.

The drive over to Moretti's only takes five minutes. I spend those minutes trying to analyse how I feel about Ben. He's a great employer. He's a nice guy. He's good-looking, maybe even handsome. Yes, definitely handsome. Going to his house for dinner has to be a date, doesn't it? I realise I'm nervous—as in butterflies-in-the-stomach nervous. Which is ridiculous, given that it's just Ben. But maybe that's because he's never been on my radar as anything other than a boss and a friend. I've only known him since I started working at Moretti's, but we clicked straight away—same sense of humour, I guess. I need to keep it that way—strictly platonic. I can't afford to lose my job, and I don't have the mental energy for a relationship. There's too much other crap going on in my life right now.

Suddenly assailed by a flurry of doubts, I use the back of my hand to wipe off my lipstick. Don't want to send out the wrong signals. I'm regretting wearing heels, too. Oh, for God's sake, Tess. Pull yourself together. I could hardly have turned up in my work fleece.

Ben welcomes me into his hallway and takes my coat. "You look lovely," he says.

I mumble a thank-you. He looks incredible in dark jeans and a bottle-green open-necked shirt, his dark hair flopping forward over one eye. Even in heels, I still only come up to his shoulder. As we lean forward to kiss on the cheek, I realise he smells good, too—citrusy and masculine. Damn, I need to get a grip.

"Really sorry," I say. "I should've brought some wine. I feel awful that I didn't get you anything."

"You offered. I told you not to," he says with a smile.

"Well, I know. It still feels rude to arrive empty-handed." I follow him into the kitchen, where he turns and places a glass of red wine in my hand.

"There," he says. "You're not empty-handed any more."

"Thanks, but I'm driving."

"No problem. I'll call you a cab later."

I pause, take a sip. "This is delicious."

He grins and pours a glass for himself. "*Saluti,*" he says, clinking my glass.

"*Saluti,*" I reply, feeling like a fraud. The extent of my Italian is *ciao* and *spaghetti*.

"You sit there and talk to me for a minute," he says, gesturing to a chair at the rustic kitchen table. "I need to check on my sauce."

"Smells gorgeous," I say, sitting down, my mouth beginning to water. I take another sip of wine. "What are you cooking?"

"Ravioli capresi," he says, standing at the range and flinging a tea towel over one shoulder. "My mum's recipe. Be ready in about five minutes."

A cream jug sits in the centre of the table filled with winter daffodils. I try to imagine Scott cooking Italian food for me and filling a vase with flowers. The closest he'd have come to that would've been a takeaway pizza and wilting carnations from the local garage. But I know I'm being uncharitable—Scott doesn't own a garden centre or have Italian parents. Maybe thinking mean things about him is my way of coping with him leaving me behind.

"Can I help at all?" I ask.

"No, it's all under control. Can't have anyone messing up my perfectly orchestrated menu." Ben narrows his eyes, then grins, and we chat about mundane things—work and the weather and such—until he brings over two terracotta bowls of ravioli garnished with basil and Parmesan. He places one of the bowls in front of me, and then sits so we're at right angles to one another. Strangely, this feels more intimate than sitting opposite him, his arm now only a hand's width from mine.

"I'm famished," I say.

"Good. Oh, hang on, I forgot the salad." He goes to the fridge, brings a bowl of red and green leaves to the table.

"From the garden?" I ask.

"Where else? Help yourself to dressing."

"Oh my God, this is like eating sunshine," I say through a mouthful of creamy pasta and tomato sauce.

"Glad you like it."

We eat in silence for a few moments. It's a little awkward, but not painfully so. I try to push all the other stuff out of my head, but it's hard to be in the moment when so much is crowding my mind.

"Not out partying on a Saturday night, then?" I ask.

"Nah. I'm not twenty-two any more."

"No, but you're not ninety-two either."

"I go out," he says defensively.

I widen my eyes and we both laugh.

"Okay, *sometimes* I go out," he amends. "*Occasionally* I go out. All right, once in a blue moon I meet the lads down the pub. You know, exciting stuff. Truth be told, I'm a bit of a workaholic. Moretti's has kind of got under my skin this past year."

I nod. "I can see how you'd want to spend all your time here. It's a pretty amazing place."

"Glad you think so."

I hope he doesn't ask me about the promotion again. I'm not quite ready to give him an answer.

"I like having you working here," he says, looking me in the eye. I stare back for a moment, but I can't hold his gaze. I'm nervous about what might be happening. The butterflies in my stomach flap their wings. I take a sip of wine and spear a cushion of ravioli.

"How come you're not married?" I ask, finding my voice again, but feeling immediately embarrassed for asking such a personal question. "Sorry," I stammer. "Tell me to mind my own business if you'd rather not answer that."

"No, I don't mind," he says with a shrug. "It's a boring story about an Italian boy and his girlfriend. The boy thought they'd live happily ever after. The girl shagged his best mate."

"No!" I say. "That's awful. What a bitch."

He smiles and nods. "Yeah."

"When did that happen, if you don't mind me asking?"

"Couple of years ago. I should've known something wasn't right between us. I asked her to marry me three times, and each time she wanted to wait." His tone is light, but I can see the pain behind his eyes.

I put a hand on his arm. "I'm really sorry."

"It's fine, all ancient history. And anyway, I didn't invite you to dinner so I could wail and gnash my teeth over ex-girlfriends."

"I don't mind. Wail away, it's better than talking about my shitty life."

There's a pause before we both dissolve into laughter.

"God, we're a right barrel of laughs," I say.

"Yeah, you can tell I don't have many dinner guests," he replies, rolling his eyes and topping up our glasses. "I need to brush up on my social skills."

I realise that I'm actually enjoying myself. It's a novel situation. "I think your social skills are just fine," I say.

He catches my eye and then takes a deep breath. "In case you haven't guessed by now, I like you, Tess."

I stop laughing and scan his features to see if he's messing with me. To see if he means what I think he means.

"I like you a lot," he murmurs. Then he leans forward and, without warning, kisses me on the mouth, his lips soft and achingly tender. The fresh, warm scent of him surrounds me.

Before I know what's happening, we're on our feet, my fingers caught up in his dark hair, his hands sliding beneath my jumper, his touch electrifying. We're kissing so hard it sets the core of my body alight.

"Tessa," he murmurs as he trails kisses down my neck and across to my ear lobe, making me shiver with pleasure.

I don't care about my earlier doubts or what happens after tonight, all I know is that I need him now.

"Let's go upstairs," I gasp.

"You sure?" He pulls away from me for a moment, his dark eyes soft and enquiring.

"Yes."

We tumble out of the kitchen and I'm hardly aware of our surroundings as Ben pushes me up against the wall. All I want is his hands, his tongue, his body hard against mine. He stops, and I pull him back towards me, but he resists. Instead, he takes my hand and leads me up the narrow staircase to his bedroom. We shed our clothes in a blur of tangled kisses, and fall onto his bed. I don't feel anything like myself: I'm hungry, angry, demanding. Skin, salt, sex—he gives me all I need to blot out the rest of the world. I don't want this to end. Not ever.

CHAPTER TWENTY-FIVE

I wake up to darkness. Hot. Panicked. Where am I? And then I remember: me and Ben. We...Oh God. I'm in his bed, his arm draped around me. I slept with my boss! That sounds so seedy. But it was more than that, wasn't it? We had a moment. A real moment together. But he's still my boss. Shit. Has this put my job in jeopardy? I inhale and try to clear my head, squint at my watch to make out the time—2:30 in the morning. I'll tell him it was a mistake—no, that sounds too harsh. I'll tell him it was an amazing night, but probably a bad idea. I'll make light of it, joke about how we got carried away. Then, hopefully, we can go back to being friends again.

I turn towards him, my eyes adjusting to the darkness, taking in his features—the strong jawline with a hint of new stubble; full lips, Roman nose, dark eyebrows, and that stray lick of hair that falls over one eye. In another lifetime, Ben and I could have been something, I'm sure of it. But in this life, things are too difficult. I can't drag him into my drama, my sadness. He'll go off me. He'll run for the hills and then I'll have lost him, too. He'll leave me heartbroken and I'll have to stop working at Moretti's, and find a crappy job in a soulless chain-store garden shop somewhere. It's better this way.

He stirs. I look away quickly and close my eyes.

"Tess? You awake?"

I stretch and open my eyes again. He turns towards me and props himself up on one elbow. Dips his head to kiss my mouth, and the fire inside me begins to glow once more. But I can't do this, I remind myself. I pull away.

"I...I'd better go," I stammer, my voice too high. "What's the time?"

"Who cares what the time is." His hand comes beneath the covers to rest on my hip, and I realise I'm naked.

"Sorry, Ben," I say, shifting away from him and out of the bed, looking around for my clothes. "I ought to get back home. I've got work tomorrow morning, in case you'd forgotten." I'm trying to keep my voice light, but it sounds a little hysterical to my ears.

"Tess, what's wrong? Come back to bed. Stay here, then you'll already be at work for tomorrow."

"Honestly, I can't. I need to go home." Where's that jokey attitude I wanted to project? Why do I sound like I want to get as far away from him as possible, when in fact the opposite is true?

Ben sits up as I awkwardly pull on my jeans and jumper, clutching my underwear in my hands. "Have I...done something wrong?" he says. "Did you not want to...?"

"Oh, Ben, no. Tonight has been amazing," I say. "More than amazing."

"So stay."

"I can't. I can't do any more than...this. We can't be together or anything. Not that I'm suggesting you want us to be together. I just mean, tonight was wonderful, but let's not make things complicated. I work for you, remember?"

"There's nothing complicated about it," he says. "I told you before, I like you. That hasn't changed."

"I like you too," I reply, taking a step towards the door. "But I have a lot going on in my life right now. Heavy stuff."

"So share it with me. I'm a good listener."

My brain is still fuzzy from sleep. I wouldn't know where to begin telling Ben what's been going on, he only knows the half of it. The rest would send him bolting in the other direction, I'm sure. "It's not something I can talk about at the moment. Let's stay friends, yeah?"

"Friends." His voice is flat, dull. "Fine."

"Ben? Are we okay?"

"Yep, fine."

Shit. "You sound... Never mind. I'll see you in a few hours, at work."

"Okay."

I've screwed up big-time. He's already pulling away from me. Why did I sleep with him? He's too nice a guy to be messed around. I can't let myself think about how it felt to be with him. How everything bad fell away for those moments. But it wasn't real. And it wouldn't last. Better to stop it now before it goes any further. I just wish I didn't like him so much, I wish I could enjoy the moment. But I know how easy it would be to fall for Ben, and after Scott... how can I trust anyone again? Anyway, once Ben realises what a mess I am, he's bound to lose interest, and I can't put myself through all that. I'm not strong enough.

"I'm sorry," I say.

"Me too."

I turn away and walk out the door.

I only had a few sips of wine, so I'm fine to drive home. The journey is short, the roads deserted. Once I'm through my front door, I trudge straight upstairs and curl up in my bed. I'm desperate to play back every wonderful moment of last night, but too scared to let myself think about it in case I do something stupid, like jump in the car again and head straight back to Ben.

* * *

At 8 a.m. I'm on my way back to Moretti's. I'm not used to being out so early on a Sunday morning. The roads are quieter than usual, dark and cold. Just the sound of my footsteps and the occasional whoosh of a car going past—maybe people going to work, but more likely coming home from a night out.

I must have had about three hours' sleep in total last night, but I'm too wired to feel tired. In addition to all the stuff going on with Fisher, I now have this extra guilt over last night, setting my guts swirling and my teeth on edge. I'm so nervous about seeing Ben this morning at work. God, I'm such a cliché. Going to bed with my boss and then regretting it. But the truth is, I don't regret it. Not at all. I'm just scared of the weirdness it's going to create between us.

At work, I keep myself busy, keep my head down, hardly stopping to draw breath, talking to customers without really hearing what they're saying, going about my daily tasks without paying any attention to what I'm actually doing. I've already said hi to Jez and Janet, and to Shanaz, a college student who only works weekends and holidays, but Ben is nowhere to be seen. He's obviously keeping a low profile—I don't blame him.

I'm half tempted to go and ring on his doorbell, to try to set things straight. But my palms go clammy at the thought of it. No, I'll probably only make things worse. Best to leave it, let the dust settle. Maybe by tomorrow the awkwardness will have passed. Or not.

Carolyn arrives at lunchtime and I'm finally able to leave. I suppose I could have swapped the whole day with her—it would have been easier—but I've never missed a Sunday at the cemetery. It's something I have to do for my children, or I'd feel I was letting them down somehow. Abandoning them. I couldn't save them in life, but I can at least be there for them in death.

The familiarity of being at the cemetery calms me a little. The weak sunshine gives out scant heat, so I walk briskly along the pathways, the crunching gravel underfoot oddly satisfying. It's a tranquil place—sixty acres of woodland cemetery, with a Victorian chapel at its heart. The pathway curves this way and that, and it's a good twenty-minute walk until I reach them, my babies, resting under a sycamore tree. They said we were lucky to get Sam a space next to his sister. If "lucky" is a word you'd use in such a circumstance.

I step off the path and up onto the frost-tipped grass, where a magpie hops away and takes flight. *One for sorrow.* I give a bitter inward laugh. But then I shake off the bolt of sadness and try to be cheerful for their sakes. They don't want to see a miserable face each week.

I tidy away last week's shrivelled snowdrops and pansies, and replace them with buttery daffodils for Lily and a bright clump of barberry for Sam, its miniature yellow flowers spilling out over shiny dark green leaves. Each week I bring them something different, taking my time to select flowers I think they would like. Pathetic, really—I know they can't see my offerings.

Maybe I'm laying the flowers for myself. For my own comfort. I have this same tussle in my head every week, never coming to any firm conclusion. There's no revelation. No sign from above. Just me standing above their graves with different bunches of flowers. Maybe if Scott had come with me each week, it would have been different. We could have talked about our children together. Brought them to life in shared memories. Recalled funny incidents from Sam's past, imagined how he and Lily would have played together. Wondered what kind of adults they would have become. Instead, it's always been me, alone with my thoughts, trying to remain positive, but failing to prevent the darkness from sneaking in.

I sit on the damp wooden bench opposite their gravestones and try to recall them: Lily's angelic sleeping face and Sam's cheeky grin, his occasional scowl, his breathless, hysterical laughter when Scott pretended to be the tickle monster. I push out the later images of his sallow-skinned bravery, lying in the hospital minus his glorious dark curls. The tubes protruding from his body giving him a few more precious weeks of life, but making him less like himself and more like there was some alien creature taking him over.

I stand up and blink away hot tears. I can't bear to leave, but I'm not strong enough to stay. Not today. I'm unable to conjure up any of my usual chatter for them, my thoughts spiralling off down dark corridors. And instead of my children's faces, I picture Fisher and his son. It was only a week ago that Harry appeared in my kitchen. Maybe tomorrow, once I've been to the clinic, I'll have more of an idea what's going on. Maybe then I'll find some peace.

I send silent kisses to their graves and hold them tight in my mind's eye before I turn away and crunch back down the gravel path. The familiar twist of guilt tugs at my guts as I leave my babies behind for another week.

CHAPTER TWENTY-SIX

Monday morning, the traffic is heavy. Maybe I shouldn't have driven. But I wanted the peace of this heated tin box, rather than the chilly, crowded bus. And with the luxury of a satnav, I barely have to concentrate on the journey—just follow the green arrows on the dashboard screen while I psych myself up for whatever it is I'm about to discover.

I park in the NCP car park and walk the two blocks to the Balmoral Clinic. Damp, cold air seeps through my clothes while dark clouds threaten rain. I quicken my pace. The building is bigger than I remember, more imposing, and I'm not prepared for the sharp memories that assail me as I approach the place. Remembering how Scott dropped me at the entrance late that night while he parked the car and then raced back. It was exciting, if a little scary. The final day that my life was still on track to be good. Before all my hopes began to collapse. The sliding doors open and I walk inside, my boots echoing on the tiled floor.

The foyer is empty, decked out with seasonal decorations. I walk straight ahead to the curved reception desk, the sudden warmth of the place a little too cloying, mingling with the scent of floral air freshener that catches in the back of my throat. A woman in a skirt suit, an ugly red bow/cravat thing around her neck, comes out of a set of swing doors to my left, her heels clacking. She looks like an air hostess and fixes me with the same brand of corporate smile.

"Good morning," she says, walking over and stepping behind the desk. "How can I help you?"

"Hi. My name's Tessa Markham. I called a couple of days ago to ask about finding out the name of the doctor who delivered my twins. It was a while ago, and I don't have his name."

"You want to know who delivered your twins?"

"Yes, please. They told me I had to either put my query in writing or come in, in person."

"Okay, hold on a minute. I'll go and ask admin." She disappears through a door behind her and I wait, trying not to think about the fact that this is the place where Lily took both her first and last breaths.

A couple of minutes later, the woman returns. "Do you have any ID on you?"

I nod, dig in my bag and pull out my photo driving licence and a council tax bill.

"Great, thanks." The woman takes them, looks at the picture on my licence, looks at me, then examines the bill. She nods, satisfied. "If you'd like to come through, our office manager, Margie Lawrence, will help you find what you're looking for." She hands me back my ID and I stuff it back in my bag while following her through the door.

It's a generic open-plan office with half a dozen staff sitting at desks, some tapping away at their computer keyboards, others on the telephone. A woman at the back of the office gets to her feet and comes over to meet me, her hand outstretched. I shake it.

"Hi, I'm Margie." She looks up at the receptionist. "Thanks, Sharon."

I mutter my thanks, too. Sharon disappears back through the door and I follow Margie over to her desk.

"Please, sit down," she says, pushing her glasses back up her nose and taking a seat opposite me. "Sharon said you wanted to know the name of the doctor who delivered your baby."

"Yes, please. It was actually twins."

"Aw, how lovely," she says.

I cut her off before she starts asking questions like *How old are they now?* and *Are they boys or girls?* I launch straight in with: "My name's Tessa Markham and the father's name is Scott Markham. The date of delivery was the third of March 2012."

Margie begins tapping into her computer. "Bear with me," she says. "The system is on go-slow today."

She's probably expecting me to come up with a response like *Well, it is Monday morning.* Then we'd both laugh and roll our eyes. But I can't bring myself to make light-hearted comments in this place. So I simply give her a wan smile and say, "No problem."

"You gave birth to Samuel and Lilian Markham, is that correct?" she asks, looking at the screen on her right. "Samuel Edward Markham born at 4:46 a.m. and Lilian Elizabeth Markham born at 5:14 a.m."

"Sorry, what time does it say she was born?" I ask.

"5:14 a.m."

"That's not right," I say. "She was only born ten minutes after Sam."

"Are you sure?" she asks.

I'm pretty sure I know when my own children were born. "Yes."

Margie sticks her chin out as she studies the screen further. "It says the doctor on the ward that night was Dr. Friedland," she says.

I frown. "No, that's not right, either."

"That's what it says here. He was your consultant, wasn't he?"

"Yes," I say. "He was my consultant, but he was ill that week and another doctor took over. I can't remember his name."

Margie frowns and taps at the keyboard some more. "I'll pull up the roster from that night. Hang on."

What if she can't find out the name? Or what if Fisher really wasn't there that night and my mind is making connections where there aren't any?

"Here we go," she says cheerily. "Found it."

My heartbeat amplifies in my head as I wait for her to tell me what she's found.

"So, the midwives were...blah-blah-blah blah-blah-blah." She skips through all the other information. "And the on-duty obstetric consultant that night was..." Her eyes skim back and forth along the screen. "Yes, here we are, same name—Dr. Friedland."

No, it can't be true! I know it wasn't him. I push a breath out through my mouth, almost like I'm in labour. I remember...I remember Friedland was ill that night. They said it was gastric flu. I remember. Don't I?

"You okay?" Margie looks up.

"Are you sure it wasn't a Dr. James Fisher?" I say. "Can you check again? It's the third of March 2012." I pray that she's looking at the wrong date, that she's made a mistake.

"Here," she says, "come and see for yourself."

I get to my feet and walk around to her side of the desk so I'm staring at the screen, at the line of text she's pointing to. I see the date and the times, and I see the name "Dr. Friedland." Tears spring to my eyes. "It can't be," I say. "I thought it would be Dr. Fisher."

"We don't have a Dr. Fisher here," she says. "You must be mistaken. Didn't you say you couldn't remember who was on duty that night?" She looks up at me. I can't tell if that's concern or mistrust in her eyes.

"Fisher moved to Dorset not long afterwards," I say.

"Oh, okay, so maybe he did practise here," she says, "but that's a bit before my time. I've only worked here for three years, although sometimes it feels like a lot longer." She smiles up at me, but I can't smile back—I'm too disappointed that my theory has been proved wrong. "Let me check our employment records." She taps on the keyboard some more. "Ah, yes, you're right, Dr. Fisher did practise here during that time. Just not on that particular night."

I realise with a dull thud in my heart that all my suspicions appear to have been wrong. "Is there any other documentation that might show the name of the consultant on duty?" I ask.

"Not that I'm aware of." She shakes her head. "Maybe you just remembered it wrong. I mean, both names start with an F. It's easy to forget something from that long ago."

I shake my head. "Dr. Friedland was sick that night."

Margie shrugs helplessly, palms splayed, as if to say she doesn't know what else she can tell me.

"Can I speak to Dr. Friedland?" I ask. "Is he here?"

"No, he retired last year. He and his wife moved to Spain."

"Do you have a contact number for him?" If I could speak to him, maybe he'd remember me. Remember having gastric flu.

"Sorry," Margie says, her expression sympathetic, "we wouldn't be able to give out that information."

I stand there for a moment, racking my brains to think of anything else that might help me prove what I know is true. But I can't. "Okay, well, thanks anyway." I leave the office, shoulders slumped, head down.

Out in the foyer, the receptionist says a cheery goodbye and asks if I found everything I was looking for. I nod, mumble a thank-you and make my way across the foyer, back through the sliding doors.

Outside, the sky is still heavy with unshed rain and I pause for a moment, suck in a breath of polluted, moisture-laden air. Am I losing the plot? Was Scott right about me? But despite what Margie told me back there, I'm still not convinced that the information on their system is correct. The time of Lily's birth is out by twenty minutes—unless I really am remembering it wrong. What if Fisher *was* working that night, but he was negligent, somehow responsible for Lily's death? He could have accessed the computer system and erased his name, changed the time of birth.

I'm starting to sound like a conspiracy theorist. Am I ignoring the truth, bending it to make it fit my own view of things? I'm sure I'm not, but when the records say one thing, how can I prove otherwise?

I slouch back to the car in a funk. Whether it was Fisher or Friedland there that night, it still doesn't explain why someone would place Fisher's son in my kitchen years later. There's some kind of link, I know it. A car horn yanks me from my thoughts and I step back onto the pavement. I'll get myself run over if I'm not careful. I wave an apology to the driver while he mouths expletives at me.

Back in the hire car, my heart still leaden, I make a decision. I really and truly believe that Dr. Friedland was sick with flu that night. I know he was, I remember it clearly. I was so upset when I heard he wouldn't be on the ward. Which means the information on the clinic's system must be wrong. But if I tell Carly what's really written on the records, she might stop pursuing the case. She might think it's a waste of her time. And I need her to stick with it. I have to find out the truth.

My call goes straight to voicemail, so I leave a message.

"Hey, Carly. It's me, Tessa. I've just come from the clinic and my hunch was right. Fisher was the doctor on duty that night. It must be connected to his son showing up at my house, don't you think? Anyway, you should ask him about it when you get there. Hope you manage to speak to him. Good luck. Let me know how you get on."

I end the call and start the car. Did my voice sound fake? Will she be able to tell I was lying? It takes me three attempts to get the car in gear. I'm all over the place. I should try to calm down or I'll end up having an accident. I just lied to Carly. I *lied* to Carly. But I had to, didn't I?

I turn on the radio and search for Classic FM, hoping to hear some soothing strings or piano, but instead there's a brass band playing "Flight of the Bumblebee." I switch it off, breathe in deeply and head to Moretti's, wondering what kind of person I'm turning into. Could Scott be right? Is there something wrong with me? Am I becoming obsessed?

CHAPTER TWENTY-SEVEN

All afternoon, I'm distracted. I don't have time to think about the Fisher thing properly, but I also can't give work my full attention, which irritates me. Usually, whatever problems I have, I can find calm here. So why is it being so damn elusive today? Janet has closed the café early, as there are hardly any customers around. Instead, she's in the shop, which means I can work in the greenhouses uninterrupted, just the steady whoosh of rain against the glass. But I'm almost decimating these vines, because I can't seem to focus on what I'm doing.

"Step away from the secateurs."

My stomach flips and I turn around. Ben is walking towards me, holding his hand out. As he comes closer, I place the secateurs in his palm, and wince.

"What did that poor grape vine ever do to you?" he asks, pushing down the hood of his navy anorak.

"I'm so sorry," I reply, looking down at the plant's amputated shoots. "I wasn't concentrating."

"I can see that," he says. But there's a mischievous smile behind his eyes. I wonder if this means he's forgiven me for running out on him the other night.

"Ben…" I begin. "I just want to say…"

He holds out his hand again, but this time it's to stop me

talking. He shakes his head. "No more explanations. Let's just not mention it again. Friends?" he says.

"Yes, please. I'd like that." My shoulders sag with relief. The last time someone asked me to be friends, it was Scott telling me about Ellie, and I had a massive meltdown. This time, it's Ben, and I'm sad, but relieved. I couldn't bear to lose his friendship.

"It's so quiet this afternoon," he says. "I've sent Janet home and I'm closing early. Want to come round for a coffee?"

I pause. Is this just an innocent coffee, or will he expect more? The thought of kissing him again makes my bones go soft, but I have to be strong.

"I won't jump on you, if that's what you're worrying about."

"Ben!" I bat his arm gently with the back of my fist. "I can't believe you just said that!"

"Why not? Just putting your mind at rest."

I'm sure I'm blushing right now. "Okay then, a coffee would be lovely."

I pull my hood up and we race around to his garden and into the kitchen, laughing at the fact that we're soaked through.

"Wait here," he says, taking off his anorak and leaving me dripping rainwater all over his kitchen floor. He disappears into the hall while I get my breath back. Memories of Saturday night assail me. My pulse quickens. *He kissed me in this kitchen.* I try to think of other things to suppress these dangerous feelings.

"Here." He returns and hands me a soft beige towel, using another to dry his hair.

"Thanks." I wipe the rain from my face and then move on to my own dripping hair. I take off my coat and hang it over the back of one of the chairs.

Ben puts his towel down and starts doing something complicated to his coffee machine. It's one of those big chrome contraptions that looks like you'd need a degree in engineering to work it. "How was your appointment this morning?" he asks.

I lean back against the kitchen counter and twiddle a strand of wet hair around my finger. "It was..." How do I even begin to explain how this morning was. "It was fine," I say.

He nods. "Good."

Sod it. He told me he wants to be friends and I'm dying to talk to someone about this. "Actually, it wasn't fine," I say. "It was...unsettling."

"Unsettling? How?"

And then I find myself telling him what happened. I tell him everything. It all comes tumbling out. About going to Cranborne and seeing Fisher. About the police warning me off. About discovering that Fisher practised at the clinic where I had my children.

"The thing is," I say, "the records showed that it was Friedland who delivered my twins, but I know it was someone else. I can't prove it was Fisher, but I know for a fact that it wasn't Friedland—he was ill that night."

Ben has stopped fiddling with the coffee machine. Instead he's staring at me like I'm some kind of freak. I've blown it. He obviously thinks I'm unhinged. I can't say I blame him.

"Sorry," I say. "I shouldn't have vented. It's all a bit heavy, I know."

"The question is," he says, ignoring my apology, "why do the records say it was Friedland when he wasn't there that night?"

"Because Fisher has something to hide?"

"Looks that way," Ben says, scratching his chin.

"So you believe me?"

"Why wouldn't I?"

I give a short laugh. "Everyone else in my life thinks I've lost the plot. Sorry, that's probably too much information."

"I don't think you've lost the plot, Tessa. I think you've had an absolutely terrible few years and you haven't been given anywhere near the support you deserve."

My throat tightens and I pray I'm not going to cry. "Thank you," I whisper. "That means a lot."

"What about your husband?" Ben asks.

"Scott? What about him?"

"I know you're separated," he says, "but what does he think about all this stuff with Fisher? He must have some theories."

"I haven't told him about going to the clinic. I don't even know if I *will* tell him."

"You should," Ben says. "He needs to know about this. They were his children too."

"He doesn't want to listen to me," I say, chewing my thumbnail. "He won't even let me have their health records. Like I said, he thinks I'm insane for worrying about any of this. He's moved on with his life—new girlfriend, new baby on the way—and he thinks I should move on too."

"Moving on is all very well," Ben says, "but it wasn't *his* kitchen where that boy turned up. It wasn't *him* being questioned by the police. You've been put under a lot of pressure, Tess. Cut yourself some slack. I really think you should make Scott listen to you about this Fisher thing. It doesn't feel right to me."

"It doesn't, does it? God, I'm glad you think so too. I thought I might be overreacting."

"Not at all," Ben says. "No wonder you're stressed out. I'm just sorry you're going through all this."

"Thanks, Ben. I really appreciate you listening and not thinking I'm a total lunatic."

"Maybe just a partial lunatic," he says.

I manage a half-smile. It feels good to have someone on my side who doesn't have an agenda.

"Now," he says, "go and tell Scott, make him listen."

I pull out of the rain-splashed yard and wave as Jez closes the gates behind me. Ben is right: Scott should be told that the clinic's records are wrong. This has nothing to do with me wanting Scott's attention, and everything to do with us finding out if something bad is going on. If Fisher was negligent at Lily's birth and he altered the records to change the time of birth and show a different doctor on duty that night, then Scott and I need to know. He should *want* to know. And we should do something about it. Report it.

I drive home, windscreen wipers going full blast, wondering how Carly got on with Fisher. Whether she managed to speak to him. She hasn't been in contact all day, but maybe by now she'll have some news for me. She's so pushy, I'm sure she'll have discovered something. I park up outside my house, still amazed and thankful that there are no journalists hanging around outside.

Before getting out of the car, I glance up and down the road, but I can't spot Carly's red Fiat. She must not be back yet. It's still quite early, and the weather is so vile, I guess she'll be taking it easy on the drive back. I give her another call, but it goes straight to voicemail. "Hi, Carly. Me again. Let me know when you have some news."

I dash from the car to my front porch, getting newly soaked in the process. Finally, I'm inside, the sound of drumming rain as loud in here as it is out there. I stand in the hallway for a moment, delaying. I realise I don't want to call Scott. I don't want to hear his frustration and annoyance. I don't like the way he makes me feel guilty and inadequate. Why did I never notice that about him before? Maybe it's because he's the opposite of Ben. Ben listens to what I have to say; he takes me seriously and doesn't patronise me.

For the first time ever I feel like it might be a good thing that Scott and I have broken up. Maybe I'm better off without him. Maybe he and Ellie are actually perfect for each other. But it doesn't change the fact that he still deserves to know what's going on with Fisher. I sigh; I'll delay calling him a little longer. First, I'm going to change into some dry clothes.

Half an hour later, I'm sitting in the kitchen in leggings, an oversized jumper and a pair of thick Fair Isle socks, cradling my mobile phone against my ear. Better to get this over with.

"Hi, Scott."

"Tessa." His voice is heavy, resigned.

I want to lay on the sarcasm and tell him: *Don't sound so happy to hear from me.* Instead, I'm polite, detached. "I've got some news," I say.

He doesn't reply.

"It's important. It's about the twins' birth."

Scott gives a loud sigh. "Not this again, Tessa. I've just got in from work and I'd really like to relax."

"But it's to do with Harry Fisher's father."

"I told you before, you need to let this fixation drop. Let it go, it's over. The boy is back with his father, that's all—"

"Just listen for one minute without interrupting," I say.

"Fine."

I take a breath. "Harry's father, James Fisher, worked at the clinic where the twins were born."

There's silence at the other end of the line.

"Did you hear what I said? He worked there, Scott. At the same clinic."

"Are you at the house?" he asks.

"Yes."

"I'm coming over," he says, and ends the call.

Finally! Finally, Scott is taking me seriously. If we can work on discovering the truth together, it will make things so much easier. I know I have Carly on the case, but she's a loose cannon; she has completely different priorities. I need someone who is truly on my side, who wants to find out the truth as much as I do—Ben was right to suggest including Scott in this.

I hate myself for doing it, but I go into the hall and check out my reflection in the mirror. I may have resigned myself to the fact that Scott and I are finished, but I still don't want him to see me looking a mess. My hair's a bit damp, but apart from that, I think I look okay.

Fifteen minutes later, the doorbell rings. When I open the door to welcome Scott in, I see that he's not alone.

He's with Ellie.

My smile falters. What the hell is she doing here? This is nothing to do with her. This is about me and Scott and our children. I can't believe he'd be so insensitive.

"Are you going to let us in, Tessa?" he says. "It's pissing down out here."

I take a step backwards, too disappointed to speak. I can't even bear to look at Ellie. I turn my back on them and mutter something about going into the lounge. Ugh, how will I be able to talk to Scott about this stuff with her here, judging me?

Scott and Ellie sit together on the large sofa, while I perch on the other one, feeling like a stranger in my own house. I glance over at her and notice she's appraising the room, taking in its sorry state—the dust, the gloomy air of neglect.

"Scott," I say. "I'd rather we talked on our own, if that's okay."

"Ellie's part of my life now, Tessa. I want her to be here."

"Well, she's not part of *my* life," I snap. "And I don't want her to be here." I hate that I sound so petulant, but I can't help it.

Scott clenches his jaw and drops a hand onto Ellie's knee, stroking it like he's telling her not to worry about his crazy ex. Ellie is the one he's there for now.

"Tessa," Ellie says, in her childlike voice. "We're here because we're worried about you."

Oh my good Lord, if I don't end up smacking this woman it will be a bloody miracle. I bite my bottom lip to stop myself saying something I'll regret.

"Did you go and see that therapist, like I asked?" Scott says.

"I don't need to see a therapist. There's nothing wrong with me other than the fact that I'm still mourning the loss of our children. You've obviously moved on, you don't want to hear anything that could upset your perfect new life. But I've found out something important. I think that clinic was negligent with Lily, I think they're trying to cover something up."

"Tessa, you promised you'd go and see a therapist."

"No, I didn't. You blackmailed me. You told me that if I didn't make an appointment, I couldn't have my children's health records. Which, by the way, if you'd looked at them like I asked, you would have seen that Harry's father was the doctor on duty that night." Okay, I don't know that the health records say that, but I'm hoping they do; I'm hoping they at least are correct.

"What does it matter who was on duty that night?" Scott says, shaking his head at me. "I know you, Tessa." He leans forward. "I know how you were after Sam died. I'm worried you're losing it again, so I'm just going to come out and say it— did you take that boy? Did you abduct that doctor's son? Just admit it, Tessa. We can get you help, but only if you admit what you did."

A momentary chill of dread scuttles down my back. What if Scott is right? What if my mind is playing tricks on me and I did this terrible thing? I'm already denying what the official records state. I even lied to Carly. Am I twisting things to fit in with my theory? Maybe I do need to speak to a professional to get everything straight in my mind. But isn't this what Scott always does? Dismisses my feelings, makes me feel like I'm not in control of my own mind. No, I won't allow him to make me second-guess myself. I didn't do what he's suggesting, I would never do that.

"Listen to me, Scott," I say. "I did not take that boy. Get that through your thick skull."

His face grows red. He's not used to me talking back to him. I don't think I've ever raised my voice to him before.

"I bet this is all your idea, isn't it?" I turn to Ellie. "Get the ex-wife off to therapy so she won't bother us any more."

"Actually, we *both* think it's for the best," she says. "We genuinely think you could do with some professional help. Look, Tessa, answer me this—if you didn't take Harry, then how did he get into your kitchen? His dad wouldn't have put him there. You're asking us to believe that some random person took a little boy all the way from Dorset and brought him to your house in London. Why would anyone do that?"

"Gosh, I don't know, Ellie." I can't help mimicking her childish voice. "I wish I'd considered that question before. Thanks for bringing it up."

"No need to be sarcastic." Her face twitches. "I'm only trying to help. You're being very…emotional."

"Well, I apologise for that, Ellie, but being emotional is an unfortunate side effect of losing one's children."

To her credit, she flushes and looks away. "We should go, Scott. We're not getting anywhere with her." She rises to her feet.

So many fitting responses come to mind, but she's not worth wasting my energy on. "You're right," I reply. "You should leave."

Ellie shakes her head as though I'm a lost cause, and a fresh plume of anger boils up in me. She's poisoned Scott's mind. I shouldn't be trying to convince him that something is wrong, he should *want* to listen. He should be experiencing the same outrage as me, the same desire to discover the truth.

I turn to him. "Scott, I was hoping to have a private conversation with you about something that I believe went terribly wrong at our children's birth. But you obviously aren't interested, so you may as well go, and take your floozy with you." It feels quite good to say the word *floozy* out loud.

"Get some help, Tessa," Scott says on his way out.

I watch them leave the room, wishing once again that he had come here without her. Maybe he would have listened to me if she hadn't been here too.

"Please, Scott," I call, trying one last time to get him to listen. "Just stop and think about what I'm telling you. There's something else going on here. Something bad. *Scott!*" But I know by the pitying look he casts over his shoulder that he isn't prepared to listen. That he's already made up his mind. In his eyes, the past is over and I'm the poor pathetic creature stuck there, trying to pull him back into the darkness.

But he's wrong. The past isn't over. It's catching up.

CHAPTER TWENTY-EIGHT

My mind is still spinning with everything that happened yesterday—the clinic's unreliable records and Scott's refusal to listen to me. I'm on my own in this, but I'm not giving up. I'm not letting it go. I'll get up, face the day—whatever it brings—and find out the truth. I feel like I'm on the verge of something. Like if I reach just a little further, I'll be able to join the dots.

In the wintry gloom of morning, I get ready for work, have a quick breakfast and zip up my raincoat, preparing myself for a mad dash through the downpour from the house to the car. Opening the front door, I see there's at least an inch of water covering the front path. I'm not sure how waterproof my boots are, so I run on tiptoe to my front gate, expecting to feel water seeping through to my socks any minute. Rain races down the road in fast-flowing rivulets, skipping over the drains and gathering in the dips and hollows of the uneven tarmac.

"Hey!"

I look up at the sound of a man's voice, and peer through the driving rain to see if it's directed at me.

"Hey! Tessa!" A dark figure is calling across the road from outside Carly's house.

Hunched against the downpour, I cross over. As I draw closer, I see that it's Vince, Carly's brother. I walk up the short gravel pathway and join him where he's standing under the dripping porch.

"Hi," I say. "Thanks again for fixing my window."

"S'okay. You seen Carly?"

"Not since Friday, when you were both at mine. But we did text on Saturday."

"She was supposed to come over last night, but she never showed," he says, wiping rain from his face. "I know she's a busy girl, but she wouldn't have missed Dad's birthday. Not without ringing."

"It was your dad's birthday?"

"Yeah. We were having steak and chips at ours. Carly said she'd be there."

I'm hit by a small stab of worry. "She went to Dorset yesterday for a story she's working on. I guess she should've been back yesterday evening. Mind you, the weather's so bad, maybe she decided to stay over at a B&B or something."

"But she would've texted me if she couldn't make it. I had to lie to Mum and Dad. Told them her car broke down. Otherwise they'd be worrying—you know what parents are like."

"Maybe her phone battery died, or she couldn't get a signal," I suggest.

"Yeah, I suppose. Anyway, I gotta get to work now. Already late."

"Me too," I reply, glancing at my watch. "If you give me your number, I'll let you know as soon as I hear anything."

We swap mobile numbers and I make my way over to the hire car, too worried about what might have happened to Carly to concern myself about the fact that I'm already soaked to the skin.

By the time I arrive at work, my anxiety over Carly's whereabouts has escalated into a full-blown panic. I park up in the yard, turn off the engine and sit for a moment trying to harness my thoughts. Carly hasn't answered any of my calls or texts and she's missed her own father's birthday. Something isn't right. Either she's had a car accident or...Or what? Could Fisher be responsible? Could he have done something to her? Is the man dangerous?

A knock on the passenger window startles me. I look up to see Ben's face. He opens the car door and slides into the passenger seat, closing the door behind him. I try to ignore the butterfly wings in my stomach at his close proximity.

"Monsoon season in Barnet," he says.

"Crazy weather," I agree.

"Not sure if it's even worth opening up today," he says. "Who in their right mind is going to come to the gardens on a day like this?"

"A good day for me to catch up on planting, I guess."

"Yeah, exciting stuff."

"I don't mind. You know I enjoy it."

He smiles. "That's why Jez is always singing your praises."

"Really?"

"He calls you conscientious, and says you've got your head screwed on right."

"Glad someone thinks I've got my head screwed on. Personally, I think it needs at least another quarter-twist." I put my hand up to my neck and pretend to lock it into place.

He shakes his head and smiles. "How did things go with Scott yesterday? You manage to speak to him?"

I place my hands on the steering wheel, gripping it tightly as I think back to our conversation. "The less said about that the better." My blood pressure soars at the mere thought of him and Ellie last night. At how patronising and insensitive they were.

"Oh, I'm sorry," Ben says. "I probably shouldn't have suggested it."

"No, it's okay. I would have ended up having to speak to him anyway." I let go of the steering wheel and rest my hands on my lap. "At least it's out of the way now, and I know his opinion."

"Which is?"

"That I'm insane and need professional help."

"Jeez."

"Yeah. But right now, I'm more worried about my neighbour."

"Your neighbour? Why?"

"You remember Carly?"

"Carly?"

"You know." I cringe, remembering how Ben saw me arguing with her. "That embarrassing scene in the café last week."

"The journalist? The one who was hassling you? She was a right piece of work."

"Yeah, that's her. Well, we've kind of come to an arrangement. A truce, if you like. She's helping me find out what's going on with Fisher. But now I think she might be in trouble."

"What's happened?"

I quickly tell him about Carly coming over to my house with her brother to fix my broken window, and how she then persuaded me to work with her.

"Wait a minute. Back up," Ben says. "She let herself into your house?"

"Yes, but it's not as bad as it sounds," I say, wondering why I'm defending Carly's actions when I was absolutely furious with her at the time. "Thing is, we used to keep an eye on each other's places whenever we were away. She knew I kept a spare key under the plant pot."

"That still doesn't give her the right to—"

"I know, I know."

"Tessa," Ben says, the tone of his voice injecting me with fresh worry. "If she can get into your house, did you ever stop to think that it could have been *Carly* who put that boy in your kitchen?"

"What? No!" I bring my hand up to my mouth, start chewing my thumbnail. "That doesn't make sense."

"Who else could have let themselves in?" Ben says. "And she has a motive."

"What motive? Why would she...?" And then the penny drops, and I push the tips of my fingers into my forehead. "For a story?"

"Exactly."

"I don't know, Ben." *Would she really do something so awful?* "She does have serious financial worries. She told me that if she doesn't get a lead soon, she might lose her house."

"There you go," Ben says. "And she looks like the type who'd sell her own grandmother for a story."

"Shi-it." What if I've been going after the wrong person? What if Fisher really has nothing to do with this, and it's all Carly's doing, using him and his son to fabricate an outrageous story? "I need to speak to her, don't I? But she's not answering her phone. She's gone AWOL."

"Since when?"

"She was supposed to have gone to Cranborne yesterday, but I haven't heard back from her since. I think I need to go and visit that housekeeper again. She's the only person I know who might actually have some useful information."

"Go and see her now."

"I can't. I've got work."

"You can carry on with the planting any time. This is important, isn't it?"

"Yes, but—"

"So, go. I can come with you if you like."

"No, she's really nervy. If she sees the two of us, there's no way she'll let us in. I don't think she'll even talk to me."

"Worth a try, though."

"Are you sure you don't mind?"

"Wouldn't have suggested it otherwise."

"I'll make up the time," I say.

"No worries."

I lean across and plant a kiss on his damp cheek without thinking. It feels like the most natural thing to do. Ben takes my hand and grazes my knuckles with his lips. Then he replaces my hand on my lap and gets out of the car back into the streaming rain.

"Let me know how you get on. And be careful," he calls out to me before closing the door with a dull thunk.

"Yes, sure." I give him a wave, but he's already a blur through the window.

The more I discover, the more confusing and conflicting everything seems. Could Ben be right? Could Carly be behind the whole thing? I guess it's a possibility, but I just don't know who to trust...

CHAPTER TWENTY-NINE

Here I am once more, outside Fisher's ex-housekeeper's flat, only this time she hasn't answered the buzzer. It's almost 9 a.m., so she's probably at work, although she was home last Friday around this time, so maybe she's up there but just not answering. I press the buzzer one more time and wait. Still no response. I'm worried Vince will call the police if he doesn't hear back from Carly soon, and that will open up a whole new can of worms.

I step back down onto the sodden pavement and gaze up at the bay window where I saw Merida Flores the last time I came. Icy rain splashes onto my upturned face, clinging to my eyelashes and running down my neck. I pay it no attention. Her curtains are open today. The room beyond is dark. My guess is that she's out. I should leave, head back to work and trust that Carly will call me when she's ready. If Ben's theory is correct, my devious neighbour could be avoiding me on purpose.

Before I go, just in case Flores is in there and can somehow see me, I stare up at her window with my palms pressed together as though in prayer, pleading. One last attempt to get her attention. To let her see my desperation. My heart jumps a beat as a shadowy figure comes into view. It's her. She's there. Our eyes lock for a brief moment. She gives a quick nod and then disappears. Does this mean she's going to let me in?

I step back up to her front door and ring the buzzer, holding my breath. This time she answers.

"Tessa Markham," she says, like a statement of fact.

"Hello," I say, trying to think of something non-threatening to add, something that will make her more likely to speak to me. "I need your help," I say. "Can we talk? Just for a few minutes?"

The door buzzes, vibrating on its hinges. I give it a push and it swings inwards, revealing a surprisingly bright and welcoming communal hallway, the smell of lemon furniture polish emanating from the woodwork. The place is cleaned to within an inch of its life, not a speck of dirt anywhere.

As I walk up the steep carpeted staircase, one of two doors opens at the top and I spy the diminutive figure of Merida Flores—and that's saying something given my own vertically challenged state.

"Hello," I say, excited and nervous to finally get to talk to this elusive person who might well hold the key to what's been going on in my life.

If I were to guess, I'd say Merida Flores is in her early forties. Her dark hair has been pulled back in a severe low ponytail, and she's wearing black jeans and a dark red sweater. Her hand clutches at a plain gold cross hanging from a chain around her neck.

As I reach the top of the stairs, she steps back into her flat and gestures to me to come in. I take a breath and do as she bids, following her through a small, dim hallway into a living room with a large bay window, beneath which sits a dark wooden table and two chairs. It's the same window through which we stared at one another moments ago. Like the entranceway, the flat smells of furniture polish.

With the heavy black clouds and the rain streaming down

outside, it's almost dark enough to feel like night in here. Flores clicks on the light switch, but that only makes the atmosphere worse, as strange shadows from the lampshade slide across the room. The two of us stand facing one another, awkward, our arms folded, her slim fingers still fiddling with her pendant.

"Thank you," I finally say, "for letting me into your home." I find myself speaking slowly, carefully, not too sure how strong her English is. I'm still surprised that she actually allowed me in—I thought there'd be more resistance after all the other times I saw her and she was so keen to get away. But I don't ask why; I don't want to give her the opportunity to change her mind.

Flores gives a small nod.

"My name is Tessa, although you already know that."

"My name is Angela," she says, her voice low and accented.

"Angela? I thought your name was Merida. Merida Flores?"

"Yes, I am Angela Merida Flores. In Spain we have two last names—the mother and the father's name together, yes?"

"Oh, okay, I didn't know that."

"Please, sit." She gestures to a green fake-leather sofa, which creaks alarmingly as I perch myself on the edge. She takes a seat on the closer of the two dining chairs by the window.

"I need to ask you some questions," I begin.

"You said you wanted my help."

Although I'm no longer sure of Carly's motives, I decide to start off by asking about her disappearance. "Yes, my neighbour is missing. She went to see Dr. James Fisher yesterday."

At the mention of his name, Angela pales and begins shaking her head. "It's not good," she mutters.

"Not good?" I repeat. Carly may not be my favourite person, but now I'm really starting to worry for her safety. "Why is it not good? Could Fisher have hurt her? The doctor, Fisher, is he dangerous?"

"Dr. Fisher? Dangerous? No."

"So why did you say 'not good'?" I ask. "When I mentioned his name just now, you looked scared."

"I'm not scared of Dr. Fisher. I don't think he would harm anyone," she says.

"You used to work for him, didn't you? Are you sure he wouldn't harm anyone? My neighbour..."—I can't bring myself to call Carly a friend—"she went to see him and now I can't get hold of her. She's not answering her phone."

"Dr. Fisher is a serious man, but not violent. Not dangerous. He wouldn't hurt your neighbour, I am sure of it."

"Why have you been following me, Angela? I saw you a few times, but you ran off."

She covers her face with her hands. Is she thinking? Crying? I can't tell.

"Are you okay?" Suddenly something clicks in my brain. I rise to my feet and take a step towards her, a sudden chill sweeping my body. "Harry said an angel brought him to me. Your name is Angela. Was it *you*? Did *you* bring Harry to my house?"

She takes her hands from her face and stares down at her knees, her expression one of dark turmoil. "Harry's mother, she used to call me her angel. God rest her soul." She makes the sign of the cross. "Harry would copy her and call me his angel, too. It was a sweet joke."

"So it *was* you!"

"Mrs. Fisher was a wonderful woman," Angela continues. "I was so sad when she died. It was such a terrible thing for the boy to lose his mother like that."

"But why did you bring him to my house?" I ask, staring down at her. "It *was* you, wasn't it?"

"You're right. It was me who brought Harry to your house."

I'm astounded by her admission and utterly confused.

"Why? Why would you do that? And you've been following me since then, maybe even before this all happened. It's something to do with Dr. Fisher, isn't it?"

Angela finally looks up at me. "Tessa, I'm sorry. I didn't know that the newspapers would say all those things about you. I didn't know that bringing Harry to you would cause so much trouble. But she wanted me to do it. I promised her I would do it."

"Who? Who did you promise? Is this something to do with Carly? Did she offer you money?"

Angela's hand flies back to the cross around her neck. "All right, please sit back down, and I will tell you."

So I do as she asks and sit back on the creaky sofa, my heart thumping wildly, wondering just what it is this woman is about to reveal.

CHAPTER THIRTY

"Dr. Fisher and his wife, they used to live in a house not too far from here, in London," Angela begins. "I started working for them as a housekeeper when she was pregnant. After their son Harry was born, they moved to the country, to Cranborne in Dorset. They moved because of Dr. Fisher's work and because they wanted Harry to grow up in the countryside. I went with them and I worked for them for almost six years. Also, I looked after Harry when Mrs. Fisher was working. She worked on the reception at Dr. Fisher's clinic. Then, earlier this year, Mrs. Fisher got very, very sick. Her doctor say she is not gonna make it. They knew she had very little time. It was cancer."

I nod, already aware of her illness. The press really milked this part of the Fishers' story, it being doubly tragic that Dr. Fisher was recently widowed when his son went missing. And doubly heart-warming when they were finally reunited.

"Her doctor said they could try surgery," Angela continues, "but the risks were high. She decided to do it anyway. Without the operation, she would die. With the operation, she had a small chance to live. Dr. Fisher did not want her to do the surgery because he said he might lose her too soon. But she insisted it was the best chance even though he did not agree.

"The day before she went into the hospital for the operation, she called me into the drawing room, where she was lying on the sofa, all covered in blankets, even though it was warm in the room, with a fire and everything. She looked like a little baby bird. I wanted so badly to cry, but I told myself: Angela, you have to be strong. This lady does not need to see your tears. You need to keep being strong. To keep being her angel."

Hearing Angela tell me about Mrs. Fisher's illness brings a lump to my own throat. I know that feeling of trying to keep it together for someone else. Trying not to let them see you're breaking inside. Putting on a mask to boost them and keep them strong for whatever they might have to face next. I shake away the memories.

"But I was not prepared for what Mrs. Fisher told me," Angela says. "I thought she might be losing her mind, I thought it was the medicine making her confused. It made no sense, what she said."

"What did she say?" I ask, leaning forward.

"She wanted me to make her a promise. She wanted me to take Harry and give him to *you*."

"Fisher's wife asked you to do that?" I don't understand what it is that Angela's telling me.

"I said to her, 'You cannot give your child to someone else just like that. What about his father?' and I told her, 'They will put me in prison if I take your child.' So she gave me a piece of paper. Wait, I will get it." Angela rises to her feet and leaves the room for a moment.

I try to digest what she's told me so far, but I can't work out why a dying woman would send her son to *me*, a complete stranger. Unless maybe her husband wasn't a fit father and she wanted to get Harry away from him. But even then, it doesn't make sense.

Seconds later, Angela returns to the room. "Here," she says, handing me a sheet of blue Basildon Bond paper, which has been folded into four. "Mrs. Fisher gave me your name—Tessa Markham—and your address and she made me swear to take Harry to you after she died. I asked her who you were. You were her friend? Relative? She said it's not important. I said, of course it is important. Of course.

"She said I must tell Harry that you are to be his new mother. That if I didn't do this, she is scared she will go to hell. She said something terrible has happened and only I can put this right. *Me*." Angela places her hand on her heart, her eyes wide, as though she still can't believe what Mrs. Fisher asked her to do.

"She made me swear on the Virgin Mary. I did not want to do this, but she begged me. She gripped my hand so tightly. I looked at her and saw this frail woman, like a little feather. You would not think she had so much strength. But she was gripping my hand so hard that it left a mark. I don't know what possessed me, but I swore to her on the Virgin Mary that I would do this thing for her.

"Mrs. Fisher, she was also Catholic like myself. Our faith is very strong. Dr. Fisher, he does not believe in any God—he says he is a scientific man. But Mrs. Fisher, she said her husband is a stubborn man, and even if he wanted to believe in God, he would rather go against his true feelings than change his mind or admit that he was wrong."

Unfolding the sheet of paper, I'm hoping for a revelation as I begin to read Fisher's wife's spidery handwriting:

12 October 2017

I, Elizabeth Fisher, request that Angela Merida Flores take my son, Harry Fisher, to Tessa Markham and leave him in her safe keeping. Tessa is to be Harry's new mother. I certify that Angela does this at my request and she should not be accused of any wrongdoing.

Below this brief message my name and address have been written out in full, followed by Fisher's wife's signature. But Elizabeth Fisher can't have been in her right mind, because I'm pretty sure this letter wouldn't legally absolve Angela of any wrongdoing. Taking a child from his widowed father without his permission has to be illegal, with or without his dead mother's approval.

"What happened to make Elizabeth Fisher think she was going to hell?" I ask. "What did she do?"

"Mrs. Fisher would not tell me anything more. I asked her and I asked her, many times, but she was so tired then. She kept closing her eyes, and in the end, she waved me away and she fell asleep. After that, I never had the chance to speak to her alone, and I had a strong feeling that she did not want Dr. Fisher to know what she had told me.

"I thought, I won't do anything until I have the chance to speak with her again after the operation. I thought that maybe when she told me this thing she was delirious. Dreaming. I don't know. But then, after the operation, she never woke up. She died a few days after that. It was so sad. I was devastated for Harry and for his father. I tried to make everything easy for them in their house. But Dr. Fisher, he was crazy with grief. I thought to myself, I cannot do what Mrs. Fisher has asked me. It is not right to take the boy away from his father.

"And then, two days after she died, Dr. Fisher called me into his office and he said to me he does not need my services any longer. He said it just like this. Cold. Finished. Like I am nothing. Like I have not been living and working in his house for all these years. 'What about Harry?' I said to him. I was thinking about the poor boy. He is going to lose his mother and his angel both together. I am like his... like his family. He is like a son to me. I pleaded with Dr. Fisher to let me stay for a few months more until Harry was not so sad. I said he does not need to pay me, I am happy to stay and look after his boy. But he did not care about this. He was too sad, too angry. He gave me money for six months' working and he told me I must leave before the end of the following week. You understand, this was less than one week's notice he gave me.

"I was heartbroken to leave Harry. I still miss him. It hurts here." She places both hands over her stomach. "And I was all the time thinking about what Mrs. Fisher asked me to do. It was terrible. For weeks I was in turmoil. I did not want to do it, but I swore to Mrs. Fisher on the Mother of Christ. And I did not want her to go to hell. I did not want to be responsible for her soul.

"So I decided I had to do it. Six weeks after Dr. Fisher asked me to leave, I took Harry from his father's house and I brought him to your house. But it's terrible, I think I made things worse for everybody. I should never have promised her. I should never have done it. I am sorry." She brings her hands to her face and rubs at her forehead with the tips of her fingers. "You are going to call the police? They will arrest me, yes? I must be punished for what I did."

My brain is whirring with all that Angela has told me. Is she mentally ill? Could she be lying? It's too outlandish a story to make up, and she'd have to be a bloody good actor to fake that kind of anguish. I do believe she's telling me the truth, but it still doesn't explain what's going on here. If it's all his wife's doing and Dr. Fisher isn't part of this, then how does it all fit together?

"I won't call the police," I say. "Not right now. But they may need to know about this eventually."

Angela nods. "Okay, thank you."

"Can I keep this piece of paper?" I ask, thinking Elizabeth Fisher's note could come in useful as evidence, should I need it.

She hesitates and then nods. "Yes, you keep it."

"Why would Elizabeth Fisher want me to have her son?" I ask. "Can you think of any reason at all? Is Dr. Fisher abusive, maybe? It's the only thing that makes any kind of sense to me."

"No, no, not abusive, no. Dr. Fisher is a good father. Strict, but not violent—never. He loves his son, of this I am sure."

"But why bring Harry to me in particular?" I ask. "Mrs. Fisher doesn't know me, has never met me. She must have told you why. Must have given you a reason."

Angela shakes her head. "She didn't give me a reason, she just made me swear. You must understand, she was sick, very weak. It was hard for her to speak, it took much energy."

"There's one other thing that's still troubling me," I say.

"Troubling you?"

"That day with Harry, how did you actually get into my house?"

"I apologise," Angela says, shaking her head. "It was terrible of me to go into your home like that."

"It's okay," I say. "I'm not angry with you. I just want to know *how* you got in."

"I used the key. You leave it under your plant pot. It's not a good thing to leave it there—dangerous. You can get burgled like that."

"But how did you know about that key?" I was so stupid to leave it there. First Angela, then Carly.

"I walked past your house many times to try and think how I will bring Harry there. I saw your neighbour, the lady who lives opposite, go into your house. She used this key."

My mouth falls open. "Carly? The woman with long brown hair?"

"Yes, she went into your house while you're at work. She's your cleaner, yes?"

"No. No, she bloody isn't my cleaner. She's the neighbour I was telling you about—the one who's gone missing." I cannot believe Carly let herself in while I was out. That's outrageous.

I sink back into the sofa, trying to digest what Angela is telling me. I realise Carly could have been snooping around my house for ages, trying to dig up some dirt on me. Or, like Ben said, has she been going over there for something more sinister? Could she be behind this whole thing? Manipulating Elizabeth Fisher somehow, creating drama for a story? She wouldn't stoop so low, would she? I realise my whole body is shaking.

Angela gets to her feet and comes over to me, taking hold of both my hands and giving them a squeeze. "I'm sorry," she says. "Forgive me for going into your home. For putting Harry in there. I should not have done it."

"It's okay, Angela," I say, my head still full of Carly's ongoing deviousness. "I forgive you, I do." At least I think I do. I can't quite marshal my thoughts. This is all too much to take in.

CHAPTER THIRTY-ONE

Around the corner from Angela's house, I sit in the hire car thinking about what I've just learned. A wave of relief sweeps across me as I realise it definitely wasn't me who abducted Harry. Subconsciously, I'd been worried I was losing my mind, blanking out things I may have done. There was always that niggle of doubt. Now that Angela has admitted it, my mind is clearer. I can trust myself once more. But there's still the dilemma of what to do next. There really is no other choice. If I want to discover the truth, I need to go back to Dorset and speak to Fisher. The thought is terrifying and yet somehow exhilarating. This could be it. This could be where I discover the truth.

First, I call Carly again, fury building in my gut as I think about how she let herself into my house while I was at work. How many times did she go in there? What was she doing? Snooping through my stuff? Trying to find something to incriminate me for a crime I didn't commit? Ugh, I'll kill her when I get hold of her. But then I remember that she could be in terrible trouble right now, and I'm hit by a wave of guilt. My call goes straight through to her voicemail once more. I end the call; I've already left enough messages.

Okay, I really don't have a choice: I'm going to have to risk arrest and go to Cranborne. I can't go to the police—not yet. Not until I've spoken to Fisher. Angela told me he wasn't dangerous, so I'll try to persuade him to speak to me. If he becomes angry and refuses, I won't run away this time; I'll show him his wife's letter—the one she gave to Angela. He won't be able to fob me off once he sees it. And if he calls the police, I'll show *them* the letter and then they can deal with the whole thing.

I also have another dilemma—Scott. Part of me wants to leave him out of the loop. He made his feelings perfectly clear. He thinks I'm unhinged and he wants me to leave him and Ellie to their new-found blissful love-in. But I need him to know that it really wasn't me who took Harry. Now that Angela has admitted she did it, maybe Scott will realise he's treated me unfairly.

Before I have the chance to talk myself out of it, I call his mobile. It rings three times and then goes to voicemail. I bet he's seen my number and diverted the call—bastard. I'm starting to see the ex-love-of-my-life in a whole new light.

"Hi, Scott. It's Tessa. Just thought you should know that I finally found out who left Harry in our house last Sunday. It was Fisher's housekeeper. She admitted it. So feel free to apologise for wrongly accusing me. Anyway, I'm going to Fisher's place today and was hoping you might want to come with me, seeing as I'm not a crazy child abductor. I'll text you the address in case you want to meet me there. I'm pretty convinced this has something to do with Fisher working at the Balmoral Clinic when we had Sam and Lily. I'm going to make him talk to me. If you want to help me find out what's going on, give me a call."

Knowing Scott, he'll probably play the voice message to Ellie and they'll convince themselves that I'm some kind of fantasist. But at least he can't say I didn't try to keep him informed. As an afterthought, I send him a photo of Elizabeth Fisher's letter. Maybe that will help convince him I'm not making this up.

* * *

Adrenalin pumps through my body as I drive the few miles to work, tyres hissing, wipers on full speed, the black sky low enough to reach out and touch.

At Moretti's, I find Ben at his desk, sorting through paperwork. He looks up, smiles and beckons me in. "How did you get on?" he asks, removing his glasses and leaning back in his chair.

I sink into the seat opposite and tell him what I've learned. About Angela being responsible for bringing Harry to my house. And about Carly letting herself into my house even before this all happened.

"Bloody hell," Ben says, shaking his head.

"I know."

"What are you going to do?" he asks. "You'll have to tell the police now that his housekeeper's admitted it."

"I don't know, Ben. I want to tell the police, I do. But I'm still worried they won't believe me, or Angela. To be honest, she's a bit intense. Very religious. Thinks she's responsible for Fisher's wife's soul, or something. They might dismiss her as unreliable."

"Why don't you just show them the letter from Harry's mother? Surely they'll take your name off the list of suspects when they see that, and then you can go back to your life without worrying about it any more. Try to put it all behind you."

With a sinking heart, it's slowly dawning on me that Angela could very well be a nutjob. She could be making the whole thing up. Maybe she even forged the letter from Elizabeth Fisher. "I really think I need to speak to Fisher first," I explain. "I want to see his reaction when I tell him what his wife and Angela did. I want to see his face. See if he knows more than he's letting on."

"But what about that PIN thing the police gave you? If you go back down there and they arrest you... It's really not a great idea, Tess."

"I know it's not a great idea," I say, my voice rising. "It's a terrible idea. I'm not stupid, I'm not doing this lightly. But if I ignore my gut, I'll end up wondering about it for the rest of my life. If there's a chance that Fisher is responsible for Lily's death in some way, I owe it to her to find out. I know I'm clutching at straws, making connections where there might be nothing. But if there's even the tiniest possibility of foul play, I need to find it. I have to do this for Lily. Can you understand?"

Ben is quiet for a moment. "I think so," he finally replies. "Look, I don't have children of my own, and I can't even imagine what you've been through, but one thing I do know is that I admire you for pushing through when everyone's been against you. You're brave, Tessa. You must have been an amazing mother. Your children, they were lucky to have you."

An unexpected tear slips down my face and I swipe at my eye, hoping Ben hasn't noticed. "Thanks," I croak. I clear my throat. "I think you're the only person in the world who agrees with me, though."

"When are you going to go?" he asks.

"Would it be okay if I left now?"

"No." He shakes his head.

My heart sinks. "I know it's cheeky of me to ask. I'll make up the time."

"I was just going to say, no, it's almost lunchtime. You need to eat before you go. You'll need all your strength."

"Oh." I exhale. "Well... thank you, Mum." I give a half-hearted smile. "I'll pick up a sandwich and eat it on the way."

"Tell you what," he says, rising to his feet, "we'll grab something from the café on our way out. I'll drive, we'll take the truck. Weather's vile—I don't like the idea of you going all that way on your own."

"You want to come with me? But what about your paperwork? And what about Moretti's?"

"I already told Carolyn we're closing the shop in half an hour. You can catch up with the planting tomorrow, or whenever. And my paperwork...well, there will always be paperwork." He grasps the thick pile of files and invoices in front of him and lets it drop back down onto the desk with a thunk.

"Are you sure?" I say, my shoulders already lighter, knowing I won't be facing this alone.

"Yes, totally. You're not driving there by yourself. What if Fisher's dangerous? You already said Carly's gone missing, although by the sounds of it, she's quite capable of taking care of herself."

"Thank you." Those two words aren't enough to convey how grateful I feel. Not just for his company on the journey ahead, but for his unwavering belief in me.

He nods. "Okay, let's go."

CHAPTER THIRTY-TWO

Ben doesn't have satnav in his truck, so I use Google Maps on my phone to navigate as we drive through rain, wind, hail and sleet. We barely talk on the journey, but it's not awkward or strained, we're simply thinking our own thoughts. I'm determined that today will be the day I get answers. I'm going to make Fisher speak to me. The hardest part will be getting him to open his front door and let us in. I clutch his wife's letter tightly—this could be my only way of getting him to listen.

At 3:30 p.m., we drive into Cranborne, its narrow streets so dark and deserted it may as well be the dead of night. I direct Ben to the road where Fisher lives and we pull up outside his house, where lights glow behind drawn curtains.

"Nice place," Ben says.

"Impressive, isn't it?"

"So, what's the plan?" he asks. "Do you have one, or is this something we should have talked about on the journey?"

"I'll go and ring the bell, I guess."

"I'll come with you."

"D'you think that's a good idea? Maybe you should wait in the truck. It might be too intimidating with both of us there."

"I'm not letting you walk into a strange man's house on your own, Tess."

"That's if he lets me over the threshold." Now that I'm here, I'm starting to doubt he'll even open the door.

"I'll be meek and mild," Ben says, bowing his head and hunching his shoulders. "I won't be intimidating at all."

"Okay." It's true I'd feel more confident with Ben by my side. "Shall we do it, then?" My insides twist at the thought of seeing Fisher once more, remembering how he yelled at me last time.

Ben must have noticed my hesitation. "You don't have to, you know. We can always go back home if you've changed your mind. It could be for the best..."

"That would be good," I say. "Making you drive a six-hour round trip for nothing."

"I don't mind. We could stop off at that inn first. Have a drink, then head home."

"I haven't changed my mind," I say, squaring my shoulders. "I want to do this."

"Okay, come on then. Let's do it."

We get out of the car, our heads bent low against the wind and rain. Ben opens the gate to Fisher's house and ushers me through it. We walk along the path and up the few steps to his front door. With my heart hammering, I place my finger on the doorbell and press down hard.

The chime sounds far away, like it's coming from another universe rather than from behind this rain-spattered red front door. After a moment, I hear the sound of a lock being turned. Ben and I glance at one another. He nods, his eyes full of encouragement, as the door is pulled open and light spills out, making me blink.

Fisher stands there, wearing jeans and a blue V-necked jumper. He looks at Ben first, and then his gaze falls on me, his quizzical eyebrows raising in disbelief and lowering almost instantly in anger.

"*You*," he says. "I'm calling the police." He pushes the door towards us, trying to slam it closed again, but Ben is too quick for him, taking a step up and wedging his shoulder into the fast-closing gap.

"Please!" Ben cries. "Hear Tessa out."

But Fisher isn't having any of it. He's pushing at the door as Ben shoves it back as hard as he can. I'm terrified I'm going to end up getting Ben arrested at this rate. "Ben!" I cry. "Leave it! You'll get hurt."

But the door now stands wide open once more, Ben in the doorway while Fisher eyes him from further back in the hall-way, panting heavily.

"Tessa only wants to talk," Ben says.

"I have nothing to say," Fisher retorts. "And I certainly don't wish to hear any more of her lies and nonsense."

"Please," I say, taking a few tentative steps up to the front door and over the threshold. "Just give me a few minutes, that's all. Then we'll leave."

"I want you to leave now," he says, glancing around as though looking for something. "I told you before, I have nothing to say to you, and if you don't leave right this second, I will call the police and have them arrest you for harassment. In fact, I'm calling them anyway." He pats at his jeans pockets—I guess he must be looking for his phone.

"Listen," I say. "You can call the police, I don't care. I think they might be very interested to hear what I have to say about your wife."

Fisher goes deathly still and his face blanches. Behind me, Ben pushes the front door closed, stilling the wind and bringing a sudden, eerie silence to the hallway.

"My wife?" Fisher says, recovering his composure. "How dare you come here and talk to me about my wife. What has she got to do with you?"

"I went to see Angela today," I say, staring at the doctor's face, at his clenched jaw, at the slightly hunted look in his eyes.

"My old housekeeper?" he says, relaxing his shoulders. "She's as nutty as a fruitcake. I had to let her go. Couldn't be trusted any longer. Too much crossing herself and talking about God and hell."

"Or maybe," I reply, "she knew things you didn't want her to know, so you fired her."

"I see she's been filling your head with nonsense, too."

"Angela admitted she left Harry in my house," I say. "So you see, this whole business has been brought to my doorstep, not the other way around. I didn't take your son. Your housekeeper brought him to me."

"And why on earth would she do that?" he says.

"You tell me."

Fisher swallows hard before snapping, "I've heard quite enough of your rubbish. Now I'd like you and your Neanderthal companion to get out of my house right this minute." He takes a step backwards, casting glances around him once more, his eyes now darting up the wooden staircase. Perhaps he's worried about his son coming down and seeing us here. I hope Harry didn't hear us yelling; I hope he's not scared.

"Listen, Dr. Fisher," I say, taking a step towards him. "Angela told me it was your wife's dying wish that she bring your son to me." I stare at him, scanning his face for a reaction.

He takes off his glasses, rubs the bridge of his nose and replaces them again. "I told you," he says, "Angela isn't to be trusted."

"Maybe she isn't," I say, "but I also have a signed letter from your wife, stating that she asked Angela to bring Harry to me."

At this, Fisher's mouth drops open and he looks at me as

though he's seeing a ghost. In this moment, I know I've touched a nerve. I know that all his bluster is covering something up.

"Get out!" he roars. "Get out of my house!"

Ben comes and stands in front of me, one arm out to Fisher, his palm down, trying to calm him. "Come on, Tess," he hisses at me. "We should go, I don't want things to get nasty."

"Why did it take you four days to report Harry missing?" I cry.

"Get out!" he yells, striding towards us.

"Were you on duty at the Balmoral Clinic when I gave birth to my twins? Were you there that night?"

Fisher stops dead in his tracks and turns around so he's facing away from us, muttering and gripping the top of his head with both hands. Then he strides out of the hallway and into one of the back rooms—the dining room, if I remember the layout correctly.

"What's he doing, Tess?" Ben asks.

"Don't know," I whisper. "But I think I'm hitting some nerves, don't you?"

"Definitely. He's guilty of something, no question. But we should go, he could be dangerous."

"We can't go now. We're so close to finding out the truth."

Seconds later, Fisher returns to the hall with a mobile phone. "I'm calling the police," he grunts.

"Where's Carly?" I ask, "The journalist who came to see you yesterday. Have you done something to her?"

Fisher flushes, whether with anger or guilt I can't tell. "I don't know who you're talking about," he cries. "There aren't any more journalists, they've all gone. Why can't you do the same and leave me alone? I'll give you one more chance to get out and then I'm calling 999."

"Call the police, then," I say. "I'll ask them about Carly, and I'll show them the letter from your wife."

Fisher lowers the phone, his shoulders drooping. "Look, I don't know what you want from me," he says, running a hand through his hair. "Why can't everyone just leave me and Harry alone? That's all we want, to be left in peace."

"Dr. Fisher," Ben says softly. "Why don't we sit somewhere and discuss this calmly? It might be better than shouting and hurling accusations at each other."

Just then, the doorbell's dull chime startles me. I catch Ben's eye and we both look at Fisher, who seems equally surprised. Has he called the police already? If he has, they'll probably arrest me. I need to prepare myself for that. Ben and I move out of Fisher's way as he walks to the door, turns the handle and pulls it open. I brace myself for trouble. Ben takes my hand and I grip it tightly.

But the person standing on Fisher's doorstep is not a police officer.

It's Scott.

CHAPTER THIRTY-THREE

"Dr. Fisher?" Scott says, extending his right hand.

Fisher shakes it, a bewildered expression on his face. "Who are you?" he asks.

"I'm here to apologise for my wife's intrusion," Scott says, standing on the doorstep, the wind tugging at his overcoat, messing up his hair. "Tessa's been under a lot of strain recently, and I'm sure she regrets coming here to disturb you and your family." He casts a puzzled glance in Ben's direction and then gives me a pointed look, jerking his head in the direction of the road, trying to indicate that I should leave.

I'm so outraged by his patronising words that I almost want to laugh. Almost, but not quite.

"Yes, well..." Fisher clears his throat. "If you could take her home, I'd be much obliged. I was actually about to call the police. She's breaking the law coming here, you know. She's already been warned to stay away from me and my son." As the wind whips through the open door once more, Scott and Fisher look at me as though I'm some naughty child who hasn't done as she's told.

"Excuse me," Ben says, stepping up to the two of them. "But Tessa and I aren't going anywhere. Not until she gets the answers she came for."

"Who are you?" Scott barks, puffing out his chest.

"I'm Tessa's friend. My name's Ben Moretti."

"Oh, right, you're the chap she works for," Scott says dismissively. "What are you doing here?"

"Moral support. You know, Scott, you should be sticking up for Tess, not apologising for her."

Scott's face turns scarlet. "Who the hell are you to tell me what I should or shouldn't be doing? I've known Tess for a lot longer than you. And she needs help. Professional help. So back off, mate."

"Scott," I snap, pushing my way forward. "If you haven't come to help me, you should just turn around and go home. When I saw you at the door, I thought you were here for *me*."

"I *am* here for you. I'm here to make sure you don't make a fool of yourself and get yourself in even more trouble. I'm not leaving here without you, Tessa. First, you abduct this poor man's son, then you come to his house and harass him. If you make another spectacle of yourself, the papers will be all over us again, and I can't put Ellie through that. Not while she's pregnant. You're just being selfish."

"Selfish!" I yell. "I'm trying to find out the truth. You're the one being selfish—worrying about your new, cosy little life. Forgetting about me and the children we had together."

"I can't live in the past any more, Tess."

"You think I want to?" I cry.

"Actually," Scott says, "yes, I do. I think you're too scared to move on. And becoming obsessed with this poor man's son is not helping anyone. Least of all yourself."

"Scott," Ben interrupts. "It wasn't Tessa who took Harry. Why won't you believe her?"

"Because she's unhinged!" he yells. "I want to believe her, God knows I do, but Tessa has a hard time differentiating between fantasy and reality."

"I think you want to believe that," Ben says, "to ease your conscience. If you tell yourself your wife has lost the plot, then it leaves you free to move on with your own life, guilt-free."

Scott barges past Fisher into his hallway and squares up to Ben. "You need to mind your own bloody business. What's this got to do with you anyway, Moretti?"

Ben gazes calmly at Scott, but doesn't reply.

"Will you all just GET OUT OF MY HOUSE!" Fisher roars as the gusting wind catches the front door, slamming it shut with an almighty bang.

I almost jump out of my skin.

Silence descends on the hallway.

"Daddy, why are you shouting? Who are all these people?"

I whip my head round to see Harry leaning over the banister, his gaze sweeping over everyone, eyes wide. Poor boy. He must be wondering what on earth is going on down here. I want to give him a reassuring hug, but Fisher would go ballistic if I approached him.

"I told you to stay in your room, Harry," Fisher says, his breathing ragged. "I thought you were watching your Thomas the Tank Engine film."

"It's finished, Daddy. But I can hear that lady upstairs in the attic. She's making a noise again."

We all turn our gazes from Harry to Fisher. He opens his mouth, but no words come out.

"What have you done?" I say to Fisher. "Who's up there?"

"Nobody," he replies. "Nobody's up there."

"Yes there is, Daddy. You said it's the lady who keeps asking too many questions."

Fisher looks as though he's about to deny it once more. But then his expression changes to an indignant frown. "She was snooping... Threatening me!"

"Are you holding her up there against her will?" Ben asks.

"No! Well, I was going to let her go..."

Ben and I turn and rush to the staircase.

"Can you show us where the lady is, Harry?" Ben asks.

"She's in the attic," Harry replies. "Daddy said she was naughty."

"Did he?" I turn to Fisher and shake my head.

"What's going on?" Scott asks, a bewildered expression on his face.

We ignore him and continue up the staircase.

"You can't go up there!" Fisher cries, making no attempt to stop us. He simply follows on behind, with Scott trailing after him, a strange procession of people led by Harry and me.

Harry takes my hand and pulls me upwards to the landing and then along to another smaller staircase with a door at the top. Dull thuds and muffled cries emanate from beyond the door. I try twisting the brass knob, but it appears to be locked.

"Key," Ben says, turning back to Fisher, holding out his hand.

"It's downstairs on my..."

But Ben doesn't wait for him to finish. Instead, he turns back and boots the door open with the back of his heel. With a splinter of wood, we tumble onto the narrow landing beyond, and I follow the sound of muffled cries through one of the painted wooden doors into an unlit room. I scan the walls until I locate the light switch and press it.

Illuminated beneath the weak ceiling light, Carly sits on a chair, her ankles tied to its legs, arms tied behind her, a gag between her teeth. I turn to glare at Fisher as Ben rushes forward to release her. She blinks, getting used to the light, and then her eyes grow wide with anger as she scowls at Fisher. Carly is not one of my favourite people at the moment, but for Fisher to have tied her up in his attic is outrageous.

I take Harry's hand and crouch down to his level. "Can you go back into your bedroom now, Harry? Your daddy will be down in a minute to see you."

"What happened to that lady?" he whispers in my ear.

"We were playing hide-and-seek, but now we've found her."

"Can I play?" His eyes light up.

"Maybe later. Go back to your room, okay? Can you do that for me?"

His face falls, but he turns and leaves the room. Good job too, as the language now flying from Carly's mouth isn't fit for a five-year-old's ears.

"You're going to jail for this!" she yells at Fisher.

"Carly? Is that you?" Scott says, his face creased in confusion. "What are you doing here? What's going on?"

"If you'd paid attention to what Tessa had to say in the first place," Ben snaps at Scott as he unties Carly's ankles, "maybe you'd have a clue."

Scott flushes and turns to me for an explanation.

"Not now, Scott," I say, giving him my best withering look. I feel a tug on the back of my coat and turn round to see that Harry has come back into the room. "Harry, sweetie, you need to go back to your room, remember?"

"You're my real mummy, aren't you?" he says in his clear, pure voice, silencing everyone and making me catch my breath.

"Angela's been filling your head with nonsense," Fisher tells his son, his voice weak, one hand against the wall, the other hand pressed to his chest. "Of course this lady isn't your mummy." He reaches out to take Harry's hand and tries to lead him away, but Harry isn't budging.

"My mummy who's in heaven told me that I had a new mummy who was my *real* mummy. She said our angel would take me to her. And I think Tessa is my new mummy because she likes trains, same as me." He stares up at me, his brown eyes meeting mine, his expression all at once strange and familiar.

I'm sure my heart has stopped beating. I'm sure the world has stopped turning and I'm sure that everyone else has frozen in time. I stare from Harry to Fisher and back to Harry again. I still don't quite understand what Harry has just said, but I understand that it is possibly momentous. Life-changing.

Everything speeds back up and my heart jump-starts itself. *Ka-boom. Ka-boom.* A deafening sound that rattles the whole house and makes my vision blur.

"What's he talking about?" Scott asks hesitantly, looking at Fisher, some kind of understanding dawning.

Fisher is quiet, pale, his face twitching, his whole body sagging like a deflating balloon. Everyone turns to him. Even Carly has stopped swearing and is studying the doctor like he's a rare specimen in a glass case.

"What's he talking about?" Scott asks again. "We're not stupid, Fisher. There's something going on here."

If I wasn't so paralysed with the possibility of what this could mean, I would have a cutting retort for Scott. But now isn't the time for *I told you so.*

"No," Fisher says. "There's nothing going on. He's just a little boy. He has an active imagination." But it's obvious that James Fisher is lying. The bluster and outrage has disappeared from his face. Instead, he now looks scared, shrunken, defeated.

"You were on duty that night, weren't you?" I say to him.

He shakes his head.

"Scott," I say, "you must remember. Fisher even changed the records to make out it was Dr. Friedland on duty. But Friedland was sick that night, remember?"

Realisation continues to spread across Scott's face. Finally, he's listening to me without his usual scepticism.

"He's covering something up, Scott. Something bad."

All the discoveries I've been trying to get Scott to pay attention to are finally beginning to sink into his resistant brain.

"No," Fisher says. "You've got it all wrong."

In a flurry of movement, Scott pushes past me, grabs Fisher by the neck of his jumper and shoves him up against the wall, his head cracking against the plaster, his glasses falling onto the wooden floor with a thin clatter.

Ben leaves Carly's side and tries to pull Scott off the doctor. "Calm down," he tells Scott. "Let him go! Let him speak."

"What have you done?" Scott asks Fisher through gritted teeth, hands at his throat, squeezing until the doctor's face begins to turn purple.

Harry has started to cry, and I swing him up into my arms so he's facing away from the awful scene in front of me.

"Stop it! Stop it!" I yell. "You're scaring Harry! Scott, is that what you want? To traumatise a little boy?"

My words seem to get through, because at last Scott releases his hold on Fisher. The doctor slides to the ground, clutching at his neck and gasping for air. Ben kneels by his side, checking he's okay.

Harry wriggles in my arms, wanting to be put down. "Daddy!" he cries, twisting out of my grasp and running over to his choking father, throwing his arms around him and burying his face in his chest. "Daddy, why are they shouting at you? Why are you shaking?" His words break down into sobs, and I feel terrible that our arrival here is the cause of this little boy's distress. But we needed to come: I have to find out the truth.

Fisher begins to sob. He encircles Harry in his arms and kisses the top of his head. "All right, I'll tell you," he says, looking up at me and Scott, his voice little more than a whisper. "I'll tell you everything."

CHAPTER THIRTY-FOUR

Carly comes and stands beside me, rubbing at her wrists and rolling her shoulders. I should ask her if she's okay, but I find myself unable to speak. I'm still in shock at the thought of what Dr. Fisher is about to reveal.

"Shall I take Harry downstairs?" Ben asks, walking over to where the little boy has pressed himself into his father's body. "Harry? Shall we go and play downstairs? Want to show me your room?"

"I don't want to go!" Harry cries. "I want to stay with Daddy."

"Did I hear you say you like trains?" Ben asks. "Have you got any good ones you can show me?"

"Show him your trains, Harry," Fisher grunts, peeling his son off his chest.

"I don't want to go," Harry wails.

"Harry," Fisher says, his voice stern despite its new hoarseness.

Harry stands, his cheeks tear-stained, his lower lip trembling, but he lets Ben take his hand.

"Come on, Carly," Ben says, turning back to her. "You too."

"I'm staying to hear this," she replies.

"No, you're not. Come on," Ben insists.

"No way. I'm not going anywh—"

"Please, Carly," I say. "Our deal still stands, but this conversation is between me, Scott and Dr. Fisher. Okay?"

She scowls, but does as I ask and goes to join Ben and Harry.

As their footsteps recede, Fisher, still huddled on the floor, begins to tremble. Tears stream down his cheeks. "My God," he murmurs. "What have I done?"

I stare at him in silence, wondering what can be so bad that he's been reduced to this snivelling wreck of a man, not daring to imagine what he's about to tell us. But at the same time, I'm almost sure I know.

"Maybe you'd better start at the beginning," I say at last, my voice not sounding like my own. I kneel opposite him, not taking my eyes from his face.

Scott remains on his feet, arms crossed over his chest, still simmering with rage.

"I...I did something terrible," Fisher says. "Beyond terrible."

"Tell me," I say.

"All right," he says quietly. "All right." He takes a breath and stares up at the ceiling for a moment, briefly clenching his fists. "You already know I'm an obstetrician. And yes, I used to practise at the Balmoral Clinic." His voice is croaky, barely more than a whisper after Scott nearly strangled him. His eyes are bloodshot and his hands quiver so much he places them between his knees to still them. "The night you gave birth, your consultant, Max Friedland, was taken ill and I was called in to cover for him. What you may not know is that my own wife, Liz, also went into labour that night. She was in the suite next to yours."

I'm listening to him with a kind of fascinated dread, barely breathing.

Fisher's eyes glaze as he remembers. "You were already in good hands with your midwife when I arrived, so I concentrated on looking after Liz. Naturally, I wanted to be with my wife during the birth of our first child, but as the clinic was short-staffed and your delivery seemed straightforward, I was happy to cover. I told your midwife that I'd come to you immediately if you got into any difficulty, but she assured me that things were progressing well.

"But then..." He looks from me to Scott, finally lowering his gaze back down to his knees. "But then, my own child got into difficulties. The umbilical cord was wrapped around the neck, cutting off blood flow and oxygen. I would normally have a midwife in the room with me, but I was overconfident—I thought I had the situation under control." His voice breaks and he clears his throat. "I tried everything I could to save her, but I panicked. I'm usually calm, professional. I deliver hundreds of healthy children every year, but this was *my* child, *my* wife. The child we'd been trying for ten years to conceive. I...I couldn't save my own baby. She died. My child died. I couldn't save her. It was my fault."

"*She?*" Scott questions immediately. "*Her?*"

"I made a decision," Fisher says. "A split-second decision that's haunted me ever since. You have to believe me, I never planned for it to happen. I wasn't thinking clearly. I didn't know how to tell Liz our baby was gone."

My heart beats in time with his words. A slow marching drum, getting faster.

Fisher turns to me. "You had already given birth to one healthy twin. The next one was coming, and that's when I did it."

I'm shaking now. My whole body, top-to-toe, my teeth chattering. I know what he's going to say, but I don't want to hear it. How will I bear it?

"Lily was *my* daughter," Fisher says. "Mine and Liz's. But she died a few moments after birth and I was grieving. I don't think I was in my right mind."

"Lily was yours?" I whisper, a chill sweeping through me.

But Fisher doesn't reply. He's intent on his confession. "Scott, you were on your phone, texting family members to say you had a son. I told you that mobiles interfered with the hospital equipment and sent you out of the room. Told you to go to the parents' lounge. I said you had about twenty minutes before your next child came along. I lied."

He turns back to me. "Just before your second child was born, I sent the midwife to check on another woman in labour. You were still woozy from the birth and from the effects of the pain relief. In a moment of utter madness, I swapped them. I swapped my dead child for your living one." He pulls at his cheeks, unable to look at me or Scott, his gaze fixed on some distant spot.

"Harry…he was Sam's brother," Fisher says. "He was your second child. He *is* your second child. I've done a terrible thing, I know. I have no excuses. At the time, I told myself that you already had one healthy child. I told myself I did it for Liz, to save her from grief. It would have destroyed her…I am so very, very sorry."

"To save her from grief?" I murmur almost to myself. "But what about *my* grief? What about *that*?" He's telling me he's sorry. He did this heinous thing and he's apologising like he took the last slice of cake, or scratched my car, or accidentally bumped me with his trolley in the supermarket. "You can't just *apologise* for this," I spit. "You can't make excuses and apologise for taking my living, breathing baby and swapping him for your dead daughter."

Fisher is still speaking. Saying the words over and over again. "I'm sorry. I'm so, so sorry."

"Stop it!" I cry. "Just stop saying sorry. Stop it!"

He closes his mouth for a moment before carrying on with his explanation, taking my life apart with his words. "My wife never knew," he says quickly. "She thought Harry was ours. She loved him like he was our own. So did I. I buried the truth deep, but the truth has sharp edges. It cut me up inside. Every day."

I want to scream at him that I know exactly how those sharp edges feel. But I will myself to stay quiet. To listen to the rest. His confession is spewing out of his mouth now like an airborne virus, infecting us all.

"When my wife was diagnosed with terminal cancer, something came over me. An epiphany. I thought, if I don't tell her about Harry now, I'll never have the chance. And so I confessed. I told her everything I'd done. She was devastated. Shocked. Disgusted. She had every right to be. She died a broken woman. I did that to her. All I ever wanted was to be a doctor. To help people. But instead..." He trails off. Buries his face in his hands.

The absolute knowledge of the truth takes the strength from my body, and I lower my head to the wooden floor, curl up and grip my knees, the truth gradually sinking in like poison from a syringe. I have no words now, only tears. My nostrils fill with the bitter odour of realisation. Of loss. Of everything that has been stripped from me. The grief for a dead daughter who was never mine to grieve for. The devastation after Sam died. Being a mother with no children to care for. All of it. All of it too much to bear, knowing that half of it need not have been borne in the first place.

And yet, didn't I know this even before now? Since that day Harry showed up in my kitchen, those brown curls so familiar, his eyes twin reflections of a lost child.

I knew. Deep down, I knew.

It's what's been driving me these past days. Pushing me on

despite the risks. That primal knowledge burnt deep into my core: a mother's knowledge.

"I'm sorry," Fisher repeats on a loop through his sobs. "I am so, so sorry."

A roar jerks me from my frozen position on the floor as Scott charges at Fisher, grabs him by his jumper and yanks him to his feet. I crawl to my knees and watch as he punches Fisher in the face, splitting his lip, sending droplets of blood spraying over him. The doctor's hands come up too late to protect himself. He doesn't even attempt to fight back. Just cowers and takes it.

"I'll kill you!" Scott cries, pulling back his fist once more and smashing it into Fisher's jaw. "I'll fucking kill you, you worthless piece of shit."

He really is going to end up killing him. "Scott!" I cry. "Please, Scott, stop."

"He's ruined our lives, Tess!" Scott says, letting another punch fly. "He took everything from us. Everything." His next punch is just as vicious. And the next and the next. "He deserves to die for what he did."

"Scott!" I yell. "Please! Stop! Think of Harry!"

He must have heeded me, for his next punch is a little less brutal. The one after that, not a punch at all. He finally turns away from Fisher, the man's face a pulpy mess of blood, tears and snot. Scott's own face is ashen with grief. I imagine that same grief etched across my features too.

I hold out my arms and Scott staggers into them. We hold each other so tightly that it hurts. Physical pain to balance the other hurt. Fresh bruises so deep and raw that I can't imagine they will ever fade.

But then it sinks in: Harry is my son. He's alive. He is here in this house.

And I am his mother.

CHAPTER THIRTY-FIVE

Eight months later

A welcome breeze blows through the trees, rippling the leaves on the horse chestnut above me. It will soon be conker season. A red-faced woman in a flowery dress sits on the other end of the bench, issuing instructions to two young boys before they scamper off towards the play park. We catch each other's eye and smile.

"At least there's a bit of shade here," the woman says, pulling a water bottle out of a rucksack and taking a long swig. "I almost melted on the walk over. Not that I'm complaining," she adds. "We'll miss the sun soon enough."

I nod and smile, then turn my attention back to the playground.

"Boy or girl?" the woman asks. "Or both?"

"Boy," I reply, my heart swelling. "Over there on the monkey bars." I point to Harry, who has made it all the way to the end and is now checking to see that I witnessed the momentous event. I clap my hands at his achievement, and the woman next to me claps too, making Harry puff his chest out with pride.

"Right," she says, rising to her feet again, "no rest for the wicked. I'd better go and give my two a push on the swings."

"Bye," I say with a smile.

"Did you see me, Mummy?" Harry runs over. I give him a

kiss and make him take a few sips of water. "I went all the way to the end without stopping!"

"You were brilliant," I say. "Super-strong muscles. Must be all those vegetables you've been eating." I pat the bench and he hops up beside me. "Want a snack?" I ask.

He nods, so I pull a small pot of grapes from my bag, remove the lid and pass it to him.

"Thank you," he says, and I kiss the top of his head, his curls damp with sweat.

"When am I going to Scott's?" he asks.

"Not until next weekend," I reply. "He's taking you to the cinema, remember?" Even though Harry calls me "Mummy," he refuses to call Scott "Daddy," which I know hurts my ex-husband a lot, but I suppose Harry already feels as though he has a father, even if he doesn't see him any more.

James Fisher has been struck off the UK medical register. He's also serving six years for child abduction and for false imprisonment for the unlawful detention of Carly Dean. Scott didn't think it was a long enough sentence, but I happen to think it's the perfect amount of time. He took almost six years of Harry's life from us, so he can have six years taken from his own life. I know what he did was terrible, but he'll have a lifetime to live with the consequences—alone.

I told the social worker that I would accept my son still having contact with Fisher if that's what Harry wanted. But it turns out Fisher doesn't want Harry to visit him in prison. He thinks it would be too upsetting. I can't say I'm not relieved.

Angela Merida Flores was prepared to go to prison for what she did, but it turns out she had nothing to worry about. For how could she be prosecuted for returning a child to his rightful parent? After a lengthy investigation, she was cleared of all wrongdoing.

I didn't tell the police about Carly's unlawful entrance to my house. She apologised to me, and I figured that in the scheme of things, she actually ended up helping me get my son back. If it wasn't for her, I would never have pursued Fisher so doggedly, and none of this would ever have come out. I'd still be plain old Tessa. Childless. Of doubtful sanity. The thought makes me shudder. So I let it go.

Carly sold her story to the newspapers with my consent, and I received a nice chunk of cash, which went towards the purchase of my new two-bedroom garden flat—a lovely light, airy place in a converted Edwardian building around the corner from Moretti's, a handy minute's stroll to work. I sold the house that was once a home for me and Scott. It was a relief to leave the hurt of that place behind. Like shedding a skin that had grown too tight.

I didn't end up taking the manager's job Ben offered me, as I want to spend as much time as I can with Harry. But I have been consulting over his plans for the new and improved garden centre, and it's been fun getting my landscape-architect head back on.

Scott also has his hands full with his and Ellie's new son, Harry's half-brother, Aiden. It's funny, but whenever I go there to drop Harry round, Ellie can't even look me in the eye. Maybe she feels guilty for accusing me, or awkward or something. She should just apologise and get over herself. I think she's finding motherhood harder than she thought she would, and Scott looks stressed every time I see him. The smug air they previously wore around me has evaporated, to be replaced by, if not respect, then maybe a little humility, although they would be the last to admit it.

It's been a wonderful yet hard few months. The adjustment for Harry has been pretty traumatic at times. He and I both still have weekly counselling. And he still misses Liz, his "other mummy." When he first came to live with me, we had a social worker visit us regularly, but she was finally satisfied that we were okay to be left alone together. That I'm a fit parent.

I'm discovering that even in the midst of grief, life can offer new joy and hope. I still grieve for the daughter who was never mine, and no one can replace my beautiful boy, Sam, but I've been given a second chance with Harry. Even though they're non-identical twins, it's like having a part of Sam back. Harry is my salvation. My reason to get up in the morning.

"Ben!" Harry cries, launching himself off the bench and flying across the playground towards the approaching figure. Ben scoops him up into his arms and swings him around before depositing him back down on the tarmac with a grin.

Those two get on like a house on fire. Ben and I are taking things slowly, but I couldn't have got through the past few months without him. I raise my hand in greeting.

"So how are my two favourite people in the world?" Ben asks as he comes closer, dipping to kiss me, his eyes shining.

"Good," Harry and I say in unison, as children's laughter from the playground drifts across on the late summer breeze.

"Fancy coming over for pizza this evening?" Ben asks. "I thought you might like to help me make it, Harry. Nothing quite like home-made pizza."

"Can we, Mummy?"

"Mm, pizza. Yes, we'll be there."

Ben takes my hand and kisses my knuckles. Then he stands and holds both his hands behind his back. "Pick a hand, Harry."

Harry stands and looks at Ben, considering his choice carefully.

"Come on, left or right, which is it to be?"

"Right!"

"Well, that's amazing," Ben says, feigning astonishment. "How did you know? You must be a magician." He brings his right hand around to reveal a Thomas the Tank Engine bouncy ball. "Want a game of catch?"

Harry nods vigorously, his curls bouncing around his face. The two of them jog over to a grassy area just beyond the playground, and I watch them tossing the ball to one another. Ben goofs around, pretending to drop it every time, making Harry roar with laughter.

I don't believe there's such a thing as a perfect life. Shit happens, as they say. And I've had more than my fair share of that. I don't believe in happy-ever-afters either. But right here, right now, watching my little fledgling family, I realise I've got something back that I thought was lost forever. A door I thought permanently shut is now wide open. Is that a happy ending? Maybe. Maybe not. But it's a good place to start.

A LETTER FROM SHALINI

I want to say a huge thank you for choosing to read *The Secret Mother*. If you enjoyed it, and would like to keep up-to-date with all my latest releases, just sign up here.

Maybe you'd be kind enough to tell your friends about it and consider posting a short review online. I'd love to hear what you think, and it makes such a difference helping new readers to discover one of my books for the first time.

I adore hearing from my readers—you can get in touch on my Facebook page, through Twitter, Goodreads or my website.

Thanks so much!
Shalini Boland x

ShaliniBolandAuthor
@ShaliniBoland
shaliniboland.co.uk

ACKNOWLEDGEMENTS

As always, I want to thank my fantastic husband Pete Boland who makes me cups of tea and smooths away my doubts while I write. You're always there to help when I'm on a deadline or there's a tricky bit of plot to be worked through. Thank you, thank you, thank you!

Having previously been self-published, this is my first novel to be written and released with the help of a publisher. I want to thank Bookouture for making the transition so enjoyable and seamless. Massive thanks to Natasha Harding, my brand new, talented and supportive publisher who is fast becoming one of my favourite people ever. Thank you for your belief in my books and for your help in making them shine.

Thanks also to the rest of the Bookouture gang. I hope to get to know you all better and I'm honoured to be part of your incredible family. PR gurus Kim Nash and Noelle Holten, you both rock. I don't know how you manage to cram so much into twenty-four hours. Thank you for being amazing!

I consider myself very lucky to have had the expert advice of police officer Sammy H. K. Smith for all the police procedural aspects of my book. Thank you for your time and patience. Any mistakes are my own. Just a heads up—you know I'm going to be firing off emails to you for my next book.

Thanks a million to Terry Harden, Julie Carey and Amara

Gillo for beta reading and proofreading. Thanks also to Tracy Fenton and Helen Boyce at TBC on Facebook and to David Gilchrist, Sarah Mackins and Caroline Maston at UK Crime Book Club—your unstoppable enthusiasm for all authors astounds me.

Finally, and most importantly, thank you to my readers who take the time to read, review or recommend my books. I'm overwhelmed some days by your tremendous support. It means the world.

ABOUT THE AUTHOR

Shalini Boland is a *USA Today* bestselling author of psychological thrillers who lives in Dorset, England, with her husband, two children and their cheeky terrier cross. Before kids, she was signed to Universal Music Publishing as a singer/songwriter, but now she spends her days writing psychological thrillers (in between school runs and hanging out endless baskets of laundry).

She is also the author of two bestselling Young Adult series as well as an atmospheric WWII novel with a time-travel twist.

Be the first to hear about her new releases here:

http://eepurl.com/b4vb45 and learn more at:
http://www.facebook.com/ShaliniBolandAuthor
http://www.shaliniboland.co.uk
https://twitter.com/ShaliniBoland